You are inside a man-made, thirty-billion-ton ice comet shooting toward the sun . . .

You are the prisoner and plaything of two bizarre un-humans on their weird planet-home . . .

You are a mangled accident victim being put together again by a computer with a sense of humor . . .

You are part of the far-out and fascinating future universe of Hal Clement . . .

HERE ARE SPELLBINDING STORYTELLING AND DAZZLING IMAGINATION—PERFECTLY PROGRAMMED TO TAKE YOU TO THE OUTER LIMITS OF SCIENCE FICTION EXCITEMENT.

SPACE LASH

(formerly: SMALL CHANGES)

by Hal Clement

A DELL BOOK

CONTENTS

"Checking out."

"Checked, Ridge. See you soon."

Ridging glanced over his shoulder at Beacon Peak, as the point where the relay station had been mounted was known. The gleaming dome of its leaden meteor shield was visible as a spark; most of the lower peaks of Harpalus were already below the horizon, and with them the last territory with which Ridging or Shandara could claim familiarity. The humming turbine tractor that carried them was the only sign of humanity except each others' faces—the thin crescent of their home world was too close to the sun to be seen easily, and Earth doesn't look very "human" from outside in any case.

The prospect ahead was not exactly strange, of course. Shandara had remarked several times in the last four weeks that a man who had seen any of the moon had seen all of it. A good many others had agreed with him. Even Ridging, whose temperament kept him normally expecting something new to happen, was beginning to get a trifle bored with the place. It wasn't even dangerous; he knew perfectly well what exposure to vacuum would mean, but checking spacesuit and air-lock valves had become a matter of habit long before.

Cosmic rays went through plastic suits and living bodies like glass, for the most part ineffective because unabsorbed; meteors blew microscopic holes through thin metal, but scarcely marked spacesuits or hulls, as far as current experiences went; the "dust-hidden crevasses" which they had expected to catch unwary men or vehicles simply didn't exist—the dust was too dry to cover any sort of hole, except by filling it completely. The closest approach to a casualty suffered so far had occurred when a man had missed his footing on the ladder outside the *Albireo*'s air lock and narrowly avoided a hundred and fifty foot fall.

Still, Shandara was being cautious. His eyes swept the

7

ground ahead of their tracks, and his gauntleted hands rested lig..tly on brake and steering controls as the tractor glided ahead.

Harpalus and the relay station were out of sight now. Another glance behind assured Ridging of that. For the first time in weeks he was out of touch with the rest of the group, and for the first time he wondered whether it was such a good idea. Orders had been strict; the radius of exploration settled on long before was not to be exceeded. Ridging had been completely in favor of this; but it was his own instruments which had triggered the change of schedule.

One question about the moon to which no one could more than guess an answer in advance was that of its magnetic field. Once the group was on the surface it had immediately become evident that there was one, and comparative readings had indicated that the south magnetic pole—or *a* south magnetic pole—lay a few hundred miles away. It had been decided to modify the program to check the region, since the last forlorn chance of finding any trace of a gaseous envelope around the moon seemed to lie in auroral investigation. Ridging found himself, to his intense astonishment, wondering why he had volunteered for the trip and then wondering how such thoughts could cross his mind. He had never considered himself a coward, and certainly had no one but himself to blame for being in the tractor. No one had made him volunteer, and any technician could have set up and operated the equipment.

"Come out of it, Ridge. Anyone would think you were worrried." Shandara's careless tones cut into his thoughts. "How about running this buggy for a while? I've had her for a hundred kilos."

"Right." Ridging slipped into the driver's seat as his companion left it without slowing the tractor. He did not need to find their location on the photographic map clipped beside the panel; he had been keeping a running check almost unconsciously between the features it showed and the landmarks appearing over the horizon. A course had been marked on it, and navigation was not expected to be a problem even without a magnetic compass.

The course was far from straight, though it led over what passed for fairly smooth territory on the moon. Even back on Sinus Roris the tractor had had to weave its way around numerous obstacles; now well onto the Mare Frigoris the situation was no better, and according to the map it was nearly time to turn south through the mountains, which would be infinitely worse. According to the photos taken during the original landing approach the journey would be possible, however, and would lead through the range at its narrowest part out onto Mare Imbrium. From that point to the vicinity of Plato, where the region to be investigated lay, there should be no trouble at all.

Oddly enough, there wasn't. Ridging was moderately surprised; Shandara seemed to take it as a matter of course. The cartographer had eaten, slept, and taken his turn at driving with only an occasional remark. Ridging was beginning to believe by the time they reached their goal that his companion was actually as bored with the moon as he claimed to be. The thought, however, was fleeting; there was work to be done.

About six hundred pounds of assorted instruments were attached to the trailer which had been improvised from discarded fuel tanks. The tractor itself could not carry them; its entire cargo space was occupied by another improvisation—an auxiliary fuel tank which had been needed to make the present journey possible. The instruments had to be removed, set up in various spots, and permitted to make their records for the next thirty hours. This would have been a minor task, and possibly even justified a little boredom, had it not been for the fact that some of the "spots" were supposed to be as high as possible. Both men had climbed Lunar mountains in the last four weeks, and neither was worried about the task; but there was some question as to which mountain would best suit their needs.

They had stopped on fairly level ground south and somewhat west of Plato—"sunset" west, that is, not astronomical. There was a number of fairly prominent elevations in sight. None seemed more than a thousand meters or so in height, however, and the men knew that Plato in one direction and the Teneriffe Mountains in the other had peaks fully twice as high. The problem was which to choose.

"We can't take the tractor either way," pointed out Shandara. "We're cutting things pretty fine on the fuel question as it is. We are going to have to pack the instruments ourselves, and it's fifty or sixty kilometers to Teneriffe before we even start climbing. Plato's a lot closer."

"The *near side* of Plato's a lot closer," admitted Ridging, "but the measured peaks in its rim must be on the east and west sides, where they can cast shadows across the crater floor. We might have to go as far for a really good peak as we would if we headed south."

"That's not quite right. Look at the map. The near rim of the crater is fairly straight, and doesn't run straight east and west; it must cast shadows that they could measure from Earth. Why can't it contain some of those two thousand meter humps mentioned in the atlas?"

"No reason why it *can't;* but we don't know that it *does.* This map doesn't show."

"It doesn't show for Teneriffe, either."

"That's true, but there isn't much choice there, and we know that there's at least one high peak in a fairly small area. Plato is well over three hundred kilometers around."

"It's still a closer walk, and I don't see why, if there are high peaks at any part of the rim, they shouldn't be fairly common all around the circumference."

"I don't see *why* either," retorted Ridging, "but I've seen several craters for which that wasn't true. So have you." Shandara had no immediate answer to this, but he had no intention of exposing himself to an unnecessarily long walk if he could help it. The instruments to be carried were admittedly light, at least on the moon; but there would be no chance of opening spacesuits until the men got back to the tractor, and spacesuits got quite uncomfortable after a while.

It was the magnetometer that won Shandara's point for him. This pleased him greatly at the time, though he was heard to express a different opinion later. The meter itself did not attract attention until the men were about ready to start, and he had resigned himself to the long walk after a good deal more argument; but a final check of the recorders already operating made Ridging stop and think.

"Say, Shan, have you noticed any sun spots lately?"

"Haven't looked at the sun, and don't plan to."

"I know. I mean, have any of the astronomers mentioned anything of the sort?"

"I didn't hear them, and we'll never be able to ask until we get back. Why?"

"I'd say there was a magnetic storm of some sort going on. The intensity, dip, and azimuth readings have all changed quite a bit in the last hour."

"I thought dip was near vertical anyway."

"It is, but that doesn't keep it from changing. You know, Shan, maybe it would be better if we went to Plato, instead."

"That's what I've been saying all along. What's changed your mind?"

"This magnetic business. On Earth, such storms are caused by charged particles from the sun, deflected by the planet's magnetic field and forming what amounts to tremendous electric currents which naturally produce fields of their own. If that's what is happening here, it would be nice to get even closer to the local magnetic vertical, if we can; and that seems to be in, or at least near, Plato."

"That suits me. I've been arguing that way all along. I'm with you."

"There's one other thing—"

"What?"

"This magnetometer ought to go along with us, as well as the stuff we were taking anyway. Do you mind helping with the extra weight?" Shandara had not considered this aspect of the matter, but since his arguments had been founded on the question of time rather than effort he agreed readily to the additional labor.

"All right. Just a few minutes while I dismount and repack this gadget, and we'll be on our way." Ridging set to work, and was ready in the specified time, since the apparatus had been designed to be handled by spacesuited men. The carrying racks that took the place of regular packs made the travelers look top-heavy, but they had long since learned to keep their balance under such loads. They turned until the nearly motionless sun was behind them and to their right, and set out for the hills ahead.

These elevations were not the peaks they expected to use; the moon's near horizon made those still invisible. They did, however, represent the outer reaches of the area which had been disturbed by whatever monstrous explosion had blown the ring of Plato in the moon's crust. As far as the men were concerned, these hills simply meant that very little of their journey would be across level ground, which pleased them just as well. Level ground was sometimes an inch or two deep in dust; and while dust could not hide deep cracks it could and sometimes did fill broader hollows and cover irregularities where one could trip. For a top-heavy man, this could be a serious nuisance. Relatively little dust had been encountered by any of the expedition up to this point, since most of their work had involved slopes or peaks; but a few annoying lessons had been learned.

Shandara and Ridging stuck to the relatively dust-free slopes, therefore. The going was easy enough for experienced men, and they traveled at pretty fair speed—some ten or twelve miles an hour, they judged. The tractor soon disappeared, and compasses were useless, but both men had a good eye for country, and were used enough to the Lunar landscape to have no particular difficulty in finding distinctive features. They said little, except to call each other's attention to particularly good landmarks.

The general ground level was going up after the first hour and a half, though there was still plenty of downhill travel. A relatively near line of peaks ahead was presumably the crater rim; there was little difficulty in deciding on the most suitable one and heading for it. Naturally the footing became worse and the slopes steeper as they approached, but nothing was dangerous even yet. Such crevasses as existed were easy both to see and to jump, and there are few loose rocks on the moon.

It was only about three and a half hours after leaving the tractor, therefore, that the two men reached the peak they had selected, and looked out over the great walled plain of Plato. They couldn't see all of it, of course; Plato is a hundred kilometers across, and even from a height of two thousand meters the farther side of the floor lies below the horizon. The opposite rim could be seen but there was no easy way to tell whether any of the peaks visible there were as high as the one from which the men saw them. It didn't really matter; this one was high enough for their purposes.

The instruments were unloaded and set up in half an hour. Ridging did most of the work, with a professional single-mindedness which Shandara made no attempt to emulate. The geophysicist scarcely glanced at the crater floor after his first look around upon their arrival, while Shandara did little else. Ridging was not surprised; he had been reasonably sure that his friend had had ulterior reasons for wanting to come this way.

"All right," he said, as he straightened up after closing the last switch, "when do we go down, and how long do we take?"

"Go down where?" asked Shandara innocently.

"Down to the crater floor, I suppose. I'm sure you don't see enough to satisfy you from here. It's just an ordinary crater, of course, but it's three times the diameter of Harpalus even if the walls are less than half as high, and you'll surely want to see every square meter of the floor."

"I'll want to see *some* of the floor, anyway." Shandara's tone carried feeling even through the suit radios. "It's nice of you to realize that we have to go down. I wish you realized why."

"You mean . . . you mean you really expect to climb down there?" Ridging, in spite of his knowledge of the other's interest, was startled. "I didn't really mean—"

"I didn't think you did. You haven't looked over the edge once."

Ridging repaired the omission, letting his gaze sweep carefully over the grayish plain at the foot of the slope. He knew that the floor of Plato was one of the darker areas on the moon, but had never supposed that this fact consti- tuted a major problem.

"I don't get it," he said at last. "I don't see anything. The floor is smoother than that of Harpalus, I'd say, but I'm not really sure even of that, from this distance. It's a couple of kilos down and I don't know how far over."

"You brought the map." It was not a question.

"Of course."

"Look at it. It's a good one." Ridging obeyed, bewil- dered. The map was good, as Shandara had said; its scale was sufficient to show Plato some fifteen centimeters across, with plenty of detail. It was basically an enlargement of a map published on Earth, from telescopic observations; but a good deal of detail had been added from photographs taken during the approach and landing of the expedition. Shandara knew that; it was largely his own work.

As a result, Ridging was not long in seeing what his companion meant. The map showed five fairly large cra- terlets *within* Plato, and nearly a hundred smaller fea- tures.

Ridging could see none of them from where he stood. He looked thoughtfully down the slope, then at the other man.

"I begin to see what you mean. Did you expect something like this? Is that why you wanted to come here? Why didn't you tell me?"

"I didn't expect it, though I had a vague hope. A good many times in the past, observers have reported that the features on the floor of this crater were obscured. Dr. Pickering, at the beginning of the century, thought of it as an active volcanic area; others have blamed the business on clouds—and others, of course, have assumed the observers themselves were at fault, though that is pretty hard to justify. I didn't really expect to get a chance to check up on the phenomenon, but I'm sure you don't expect me to stay up here now."

"I suppose not." Ridging spoke in a tone of mock resignation. The problem did not seem to concern his field directly, but he judged rightly that the present situation affected Shandara the way an offer of a genuine fragment of Terrestrial core material would influence Ridging himself. "What do you plan to take down? I suppose you want to get measures of some sort."

"Well, there isn't too much here that will apply, I'm afraid. I have my own camera and some filters, which may do some good. I can't see that the magnetic stuff will be any use down there. We don't have any pressure measuring or gas collecting gadgetry; I suppose if we'd brought a spare water container from the tractor we could dump it, but we didn't and I'd bet that nothing would be found in it but water vapor if we did. We'll just have to go down and see what our eyes will tell us, and record anything that seems recordable on film. Are you ready?"

"Ready as I ever will be." Ridging knew the remark was neither original nor brilliant, but nothing else seemed to fit.

The inner wall of the crater was a good deal steeper than the one they had climbed, but still did not present a serious obstacle. The principal trouble was that much of the way led through clefts where the sun did not shine, and the only light was reflected from distant slopes. There wasn't much of it, and the men had to be careful of their footings—there was an occasional loose fragment here, and a thousand-meter fall is no joke even on the moon. The way did not lead directly toward the crater floor; the serrated rim offered better ways between its peaks, hair-pinning back and forth so that sometimes the central plain was not visible at all. No floor details appeared as they descended, but whatever covered them was still below; the stars, whenever the mountains cut off enough sidelight, were clear as ever. Time and again Shandara stopped to look over the great plain, which seemed limitless now that the peaks on the farther side had dropped below the horizon, but nothing in the way of information rewarded the effort.

It was the last few hundred meters of descent that began to furnish something of interest. Shandara was picking his way down an unusually uninviting bit of slope when Ridging, who had already negotiated it, spoke up sharply.

"Shan! Look at the stars over the northern horizon! Isn't there some sort of haze? The sky around them looks a bit lighter." The other paused and looked.

"You're right. But how could that be? There couldn't suddenly be enough air at this level—gases don't behave that way. Van Maanen's star might have an atmosphere twenty meters deep, but the moon doesn't and never could have."

"There's *something* between us and the sky."

"That I admit; but I still say it isn't gas. Maybe dust—"

"What would hold it up? Dust is just as impossible as air."

"I don't know. The floor's only a few yards down—let's not stand here guessing." They resumed their descent.

The crater floor was fairly level, and sharply distinguished from the inner slope of the crater wall. Something had certainly filled, partly at least, the vast pit after the original explosion; but neither man was disposed to renew the argument about the origin of Lunar craters just then. They scrambled down the remaining few yards of the journey and stopped where they were, silently.

There *was* something blocking vision; the horizon was no longer visible, nor could the stars be seen for a few degrees above where it should have been. Neither man would have had the slightest doubt about the nature of the obscuring matter had he been on Earth; it bore every resemblance to dust. It *had* to be dust.

But it couldn't be. Granted that dust can be fine enough

to remain suspended for weeks or months in Earth's atmosphere when a volcano like Krakatoa hurls a few cubic miles of it aloft, the moon had not enough gas molecules around it to interfere with the trajectory of a healthy virus particle—and no seismometer in the last four weeks had registered crustal activity even approaching the scale of vulcanism. There was nothing on the moon to throw the dust up, and even less to keep it there.

"Meteor splash?" Shandara made the suggestion hesitantly, fully aware that while a meteor might raise dust it could never keep it aloft. Ridging did not bother to answer, and his friend did not repeat the suggestion.

The sky straight overhead seemed clear as ever; whatever the absorbing material was it apparently took more than the few feet above them to show much effect. That could not be right, though, Ridging reflected, if this stuff was responsible for hiding the features which should have been visible from the crater rim. Maybe it was thicker farther in. If so, they'd better go on—there might be some chance of collecting samples after all.

He put this to Shandara, who agreed; and the two started out across the hundred kilometer plain.

The surface *was* fairly smooth, though a pattern of minute cracks suggestive of the joints formed in cooling basalt covered it almost completely. These were not wide enough even to constitute a tripping danger, and the men ignored them for the time being, though Ridging made a mental note to get a sample of the rock if he could detach one.

The obscuration did thicken as they progressed, and by the time they had gone half a dozen kilometers it was difficult to see the crater wall behind them. Looking up, they saw that all but the brighter stars had faded from view even when the men shaded their eyes from the sunlit rock around them.

"Maybe gas is coming from these cracks, carrying dust up with it?" Shandara was no geologist, but had an imagination. He had also read most of the serious articles which had ever been published about the moon.

"We could check. If that were the case, it should be possible to see currents coming from them; the dust would be thicker just above a crack than a few centimeters away.

If we had something light, like a piece of paper, it might be picked up."

"Worth trying. We have the map," Shandara pointed out. "That should do for paper; the plastic is thin enough." Ridging agreed. With some difficulty—spacesuit gloves were not designed for that purpose—he tore a tiny corner off the sheet on which the map was printed, knelt down, and held the fragment over one of the numerous cracks. It showed no tendency to flutter in his grasp, and when he let go it dropped as rapidly as anything ever did on the moon, to lie quietly directly across the crack he had been testing. He tried to pick it up, but could not get a grip on it with his stiff gloves.

"That one didn't seem to pan out," he remarked, standing up once more.

"Maybe the paper was too heavy—this stuff must be awfully fine—or else it's coming from only a few of the cracks."

"Possibly; but I don't think it's practical to try them all. It would be smarter to figure some way to get a sample of this stuff, and let people with better lab facilities figure out what it is and what holds it off the surface."

"I've been trying to think of a way to do that. If we laid the map out on the ground, some of the material might settle on it."

"Worth trying. If it does, though, we'll have another question—why does it settle there and yet remain suspended long enough to do what is being done? We've been more than an hour coming down the slope, and I'll bet your astronomical friends of the past have reported obscurations longer lasting even than that."

"They have. Well, even if it does raise more problems it's worth trying. Spread out the map, and we'll wait a few minutes." Ridging obeyed; then, to keep the score even, came up with an idea of his own.

"Why don't you lay your camera on the ground pointing up and make a couple of time exposures of the stars? You could repeat them after we get back in the clear, and maybe get some data on the obscuring power of this material."

"Good enough." Shandara removed the camera from its case, clipped a sun shade over its lens, and looked up to find a section of sky with a good selection of stars. As usual, he had to shield his eyes both from sunlight and from the glare of the nearby hills; but even then he did not seem satisfied.

"This stuff is getting thicker, I think," he said. "It's scattering enough light so that it's hard to see any stars at all—harder than it was a few minutes ago, I'd say," Ridging imitated his maneuver, and agreed.

"That's worth recording, too," he pointed out. "Better stay here a while and get several shots at different times." He looked down again. "It certainly *is* getting thicker. I'm having trouble seeing you, now."

Human instincts being what they are, the solution to the mystery followed automatically and immediately. A man who fails, for any reason, to see as clearly as he expects usually rubs his eyes—if he can get at them. A man wearing goggles or a space helmet may just possibly control this impulse, but he follows the practically identical one of wiping the panes through which he looks. Ridging did not have a handkerchief within reach, of course, and the gauntlet of a spacesuit is not one of the best windshield wipers imaginable; but without giving a single thought to the action, he wiped his face plate with his gauntlet.

Had there been no results he would not have been surprised; he had no reason to expect any. He would probably have dismissed the matter, perhaps with a faint hope that his companion might not have noticed the futile gesture. However, there were results. Very marked ones.

The points where the plastic of the gauntlet actually touched the face plate were few; but they left trails all the way across—opaque trails. Surprised and still not thinking, Ridging repeated the gesture in an automatic effort to wipe the smears of whatever it was from his helmet; he only made matters worse. He did not quite cover the supposedly transparent area with glove trails—but in the few seconds after he got control of his hand the streaks spread and merged until nothing whatever was visible. He was not quite in darkness; sunlight penetrated the obscuring layer, but he could not see any details.

"Shan!" The cry contained almost a note of panic. "I can't see at all. Something's covering my helmet!" The cartographer straightened up from his camera and turned toward his friend.

"How come? You look all right from here. I can't see too clearly, though——"

Reflexes are wonderful. It took about five seconds to blind Shandara as thoroughly as Ridging. He couldn't even find his camera to close the shutter.

"You know," said Ridging thoughtfully after two or three minutes of heavy silence, "we should have been able to figure all this out without coming down here."

"Why?"

"Oh, it's plain as anything——"

"Nothing, and I mean *nothing*, is plain right now."

"I suppose a map maker would joke while he was surveying Gehenna. Look, Shan, we have reason to believe there's a magnetic storm going on, which strongly suggests charged particles from the sun. We are standing, for practical purposes, on the moon's south magnetic pole. Most level parts of the moon are covered with dust—but we walked over bare rock from the foot of the rim to here. Don't those items add up to something?"

"Not to me."

"Well, then, add the fact that electrical attraction and repulsion are inverse square forces like gravity, but involve a vastly bigger proportionality constant."

"If you're talking about scale I know all about it, but you still don't paint me a picture."

"All right. There are, at a guess, protons coming from the sun. They are reaching the moon's surface here—virtually all of them, since the moon has a magnetic field but no atmosphere. The surface material is one of the lousiest imaginable electrical conductors, so the dust normally on the surface picks up *and keeps* a charge. And what, dear student, happens to particles carrying like electrical charges?"

"They are repelled from each other."

"Head of the class. And if a hundred-kilometer circle with a rim a couple of kilos high is charged all over, what happens to the dust lying on it?"

Shandara did not answer; the question was too obviously rhetorical. He thought for a moment or two, instead, then asked, "How about our face plates?"

Ridging shrugged—a rather useless gesture, but the time for fighting bad habits had passed some minutes before.

"Bad luck. Whenever two materials rub against each other, electrons come loose. Remember your rubber-and-cat-fur demonstrations in grade school. Unless the materials are of identical electronic make-up, which for practical purposes means unless they are the same substance, one of them will hang onto the electrons a little—or a lot—better than the other, so one will have a negative net charge and the other a positive one. It's our misfortune that the difference between the plastic in our face plates and that in the rest of the suits is the wrong way; when we rubbed the two, the face plates picked up a charge opposite to that of the surrounding dust—probably negative, since I suppose the dust is positive and a transparent material should have a good grip on its electrons."

"Then the rest of our suits, and the gloves we wiped with in particular, ought to be clean."

"Ought to be. I'd like nothing better than a chance to check the point."

"Well, the old cat's fur didn't stay charged very long, as I remember. How long will it take this to leak off, do you think?"

"Why should it leak off at all?"

"What? Why, I should think— Hm-m-m." Shandara was silent for a moment. "Water *is* pretty wonderful stuff, isn't it?"

"Yep. And air has its uses, too."

"Then we're . . . Ridge, we've got to *do* something. Our air will last indefinitely, but you still can't stay in a space-suit too long."

"I agree that we should do something; I just haven't figured out what. Incidentally, just how sure are you that our air will last? The windows of the regenerators are made, as far as I know, of the same plastic our face plates are. What'll you bet you're not using emergency oxygen right now?"

"I don't know—I haven't checked the gauges."

"I'll say you haven't. You won't, either; they're outside your helmet."

"But if we're on emergency now, we could hardly get back to the tractor starting this minute. We've got to get going."

"Which way?"

"Toward the rim!"

"Be specific, son. Just which way is that? And please

don't point; it's rude, and I can't see you anyway."

"All right, don't rub it in. But Ridge, what *can* we do?"

"While this stuff is on our helmets, and possibly our air windows, nothing. We couldn't climb even if we knew which way the hills were. The only thing which will do us the least good is to get this dust off us; and that will do the trick. As my mathematical friends would say, it is necessary and sufficient."

"All right, I'll go along with that. We know that the material the suits are made of is worse than useless for wiping, but wiping and electrical discharge seem to be the only methods possible. What do we have which by any stretch of the imagination might do either job?"

"What is your camera case made of?" asked Ridging.

"As far as I know, same as the suits. It's a regular clip-on carrier, the sort that came with the suits—remember Tazewell's remarks about the dividends AirTight must have paid when they sold the suits to the Project? It reminded me of the old days when you had to buy a lot of accessories with your automobile whether you wanted them or not—"

"All right, you've made your point. The case is the same plastic. It would be a pretty poor wiper anyway; it's a box rather than a bag, as I remember. What else is there?"

The silence following this question was rather lengthy. The sad fact is that spacesuits don't have outside pockets for handkerchiefs. It did occur to Ridging after a time that he was carrying a set of geological specimen bags; but when he finally did think of these and took one out to use as a wiper, the unfortunate fact developed that it, too, left the wrong charge on the face plate of his helmet. He could see the clear, smooth plastic of the bag as it passed across the plate, but the dust collected so fast behind it that he saw nothing of his surroundings. He reflected ruefully that the charge to be removed was now greater than ever. He also thought of using the map, until he remembered that he had put it on the ground and could never find it by touch.

"I never thought," Shandara remarked after another lengthy silence, "that I'd ever miss a damp rag so badly. Blast it, Ridge, there must be *something*."

"Why? We've both been thinking without any result that I can see. Don't tell me you're one of those fellows who think there's an answer to every problem."

"I am. It may not be the answer we want, but there is one. Come on, Ridge, you're the physicist; I'm just a high-priced picture-copier. Whatever answer there is, you're going to have to furnish it: all my ideas deal with maps, and we've done about all we can with those at the moment."

"Hm-m-m. The more I think, the more I remember that there isn't enough fuel on the moon to get a rescue tractor out here, even if anyone knew we were in trouble and could make the trip in time. Still—wait a minute; you said something just then. What was it?"

"I said all my ideas dealt with maps, but—"

"No; before that."

"I don't recall, unless it was that crack about damp rags, which we don't have."

"That was it. That's it, Shan; we don't have any rags, but we do have *water*."

"Yes—inside our spacesuits. Which of us opens up to save the other?"

"Neither one. Be sensible. You know as well as I do that the amount of water in a closed system containing a living person is constantly increasing; we produce it, oxidizing hydrogen in the food we eat. The suits have driers in the air cycler or we couldn't last two hours in them."

"That's right; but how do you get the water out? You can't open your air system."

"You can shut it off, and the check valve will keep air in your suit—remember, there's always the chance someone will have to change emergency tanks. It'll be a job, because we won't be able to see what we're doing, and working by touch through spacesuit gauntlets will be awkward as anything I've ever done. Still, I don't see anything else."

"That means you'll have to work on my suit, then, since I don't know what to do after the line is disconnected. How long can I last before you reconnect? And what do you do, anyway? You don't mean there's a reservoir of liquid water there, do you?"

"No, it's a calcium chloride drier; and it should be fairly moist by now— You've been in the suit for several hours. It's in several sections, and I can take out one and leave you the others, so you won't suffer from its lack. The air in your suit should do you for four or five minutes, and if I can't make the disconnection and disassembly in that time I can't do it at all. Still, it's your suit, and if I do make a mistake it's your life; do you want to take the chance?"

"What have I to lose? Besides, you always were a pretty good mechanic—or if you weren't, please don't tell me. Get to work."

"All right."

As it happened, the job was not started right away, for there was the minor problem of finding Shandara to be solved first. The two men had been perhaps five yards apart when their face plates were first blanked out, but neither could now be sure that he hadn't moved in the meantime, or at least shifted around to face a new direction. After some discussion of the problem, it was agreed that Shandara should stand still, while Ridging walked in what he hoped was the right direction for what he hoped was five yards, and then start from wherever he found himself to quarter the area as well as he could by length of stride. He would have to guess at his turns, since even the sun no longer could penetrate the layer of dust on the helmets.

It took a full ten minutes to bump into his companion, and even then he felt undeservedly lucky.

Shandara lay down, so as to use a minimum of energy while the work was being done. Ridging felt over the connection several times until he was sure he had them right—they were, of course, designed to be handled by spacesuit gauntlets, though not by a blindfolded operator. Then he warned the cartographer, closed the main cutoffs at helmet and emergency tanks to isolate the renewer mechanism, and opened the latter. It was a simple device, designed in throwaway units like a piece of electronic gear, with each unit automatically sealing as it was removed—a fortunate fact if the alga culture on which Shandara's life for the next few hours depended was to survive the operation.

The calcium chloride cells were easy to locate; Ridging removed two of the half dozen to be on the safe side, replaced and reassembled the renewer, tightened the connections, and reopened the valves.

Ridging now had two cans of calcium chloride. He could not tell whether it had yet absorbed enough water actually to go into solution, though he doubted it; but he took no chances. Holding one of the little containers carefully right side up, he opened its perforated top, took a specimen bag and pushed it into the contents. The plastic was not, of course, absorptive—it was not the first time in the past hour he had regretted the change from cloth bags—but the damp crystal should adhere, and the solution if there was any would wet it. He pulled out the material and applied it to his face plate.

It was not until much later that he became sure whether there was any liquid. For the moment it worked, and he found that he could see; he asked no more. Hastily he repeated the process on Shandara's helmet, and the two set out rapidly for the rim. They did not stop to pick up camera or map.

Travel is fast on the moon, but they made less than four hundred meters. Then the face plates were covered again. With a feeling of annoyance they stopped, and Ridging repeated the treatment.

This time it didn't work.

"I supposed you emptied the can while you were jumping," Shandara remarked in an annoyed tone. "Try the other one."

"I didn't empty anything; but I'll try." The contents of the other container proved equally useless, and the cartographer's morale took another slump.

"What happened?" he asked. "And please don't tell me it's obvious, because you certainly didn't foresee it."

"I didn't, but it is. The chloride dried out again."

"I thought it held onto water."

"It does, under certain conditions. Unfortunately its equilibrium vapor pressure at this temperature is higher than the local barometer reading. I don't suppose that every last molecule of water has gone, but what's left isn't sufficient to make a conductor. Our face plates are holding charge again—maybe better than before; there must be some calcium chloride dust on them now, though I don't know offhand what effect it would have."

"There are more chloride cartridges in the cyclers."

"You have four left, which should get us maybe two kilos at the present rate. We can't use mine, since you can't get them out; and if we use all yours you'd never get up the rim. Drying your air isn't just a matter of comfort, you know; that suit has no temperature controls—it depends on radiation balance and insulation. If your perspiration stops evaporating, your inner insulation is done; and in any case, the cartridges won't get us to the rim."

"In other words you think we're done—again."

"I certainly don't have any more ideas."

"Then I suppose I'll have to do some more pointless chattering. If it gave you the last idea, maybe it will work again."

"Go ahead. It won't bother me. I'm going to spend my last hours cursing the character who used a different plastic for the face plate than he did for the rest of these suits."

"All right," Commander Tazewell snapped as the geophysicist paused. "I'm supposed to ask you what you did then. You've just told me that that handkerchief of yours is a good windshield wiper; I'll admit I don't see how. I'll even admit I'm curious, if it'll make you happy."

"It's not a handkerchief, as I said. It's a specimen bag."

"I thought you tried those and found they didn't work —left a charge on your face plate like the glove."

"It did. But a remark I made myself about different kinds of plastic in the suits gave me another idea. It occurred to me that if the dust was, say, positively charged—"

"Probably was. Protons from the sun."

"All right. Then my face plate picked up a negative, and my suit glove a positive, so the dust was attracted to the plate.

"Then when we first tried the specimen bag, it also charged positively and left negative on the face plate.

"Then it occurred to me that the specimen bag *rubbed by the suit* might go negative; and since it was fairly transparent, I could—"

"I get it! You could tie it over your face plate and have a windshield you could see through which would repel the dust."

"That was the idea. Of course, I had nothing to tie it with; I had to hold it."

"Good enough. So you got a good idea out of an idle remark."

"Two of them. The moisture one came from Shan the same way."

"But yours worked." Ridging grinned.

"Sorry. It didn't. The specimen bag still came out negative when rubbed on the suit plastic—at least it didn't do the face plate any good."

Tazewell stared blankly, then looked as though he were about to use violence.

"All right! Let's have it, once and for all."

"Oh, it was simple enough. I worked the specimen bag —I tore it open so it would cover more area—across my face plate, pressing tight so there wouldn't be any dust under it."

"What good would that do? You must have collected more over it right away."

"Sure. Then I rubbed my face plate, dust rag and all, against Shandara's. We couldn't lose; one of them was bound to go positive. I won, and led him up the rim until the ground charge dropped enough to let the dust stick to the surface instead of us. I'm glad no one was there to take pictures, though; I'd hate to have a photo around which could be interpreted as my kissing Shandara's ugly face— even through a space helmet."

Ron Sacco's hand reached gently toward his switch, and paused. He glanced over at the commander, saw the latter's eyes on him, and took a quick look at the clock. Welland turned his own face away—to hide a smile?—and Sacco almost angrily thumbed the switch.

Only one of the watchers could follow the consequences in real detail. To most, the closing of the circuit was marked a split second later by a meaningless pattern on an oscilloscope screen; to "Grumpy" Ries, who had built and installed the instrument, a great deal more occurred between the two events. His mind's eye could see the snapping of relays, the pulsing of electrical energy into the transducers in the ice outside and the hurrying sound waves radiating out through the frozen material; he could visualize their trip, and the equally hasty return as they echoed back from the vacuum that bounded the flying iceberg. He could follow them step by step back through the electronic gear, and interpret the oscilloscope picture almost as well as Sacco. He saw it, and turned away. The others kept their eyes on the physicist.

Sacco said nothing for a moment. He had moved several manual pointers to the limits of the weird shadow on the screen, and was using his slide rule on the resulting numbers. Several seconds passed before he nodded and put the instrument back in its case.

"Well?" sounded several voices at once.

"We're not boiling off uniformly. The maximum loss is at the south pole, as you'd expect; it's about sixty centimeters since the last reading. It decreases almost uniformly to zero at about fifteen degrees north; any loss north of that has been too small for this gear to measure. You'll have to go out and use one of Grumpy's stakes if you want a reading there."

No one answered this directly; the dozen scientists drifting in the air of the instrument room had already started arguments with each other. Most of them bristled with the phrase "I told you—" The commander was listening intently now; it was this sort of thing which had led him, days before, to schedule the radius measurements only once in twelve hours. He had been tempted to stop them altogether, but realized that it would be both impolite and impractical. Men riding a snowball into a blast furnace may not be any better off for knowing how fast the snowball is melting, but being men they *have to know*.

Sacco turned from his panel and called across the room. "What are the odds now?"

"Just what they were before," snapped Ries. "How could they have changed? We've buried ourselves, changed the orbit of this overgrown ice cake until the astronomers were happy, and then spent our time shoveling snow until the exhaust tunnels were full so that we couldn't change course again if we wanted to. Our chances have been nailed down ever since the last second the motors operated, and you know it as well as I do."

"I stand . . . pardon me, float . . . corrected. May I ask what our *knowledge* of the odds is now?" Ries grimaced, and jerked his head toward the commander.

"Probably classified information. You'd better ask the chief executive of Earth's first manned comet how long he expects his command to last."

Welland managed to maintain his unperturbed expression, though this was as close to outright insolence as Ries had come yet. The instrument man was a malcontent by nature, at least as far as speech went; Welland, who was something of a psychologist, was fairly sure that the matter went no deeper. He was rather glad of Ries' presence, which served to bring into the open a lot of worrying which might otherwise have simmered under cover, but that didn't mean that he liked the fellow; few people did. "Grumpy" Ries had earned his nickname well. Welland, on the present occasion, didn't wait for Sacco to repeat the question; he answered it as though Ries had asked him directly—and politely.

"We'll make it," he said calmly. "We knew that long ago, and none of the measures have changed the fact. This comet is over two miles in diameter, and even after our using a good deal of it for reaction mass it still contains over thirty billion tons of ice. I may be no physicist, but I can integrate, and I know how much radiant heat this iceberg is going to intercept in the next week. It's not enough, by a good big factor, to boil off any thirty billion tons of the stuff around us. You all know that—you've been wasting time making a book on how much we'd still have around us after perihelion, and not one of you has figured that we lose more than three or four hundred meters from the outside. If that's not a safe margin, I don't know what is."

"You don't know, and neither do I," retorted Ries. "We're supposed to pass something like a hundred thousand miles from the photosphere. You know as well as I do that the only comet ever to do that came away from the sun as two comets. Nobody ever claimed that it *boiled* away."

"You knew that when you signed up. No one blackmailed you. No one would—at least, no one who's here now." The commander regretted that remark the instant he had made it, but saw no way to retract it. He was afraid for a moment that Ries might make a retort which he couldn't possibly ignore, and was relieved when the instrument man reached for a handhold and propelled himself out of the room. A moment later he forgot the whole incident as a physicist at one of the panels suddenly called out.

"On your toes, all of you! X-ray count is going up— maybe a flare. Anyone who cares, get his gear grinding!" For a moment there was a scene of confusion. Some of the men were drifting free, out of reach of handholds; it took these some seconds to get swimming. Others, more skilled in weightless maneuvering, had kicked off from the nearest wall in the direction of whatever piece of recording machinery they most cherished, but not all of these had made due allowance for the traffic. By the time everyone was strapped in his proper place, Ries was back in the room, his face as expressionless as though nothing had been said a few moments before. His eyes kept swiveling from one station to another; if anyone had been looking at him, they would have supposed he was just waiting for something to break down. He was.

To his surprise, nothing did. The flare ran its course, with instruments humming and clicking serenely and no word of complaint from their attendants. Ries seemed almost disappointed; at least Pawlak, the power plant engineer who was about the only man on board who really liked the instrument specialist, suspected that he was.

"C'mon, Grump," was this individual's remark when everything seemed to have settled down once more. "Let's go outside and bring in the magazine from the monitor camera. Maybe something will have gone wrong with *it;* you said you didn't trust that remote-control system."

Ries almost brightened.

"All right. These astronomers will probably be howling for pictures in five minutes anyway, so they can tell each other they predicted everything correctly. Suit up." They left the room together with no one but the commander noting their departure.

There was little space outside the ship's air lock. The rocket had been brought as close to the center of the comet as measurement would permit, through a tunnel just barely big enough for the purpose. Five more smaller tunnels had been drilled, along three mutually perpendicular axes, to let out the exhaust of the fusion-powered reaction motors which were to use the comet's own mass to change its course. One other passageway, deliberately and carefully zigzagged, had been cut for personnel. Once the sunward course had been established all the tunnels except the last had been filled with "snow"—crushed comet material from near the ship. The cavern left by the removal of this and the exhaust mass was the only open space near the vessel, and even that was not too near. No one had dared weaken the structure of the big iceberg *too* close to the rocket; after all, one comet *had* been seen to divide as it passed the sun.

The monitor camera was some distance from the mouth of the tunnel—necessarily; the passage had been located very carefully. It opened in the "northern" hemisphere, as determined by direction of rotation, so that the camera could be placed at its mouth during perihelion passage and get continuous coverage. This meant, however, that in the comet's present orbital position the sun did not rise at all at the tunnel mouth. Since pictures had to be taken anyway, the camera was at the moment in the southern hemisphere, about a mile from the tunnel mouth.

Some care was needed in reaching it. A space-suited man with a mass of two hundred fifty pounds weighed something like a quarter of an ounce at the comet's surface, and could step away at several times the local escape velocity if he wished—or, for that matter, if he merely forgot himself. A dropped tool, given only the slightest accidental shove sideways, could easily go into orbit about the comet—or leave it permanently. That problem had been solved, though, after a fashion. Ries and Pawlak attached their suits together with a snap-ended coiled length of cable; then they picked up the end of something resembling a length of fine-linked chain which extended off to the southwest and disappeared quickly over the near horizon —or was it around the corner? Was the comet's surface below them, or beside or above? There was not enough weight to give a man the comforting sensation of a definite "up" and "down." The chain had a loop at the end, and both men put one arm through this. Then Ries waved his free arm three times as a signal, and they jumped straight up together on the third wave.

It was not such a ridiculous maneuver if one remembered the chain. This remained tight as the men rose, and pulled them gradually into an arc toward the southwest.

Partway up, they emerged from the comet's shadow, the metal suits glowing like miniature suns themselves. The great, gaseous envelope of a comet looks impressive from outside, seen against a background of black space; but it means exactly nothing as protection from sunlight even at Earth's distance from the sun. At twenty million miles it is much less, if such a thing is possible. The suits were excellent reflectors, but as a necessary consequence they were very poor radiators. Their temperature climbed more slowly than that of the proverbial black body, but it would climb much higher if given time. There would be perhaps thirty minutes before the suits would be too hot for life; and that, of course, was the reason for the leap.

A one-mile walk on the surface of the comet would take far more than half an hour if one intended to stay below circular velocity; swinging to their goal as the bobs on an inverted pendulum, speed limited only by the strength of their legs, should take between ten and twelve minutes. There were rockets on their suits which could have cut even that time down by quite a factor, but neither man thought of using them. They were for *emergency;* if the line holding them to the comet were to part, for example, the motors would come in handy. Not until.

They reached the peak of their arc, the chain pointing straight "down" toward the comet. Their goal had been visible for several minutes, and they had been trying to judge how close to it they would land. A direct hit was nearly impossible; even if they had been good enough to jump exactly straight up, the problem was complicated by the comet's rotation. As it turned out, the error was about two hundred yards, fairly small as such things went.

The landing maneuver was complicated-looking but logical. Half a minute before touchdown, Ries braced his feet against Pawlak and pushed. The engineer kept his grip on the chain and stayed in "orbit" while his companion left him in an apparently straight line. About fifteen seconds sufficed to separate them by the full length of the connecting snap line; the elasticity of this promptly started them back together, though at a much lower speed than they had moved apart. Just before they touched the surface, Ries noted which side of the camera the snap line was about to land on, and deliberately whipped it so that it fell on the other side; then, when both men took up slack, it snubbed against the camera mounting. Even though both men bounced on landing—it was nearly impossible to take up exactly the right amount of energy by muscle control alone—they were secure. Ries sent a couple of more loops rippling down the line and around the camera mount—a trick which had taken some practice to perfect, where there was no gravity to help—and the two men pulled themselves over to their goal. The tendency to whip around it like a mishandled yo-yo as they drew closer was a nuisance but not a catastrophe; both were perfectly familiar with the conservation of angular momentum.

Ries quickly opened the camera, removed the exposed part of the film in its take-up cartridge and replaced and rethreaded another, checked the mounting for several seconds, and the job was done. The trip back was like that out, except for the complication that their landing spot was not in sunlight and control was harder. Five minutes after getting their rope around the pole at the tunnel mouth, they were in the ship. There was no speed limit *inside* the comet.

Once they were inside the air lock, Ries' prophecy was promptly fulfilled. Someone called for pictures before his suit had been off for two minutes. Pawlak watched his friend's blood pressure start up, and after a moment's calculation decided that intervention was in order— Grumpy couldn't be allowed *too* many fights.

"Go develop the stuff," he said. "I'll calm this idiot down."

For a moment it looked as though Ries would rather do his own arguing; then he relaxed, and vanished toward the instrument shop. Pawlak homed on the voice of the complaining astrophysicist, and in the three minutes it took Ries to process the film managed to make the fellow feel properly apologetic. This state of affairs lasted for about ten seconds after the film was delivered.

A group of six or seven scientists were waiting eagerly and had it in a projector almost instantly. For a few seconds after the run started there was silence; then a babble of expostulating voices arose. The general theme seemed to be, "Where's that instrument maker?"

Ries had not gone far, and when he appeared did not seem surprised. He didn't wait to be asked any questions, but took advantage of the instant silence which greeted his entrance.

"Didn't get your flare, did you? I didn't think so. That camera has a half-degree field, and the sun is over two degrees wide seen from here—"

"We know that!" Sacco and two or three others spoke almost together. "But the camera was supposed to scan the whole sun automatically whenever it was turned on from here, and keep doing it until we turned it off!"

"I know. And it didn't scan. I thought it hadn't when I was getting the film—"

"How could you tell? Why didn't you fix it? Or did you? What was wrong, anyway? Why didn't you set it up right in the first place?"

"I could tell that there hadn't been enough film exposed for the time it was supposed to be on. As for fixing it out there, or even finding out what was wrong—don't sound any more idiotic than you can help. It'll have to be brought into the shop. I can't promise how long it'll take to fix it until I know what's wrong."

The expostulation rose almost to a roar at this last remark. The commander, who alone of the group had been silent until now, made a gesture which stilled the others.

"I know it's hard to promise, but please remember one thing," he said. "We're twenty million miles from the sun; we'll be at perihelion in sixty-seven hours. If we pass it without that camera, we'll be missing our principal means

of correlating any new observations with the old ones. I
don't say that without the camera we might as well not be
here, but—"

"I know it," growled Ries. "All right. I knew we should
have laid down a walk cable between here and the blasted
thing when we first set it up, but with people talking about
time and shortage of anchoring pins and all that tripe—"

"I think that last was one of your own points," interjected the commander. "However, we have better things to
do than fix blame. Tell us what help you need in getting the
camera back to the ship."

An hour later, the device came in through the air lock.
Its mass had demanded a slight modification in travel technique; if the chain had broken during a "swing" the rockets would not have been able to return men and camera
both to the comet, in all likelihood. Instead of swinging,
therefore, the workers had pulled straight along the chain,
building up speed until they reached its anchorage and
then slowing down on the other side by applying friction to
the chain as it unwound behind them. An extra man with a
line at the tunnel mouth had simplified the stopping problem on the return trip with the camera.

Four hours later still, Ries had taken the camera completely apart and put it together again, and was in a position
to say that there had been nothing wrong with it. He was
not happy about this discovery, and the scientists who
heard his report were less so. They were rather abusive
about it; and that, of course detonated the instrument
man's temper.

"All right, *you* tell *me* what's wrong!" he snapped at
last. "I can say flatly that nothing is broken or out of
adjustment, and it works perfectly in here. Any genius
who's about to tell me that *in here* isn't *out there* can save
his breath. I know it, and I know that the next thing to do
is take it back out and see if it still works. That's what I'm
doing, if I can spare the time from listening to your
helpful comments." He departed abruptly, donned his suit,
and went outside with the instrument but without Pawlak.
He had no intention of returning to the original camera
site, and needed no help. The tunnel mouth was "outside"
enough, he felt.

It took several more hours to prove that he was right.
At first, the trouble refused to show itself. The camera

tracked beautifully over any sized square of sky that Ries chose to set into its control. Then after half an hour or more, the size of the square began to grow smaller no matter what he did with the controls. Eventually it reached zero. This led him into its interior, as well as he could penetrate it in a spacesuit, but no information was forthcoming. Then, just to be tantalizing, the thing started to work again. On its own, as far as Ries could tell. He was some time longer in figuring out why.

Eventually he came storming back into the ship, fulminating against anyone who had had anything to do either with designing or selecting the device. He was a little happier, since the trouble was demonstrably not his own fault, but not much. He made this very clear to the waiting group as soon as his helmet was off.

"I don't know what genius indulged his yen for subminiaturization," be began, "but he carried it too far. I suppose using a balanced resistance circuit in a control is sensible enough; it'll work at regular temperatures, and it'll work at comet temperatures. The trouble is it won't work unless the different segments are near the *same* temperature; otherwise the resistors can't possibly balance. When I first took the thing outside, it worked fine; it was at ship's temperature. Then it began to leak heat into the comet, and went crazy. Later on, with the whole thing cooled down to comet temperature, it worked again. Nice design!"

"But it had been outside for days before—" began someone, and stopped as he realized what had happened. Ries pounced on him just the same.

"Sure—outside *in the sunlight*. Picking up radiant heat on one side, doing its best to get to equilibrium at a couple of hundred degrees. Conducting heat out into the ice four or five hundred degrees colder on the other side. Nice, uniform—aach!"

"Can't a substitute control be devised?" cut in the commander mildly. "That's your field, after all. Surely you can put something together—"

"Oh, sure. In a minute. We're just loaded with spare parts and gear; rockets always are. While I'm at it I'll try to make the thing wrist-watch size so it will fit in the available space—all we need is a research lab's machine shop. I'll do what I can, but you won't like it. Neither will I." He stormed out to his own shop.

"I'll buy his last remark, anyway," muttered someone. Agreement was general but not too loud.

At fifteen million miles from the sun, with another meter or so boiled off the comet's sunlit surface, Ries emerged with his makeshift. He was plainly in need of sleep, and in even worse temper than usual. He had only one question to ask before getting into his suit.

"Shouldn't the sun be starting to show near the tunnel mouth by now?"

One of the astronomers did a little mental arithmetic. "Yes," he answered. "You won't need to travel anywhere to test the thing. Do you need any help?"

"What for?" growled Ries in his usual pleasant fashion, and disappeared again. The astronomer shrugged. By the time conversation had gotten back to normal the instrument specialist and his camera were in the air lock.

Taking the heavy device out through the tunnel offered only one danger, and that only in the last section—the usual one of going too fast and leaving the comet permanently. To forestall the risk of forcing people to pay final respects to him and regret the camera, he made full use of the loops of safety cable which had been anchored in the tunnel wall. He propped the instrument at the tunnel mouth facing roughly north, and waited for sunrise. This came soon enough. It was the display characteristic of an airless world, since the coma was not dense enough to scatter any light to speak of. The zodiacal light brightened near the horizon; then it merged into pearly corona; then a brilliant crimson eruptive arch prominence appeared, which seemed worth a picture or two to the nonprofessional; and finally came the glaring photosphere on which the test had to be made. It was here that another minor problem developed.

The photosphere, area for angular area, was of course no brighter than when seen from just above Earth's atmosphere; but it was no fainter either, and Ries could not look at it to aim his camera. The only finder on the latter was a direct-view collimating sight, since it was designed for automatic control. After a moment's thought, Ries decided that he could handle this situation too, but, since his solution would probably take longer than the sun would be above the horizon, he simply ran the camera through a few scanning cycles, aiming it by the shape of its own shadow. Then he anchored the machine in the tunnel mouth and made his way back to the ship.

Here he found what he wanted with little difficulty—a three-inch-square interference filter. It was not of the tunable sort, though of course its transmission depended on the angle of incidence of the light striking it, but it was designed for sixty-five hundred Angstroms and would do perfectly well for what he had in mind.

Before he could use it, though, another problem had to be solved. Almost certainly the lining up of the camera and its new control—that is, making sure that the center of its sweep field agreed with the line laid down by the collimator sight—would take quite a while. At fifteen million miles from the sun, one simply doesn't work for long with only a spacesuit as protection. The expedition had, of course, been carefully planned so that no one would have to do any such thing; but the plans had just graduated from history to mythology. Grumpy Ries was either going to work undisturbed in full sunlight, probably for one or two whole hours, or spend twenty minutes cooling off in the tunnel for every ten he spent warming up outside it; and that last would add hours and hours to the job time—with the heating period growing shorter with each hour that passed. A parabolic orbit has one very marked feature; its downhill half is very *steeply* downhill, and speed builds up far too quickly for comfort. It seemed that some means of working outside, if one could be found, would pay for itself. Ries thought he could find one.

He was an artisan rather than a scientist, but he was a good artisan. A painter knows pigments and surfaces, a sculptor knows metal and stone; Ries knew basic physics. He used his knowledge.

Limited as the spare supplies were, they included a number of large rolls of aluminum foil and many spools of wire. He put these to use, and in an hour was ready with a six-foot-square shield of foil, made in two layers a couple of inches apart, the space between them stuffed with pulverized ice from the cavern. In its center was mounted the filter, and besides this a hole big enough to take the camera barrel. The distance between the two openings had been measured carefully; the filter would be in front of the camera sight.

Characteristically, he showed the device to no one. He

made most of it outside the ship, as a matter of fact; and when it was done he towed it rather awkwardly up the tunnel to the place where the camera was stored. Incredibly, twenty minutes later the new control was aligned, the camera mounted firmly on its planned second base at the tunnel mouth, and a control line was being run down the tunnel to the ship. With his usual curtness he reported completion of the job; when the control system had been tested from inside, and the method Ries had used to accomplish the task wormed out of him, the reaction of the scientists almost had him smiling.

Almost; but a hardened grouch doesn't change all at once—if ever.

Ten million miles from Sol's center. Twenty-one hours to go—people were not yet counting minutes. The sun was climbing a little higher above the northern horizon as seen from the tunnel mouth, and remaining correspondingly longer in view each time it rose. Some really good pictures were being obtained; nothing yet which couldn't have been taken from one of the orbital stations near Earth.

Five million miles. Ten hours and fifty minutes. Ries stayed inside, now, and tried to sleep. No one else had time to. Going outside, even to the mouth of the tunnel, was presumed impossible, though the instrument maker had made several more shields. Technically, they were within the corona of the sun, though only of its most tenuous outlying zones—there is, of course, a school of thought that considers the corona as extending well past the Earth's orbit. None of the physicists were wasting time trying to decide what was essentially a matter of definition; they were simply reading and recording every instrument whose field of sensitivity seemed to have the slightest bearing on their current environment, and a good many which seemed unlikely to be useful, but who could tell?

Ries was awake again when they reached the ninety degree point—one quarter of the way around the sun from perihelion. The angular distance the earth travels in three months. Slightly over one million miles from the sun's center. Six hundred thousand miles from the photosphere. Well within *anyone's* definition of the corona; within reach of a really healthy eruptive prominence, had any been in the way. One hour and eighteen minutes from their closest approach—or deepest penetration, if one preferred to put it that way. Few did.

They were hurtling, at some three hundred ten miles per second, into a region where the spectroscope claimed temperatures above two million degrees to exist, where ions of iron and nickle and calcium wandered about with a dozen and more of their electrons stripped away, and where the electrons themselves formed almost a gas in their own right, albeit a highly tenuous one.

It was that lack of density on which the men were counting. A single ion at a "temperature" of two million degrees means nothing; there isn't a human being alive who hasn't been struck by vast numbers of far more energetic particles. No one expected to pick up any serious amount of heat from the corona itself.

The photosphere was another matter. It was an opaque, if still gaseous, "surface" which they would approach within one hundred fifty thousand miles—less than its own diameter by a healthy factor. It had a radiation equilibrium temperature of some six thousand degrees, and would fill a large solid angle of sky; this meant that blackbody equilibrium temperature at their location would not be much below the same value. The comet, of course, was not a black body—and did not retain even the heat which it failed to reflect. The moment a portion of its surface was warmed seriously, that portion evaporated, taking the newly acquired heat energy with it. A new layer, still only a few degrees above absolute zero, was exposed in its turn to the flood of radiation.

That flood was inconceivably intense, of course; careless, non-quantitative thought could picture the comet's vanishing under that bombardment like a snowball in a blast furnace—but the flood wasn't infinite. A definite, measurable amount of energy struck the giant snowball; a definite amount was reflected; a definite, measurable amount was absorbed and warmed up and boiled away the ices of water and ammonia and methane that made it up.

And there was a lot to boil away. Thrust-acceleration ratios had long ago given the scientists the mass of their shelter, and even at a hundred and fifty thousand miles a two and a half mile thick bar of sunlight will take some time to evaporate thirty-five billion tons of ice. The comet would spend only a little over twenty-one hours within five million miles of the sun, and unless several physicists had misplaced the same decimal point, it should last with plenty to spare. The twelve-hour rule on Sacco's echo sounder had been canceled now, and its readings were common knowledge; but none of them caused anxiety.

In they drove. No one could see out, of course; there was nothing like the awed watching of an approaching prominence or gazing into the deceptively pitlike area of a sunspot of which many of them had unthinkingly dreamed. If they could have seen a sunspot at all, it would have been as blinding as the rest of the photosphere—human eyes couldn't discriminate between the two orders of overload. For all any of them knew, they might be going through a prominence at any given second; they wouldn't be able to tell until the instrument records were developed and reduced. The only people who could "see" in any sense at all were the ones whose instruments gave visible as well as recorded readings. Photometers and radiometers did convey a picture to those who understood them; magnetometers and ionization gauges and particle counters meant almost as much; but spectrographs and interferometers and cameras hummed and clicked and whirred without giving any clues to the nature of the meals they were digesting. The accelerometers claimed their share of watchful eyes—if there were any noticeable drag to the medium outside all bets on the comet's future and their own were off—but nothing had shown so far.

They were nineteen minutes from perihelion when a growing sense of complacency was rudely shattered. There was no warning—one could hardly be expected at three hundred twenty-five miles a second.

One instant they were floating at their instruments, doing their allotted work, at peace with the universe; the next there was a violent jolt, sparks flew from exposed metal terminals, and every remote indicator in the vessel went dead.

For a moment there was silence; the phenomenon ended as abruptly as it had started. Then there was a mixed chorus of yells, mostly of surprise and dismay, a few of pain. Some of the men had been burned by spark discharges. One had also been knocked out by an electric shock, and it was fortunate that the emergency lights had not been affected; they sprang automatically to life as the main ones failed, and order was quickly restored. One of the engineers applied mouth-to-mouth respiration to the shock victim—aesthetic or not, it is the only sort practical in the weightless condition—and each of the scientists began trouble shooting.

None of the remote gear registered in any way, but much of the apparatus inside the ship was still functioning, and a tentative explanation was quickly reached.

"Magnetic field," was Mallion's terse comment, "size impossible to tell, just as impossible to tell what formed or maintained it. We went through it at three hundred twenty miles a second, plus. If this ship had been metal, it would probably have exploded; as it was, this general sort of thing was a considered possibility and there are no long conducting paths anywhere in the ship—except the instrument controls. The field intensity was between ten and a hundred Gauss. We've taken all the outside readings we're going to, I'm afraid."

"But we can't stop now!" howled Donegan. "We need pictures—hundreds more of them. How do we correlate all the stuff we have, and the things that will still show on the inside instruments we can still use, unless there are pictures—it's fine to say that this or that or the other thing comes from a prominence, or a flare, or what have you, but we won't *know* it does, or anything about the size of the flare. . . ."

"I understand, sympathize, and agree; but what do you propose to do about it? I'd bet a small but significant sum that the cable coming in through the access tunnel *did* explode. Something certainly stopped the current surge before all the instruments here burned up."

"Come on, Dr. Donegan. Get your suit." It was Ries, of course. The physicist looked at him, must have read his mind, and leaped toward his locker.

"What are you madmen up to?" shouted Mallion. "You can't go out to that camera—you'd be a couple of moths in a candle flame, to put it mildly!"

"Use your brain, not your thalamus, Doc," Ries called over his shoulder. Welland said nothing. Two minutes later the pair of madmen were in the air lock, and sixty seconds after that were floating as rapidly as they dared out the tunnel.

The lights were out, but seeing was easy. There was plenty of illumination from the mouth of the tunnel, crooked as the passage was; and the two had to use the filters on their face plates long before they reached the opening. By that time, the very snow around them seemed to be glowing—and may very well have been doing just that, since light must have filtered for some distance in through the packed crystalloids as well as bounced its way around the tunnel bends.

Ries had left his foil shelters at the first bend. There was some loose snow still on hand from his earlier experiments, and they stuffed as much of this as they could between the thin metal layers, and took several of the sandwiched slabs with them as they gingerly approached the opening. They held one of the larger of these—about four feet square—ahead of them as they went; but it proved insufficient when they got within a few yards of the mouth. The trouble was not that the shield failed, but that it wasn't big enough; no matter how close to the opening they came, the entire sky remained a sea of flame. They retreated a little way and Ries rapidly altered the foil armor, bending the sheets and wiring them together until he had a beehive-shaped affair large enough to shield a man. He used the last of their snow in this assembly.

Covered almost completely, he went alone to the tunnel mouth, and this time had no trouble. He was able to use a loop of control wire as a safety, and by hooking his toes under this reached the instrument. It had settled quite a bit —its case and mounting had transmitted heat as planned to the broad silver feet, and these had maintained good surface contact. Naturally a good deal of comet material had boiled away from under them, and the whole installation was in a pit over two feet deep and eight in width. The general lowering of the comet's surface was less obvious.

The vanes of the legs were fairly well sunk into the surface, but with gravity as it was, the only difficulty in freeing them was the perennial one—the risk of giving too much upward momentum. Ries avoided this, got camera and mounting loose, and as quickly as possible brought them back into the tunnel. There was no need to disconnect the control wire from the main cable; as Mallion had predicted, both had disappeared. Their explosion had scarred a deep groove along the tunnel wall at several points where they had been close to the side. Ries regretted their loss; without them he had some difficulty getting himself and his burden started downward, and he wanted the camera into the tunnel's relative shelter as quickly as possible. With its heat-shedding "feet" out of contact with the ground, it would not take long to heat up dangerously. Also, with the comet now whipping closer and closer to perihelion, there was already an annoyingly large gap in the photographic record.

Back in the tunnel, Ries improvised another set of shields for the camera and its operator, and checked the one he had used to see how much snow remained in it. There was some, but discouragingly little. He placed his helmet against that of Donegan and spoke—the radios were useless in the sun's static.

"You can't go out until we get more snow for this thing, and you'll have to come back every few minutes for a refill. I'd do the photography, but you know better than I what has to be taken. I hope you can make out what you need to see through the sixty-five hundred filter in the shield I made for the finder. I'll be back."

He started back down the tunnel, but at the second turn met another suited figure coming out—with a large bag of snow. He recognized Pawlak by the number on the suit, since the face of the occupant was invisible behind the filter. Ries took the bag and gestured his thanks; Pawlak indicated that he would go back and bring more, and started on this errand. Ries reappeared at the camera soon enough to surprise his companion, but the physicist wasted no time in questions. The two men restuffed the shields with snow, and Donegan went back to the tunnel mouth to do his job.

Through the filter, the angry surface of the sun blazed a fiery orange. Features were clear enough, though not always easy to interpret. Individual "rice grains" were clearly visible; a small spot, badly foreshortened, showed far to one side. By moving his head as far as the shield allowed, the observer could see well away from the camera's line of sight; doing this, of course, blued the sun as the ray path difference between the reflecting layers in the filter was shortened. He could not tell exactly what wavelength he was using at any given angle, but he quickly learned to make use of the rather crude "tuning" that angle change afforded. He began shooting, first the spot and its neighborhood, altering the camera filter wavelength regularly as he did so. Then he found something that might have been a calcium flocculus and took a series around it; then feature after feature caught his eye, and he

shot and shot, trying to get each field through the full
wavelength range of the camera at about fifty Angstrom
intervals plus definite lengths which he knew should be
there—the various series lines of hydrogen and of neutral
and ionized helium particularly, though he did not neglect
such metals as calcium and sodium.

He was distracted by a pull on his armored foot; Ries
had come up, inadequately protected by the single remaining sheet of "parasol," to warn him to recharge his own
shield. Reluctantly he did so, grudging the time. Ries
packed snow against the feet of the camera mounting while
Donegan stuffed it between the foil layers of his shield as
rapidly as his spacesuited hands could work. The moment
this was done he headed back to the tunnel mouth, now
not so far away as it had been, and resumed operations.

They must have been almost exactly at perihelion then.
Donegan neither knew nor cared. He knew that the camera held film enough to let him take one picture a second
for about ninety minutes, and he intended to use all of it if
he could. He simply scanned the sun as completely as his
eyesight, the protecting filter, and his own knowledge permitted, and recorded as completely as possible everything
even slightly out of the ordinary that he saw. He knew that
many instruments were still at work in the ship, even
though many were not, and he knew that some of the
devices on the comet's surface would function—or should
function—automatically even though remote control was
gone; and he intended that there should be a complete
record in pictures of everything which might be responsible for whatever those machines recorded. He did a good
job.

Not too many—in fact, as time went on, too few—yards
below him Ries also worked. If being an instrument
maintenance specialist involved moving snow, and in this
part of the universe it seemed to involve little else, then he
would move snow. He had plenty of it; Pawlak kept bringing more and more bags of the stuff. Also, on his second
trip, the engineer produced a lengthy coil of wire; and at
the first opportunity Ries fastened one end of this to
Donegan's ankle. It served two purposes—it was no longer
necessary to go out to let the fellow know by physical
contact that his time was getting short, and it let the
observer get back to work more quickly. Since he was
belayed to Ries, who could brace himself against the tunnel

walls beyond the bend, there was no worry of going back to the surface too rapidly and being unable to stop.

Ries kept busy. No one ever knew whether he did it silently or not, since the radios were unavailable. It was generally taken for granted that he grumbled as usual, and he may very well have done just that, or even surpassed himself. Hanging weightless in a white-glowing tunnel, trying to read a watch through the heaviest solar filter made for space helmets, holding one end of a line whose other end was keeping a man and a fantastically valuable camera from drifting away and becoming part of the solar corona, all the while trying to organize a number of large plastic sacks of pulverized frozen water, ammonia, and methane which persistently gathered around him would have driven a more self-controlled man than Ries to bad language.

Of course, Donegan didn't map the whole surface. This would take quite a while, using a camera with a half degree field on a surface over ninety-five degrees across, even when the surface in question is partly hidden by the local horizon. It was made even more impossible by their rate of motion; parabolic velocity at a distance of five hundred eighty thousand miles from Sol's center is just about three hundred thirty miles per second, and that produced noticeable relative motion even against a background a hundred and fifty thousand miles away. Features were disappearing below the solar horizon, sometimes, before Donegan could get around to them. Even Ries could think of no solution to this difficulty, when the physicist complained of it on one of his trips for more snow.

At this point, the sun's apparent motion in latitude was more rapid than that in longitude—the comet was changing its direction from the sun more rapidly than it was rotating. The resultant motion across the sky was a little hard to predict, but the physicist knew that the center of the solar disk would set permanently at the latitude of the tunnel mouth an hour and three-quarters after perihelion. The angular size of the disk being what it was, there would be *some* observing after that, but how much depended on what might be called the local time of day, and he had not attempted to figure that out. He simply observed and photographed, except when Ries dragged him forcibly back to get his shield recharged.

Gradually the gigantic disk shrank. It never was far above the local horizon, so there was always something with which to compare it, and the shrinking could be noticed. Also, Ries could tell as time went on that there was a little more snow left in Donegan's shield each time it came back for refilling. Evidently they were past the worst.

But the sun had taken its toll. The mouth of the tunnel was much closer to the ship than it had been; several times Ries had been forced back to another section of tunnel with his snow bags, and each resumption of observation by Donegan had involved a shorter trip than before to the surface. Ries, Donegan, and Pawlak were the only members of the expedition to know just how far the evaporation was progressing, since the echo-sounder had been wrecked by the magnetic field; they were never sure afterward whether this was good or not. Those inside were sustained, presumably, by their faith in mathematics. For the physicists this was adequate, but it might not have been for Ries if he had been with them. In any case, he didn't worry much about the fate of the comet after perihelion had been passed; he had too many other troubles, even though his activity had quickly become routine. This left him free to complain—strictly to himself.

Donegan was furious when he finally realized that the sun was going to set at his observing station while it was still close enough to photograph. Like Ries, however, he had no way of expressing his annoyance so that anyone could hear him; and as it turned out, it would have been wasted breath. Observation was cut even shorter by something else.

They had been driven down to what had been originally the third bend in the tunnel, and at this point the passage ran horizontally for a time. Pawlak had just come to the other end of this straight stretch with what he hoped would be his last load of snow when something settled gently through its roof between him and Ries. He leaped toward it, dropping his burden, and discovered that it was one of the instruments which had been on the surface. Its silver cover was slightly corroded, and the feet of its mounting badly so. Apparently its reflecting powers had been lowered by the surface change, and it was absorbing more energy than an equivalent area of comet; so its temperature had gone up accordingly, and it had melted its way below the rest of the surface.

Low as the sun was, it was shining into the hole left by the instrument; evidently the pit it had made was very broad and shallow. Pawlak made his way around the piece of gear and up to Ries, whose attention was directed elsewhere, and reported what had happened. The instrument man looked back down the tunnel and began to haul in on the line attached to Donegan. The physicist was furious when he arrived, and the fact became evident when the three helmets were brought together.

"What in blazes is going on here?" he fulminated. "You can't make me believe my shield had boiled dry again—I haven't been out five minutes, and the loads are lasting longer now. We're losing the sun, you idiot; I can't come back because someone had a brainstorm or can't read a watch—"

Pawlak interrupted by repeating his report. It did not affect Donegan.

"So what?" he blazed. "We expected that. All the gear around the tunnel mouth has sunk—we're in a big pit now anyway. That's making things still worse—we'll lose sight of the sun that much sooner. Now let me get back and work!"

"Go back and work if you want, provided you can do anything with the naked eye," retorted Ries, "but the camera's going back to the ship pronto. That's one thing we forgot—or maybe it was just assumed that gaseous ammonia in this concentration and at this temperature wouldn't do anything to silver. Maybe it isn't the ammonia, for all I know; maybe it's something we've been picking up from the corona; but look at that camera of yours! The polish is gone; it's picking up heat much faster than it was expected to, and not getting rid of it any quicker. If that magazine of exposed film you have in there gets too hot, you'll have wasted a lot of work. Now come on, or else let me take the camera back." Ries started along the tunnel without further words, and the physicist followed reluctantly.

Inside, Donegan disappeared with his precious film magazine, without taking time to thank Ries.

"Self-centered character," he muttered. "Not a word to anyone—just off to develop his film before somebody opens the cartridge, I suppose."

"You can't blame him," Ries said mildly. "He did a lot of work for it."

"*He* did a lot of work? How about us? How about you; it was all your idea in the first place—"

"Careful, Joe, or they'll be taking my nickname away from me and giving it to you. Come on; I want to see Doc Sonne. My feet hurt." He made his way to the main deck, and Pawlak drifted after him, grumbling. By the time the engineer arrived, the rest of the group was overwhelming Ries with compliments, and the fellow was grinning broadly. It began to look as though the name "Grumpy" *would* have to find a new owner.

But habit is hard to break. The doctor approached, and without removing his patient's shoes dredged a tube of ointment out of his equipment bag.

"Burn ointment," the doctor replied. "It'll probably be enough; you shouldn't have taken too bad a dose. I'll have you patched up in a minute. Let's get those shoes off."

"Now wouldn't you know it," said Ries aloud. "Not even the doctor around here can do the right thing at the right time. Physicists who want A's gear fixed on B's time— won't let a man go out to do a job in the only way it can be done—won't give a person time to rest—and now," it was the old Grumpy back again, "a man spends two hours or so swimming around among sacks of frozen methane, which melts at about a hundred and eighty-five degrees Centigrade below zero—that's about two hundred and ninety below, Fahrenheit, doctor—and the doctor wants to use *burn ointment*. Break out the frostbite remedy, will you, please? My feet hurt."

"So you've left us, Mr. Cunningham!" Malmeson's voice sounded rougher than usual, even allowing for headphone distortion and the ever-present Denebian static. "Now, that's too bad. If you'd chosen to stick around, we would have put you off on some world where you could live, at least. Now you can stay here and fry. And I hope you live long enough to watch us take off—without you!"

Laird Cunningham did not bother to reply. The ship's radio compass should still be in working order, and it was just possible that his erstwhile assistants might start hunting for him, if they were given some idea of the proper direction to begin a search. Cunningham was too satisfied with his present shelter to be very anxious for a change. He was scarcely half a mile from the grounded ship, in a cavern deep enough to afford shelter from Deneb's rays when it rose, and located in the side of a small hill, so that he could watch the activities of Malmeson and his companion without exposing himself to their view.

In a way, of course, the villain was right. If Cunningham permitted the ship to take off without him, he might as well open his face plate; for, while he had food and oxygen for several days' normal consumption, a planet scarcely larger than Luna, baked in rays of one of the fiercest radiating bodies in the galaxy, was most unlikely to provide further supplies when these ran out. He wondered how long it would take the men to discover the damage he had done to the drive units in the few minutes that had elapsed between the crash landing and their breaking through the control room door, which Cunningham had welded shut when he had discovered their intentions. They might not notice it at all; he had severed a number of inconspicuous connections at odd points. Perhaps they would not even test the drivers until they had completed repairs to the cracked hull. If they didn't, so much the better.

Cunningham crawled to the mouth of his cave and

looked out across the shallow valley in which the ship lay.
It was barely visible in the starlight, and there was no sign
of artificial luminosity to suggest that Malmeson might
have started repairs at night. Cunningham had not expected that they would, but it was well to be sure. Nothing
more had come over his suit radio since the initial out-
burst, when the men had discovered his departure; he
decided that they must be waiting for sunrise, to enable
them to take more accurate stock of the damage suffered
by the hull.

He spent the next few minutes looking at the stars,
trying to arrange them into patterns he could remember.
He had no watch, and it would help to have some warning
of approaching sunrise on succeeding nights. It would not
do to be caught away from his cave, with the flimsy protection his suit could afford from Deneb's radiation. He
wished he could have filched one of the heavier work suits;
but they were kept in a compartment forward of the
control room, from which he had barred himself when he
had sealed the door of the latter chamber.

He remained at the cave mouth, lying motionless and
watching alternately the sky and the ship. Once or twice he
may have dozed; but he was awake and alert when the low
hills beyond the ship's hull caught the first rays of the
rising sun. For a minute or two they seemed to hang
detached in a black void, while the flood of blue-white light
crept down their slopes; then, one by one, their bases
merged with each other and the ground below to form a
connected landscape. The silvery hull gleamed brilliantly,
the reflection from it lighting the cave behind Cunningham
and making his eyes water when he tried to watch for the
opening of the air lock.

He was forced to keep his eyes elsewhere most of the
time, and look only in brief glimpses at the dazzling metal;
and in consequence, he paid more attention to the details of
his environment than he might otherwise have done. At the
time, this circumstance annoyed him; he has since been
heard to bless it fervently and frequently.

Although the planet had much in common with Luna as
regarded size, mass, and airlessness, its landscape was
extremely different. The daily terrific heatings which it
underwent, followed by abrupt and equally intense temperature drops each night, had formed an excellent substitute
for weather; and elevations that might at one time have

rivaled the Lunar ranges were now mere rounded hill-
ocks, like that containing Cunningham's cave. As on the
Earth's moon, the products of the age-long spalling had
taken the form of fine dust, which lay in drifts everywhere. What could have drifted it, on an airless and consequently windless planet, struck Cunningham as a puzzle of
the first magnitude; and it bothered him for some time
until his attention was taken by certain other objects upon
and between the drifts. These he had thought at first to be
outcroppings of rock; but he was at last convinced that
they were specimens of vegetable life—miserable, lichenous specimens, but nevertheless vegetation. He wondered
what liquid they contained, in an environment at a temperature well above the melting point of lead.

The discovery of animal life—medium-sized, crablike
things, covered with jet-black integument, that began to dig
their way out of the drifts as the sun warmed them—
completed the job of dragging Cunningham's attention
from his immediate problems. He was not a zoologist by
training, but the subject had fascinated for years; and he
had always had money enough to indulge his hobby. He
had spent years wandering the Galaxy in search of bizarre
life forms—proof, if any were needed, of a lack of scientific training—and terrestrial museums had always been
more than glad to accept the collections that resulted from
each trip and usually to send scientists of their own in his
footsteps. He had been in physical danger often enough,
but it had always been from the life he studied or from the
forces which make up the interstellar traveler's regular
diet, until he had overheard the conversation which informed him that his two assistants were planning to do
away with him and appropriate the ship for unspecified
purposes of their own. He liked to think that the prompt-
ness of his action following the discovery at least indicated
that he was not growing old.

But he did let his attention wander to the Denebian life
forms.

Several of the creatures were emerging from the dust
mounds within twenty or thirty yards of Cunningham's
hiding place, giving rise to the hope that they would come
near enough for a close examination. At that distance, they
were more crablike than ever, with round, flat bodies
twelve to eighteen inches across, and several pairs of legs.

They scuttled rapidly about, stopping at first one of the lichenous plants and then another, apparently taking a few tentative nibbles from each, as though they had delicate tastes which needed pampering. Once or twice there were fights when the same tidbit attracted the attention of more than one claimant; but little apparent damage was done on either side, and the victor spent no more time on the meal he won than on that which came uncontested.

Cunningham became deeply absorbed in watching the antics of the little creatures, and completely forgot for a time his own rather precarious situation. He was recalled to it by the sound of Malmeson's voice in his headphones.

"Don't look up, you fool; the shields will save your skin, but not your eyes. Get under the shadow of the hull, and we'll look over the damage."

Cunningham instantly transferred his attention to the ship. The air lock on the side toward him—the port—was open, and the bulky figures of his two ex-assistants were visible standing on the ground beneath it. They were clad in the heavy utility suits which Cunningham had regretted leaving, and appeared to be suffering little or no inconvenience from the heat, though they were still standing full in Deneb's light when he looked. He knew that hard radiation burns would not appear for some time, but he held little hope of Deneb's more deadly output coming to his assistance; for the suits were supposed to afford protection against this danger as well. Between heat insulation, cooling equipment, radiation shielding, and plain mechanical armor, the garments were so heavy and bulky as to be an almost insufferable burden on any major planet. They were more often used in performing exterior repairs in space.

Cunningham watched and listened carefully as the men stooped under the lower curve of the hull to make an inspection of the damage. It seemed, from their conversation, to consist of a dent about three yards long and half as wide, about which nothing could be done, and a series of radially arranged cracks in the metal around it. These represented a definite threat to the solidity of the ship, and would have to be welded along their full lengths before it would be safe to apply the stresses incident to second-order flight. Malmeson was too good an engineer not to realize this fact, and Cunningham heard him lay plans for bringing power lines outside for the welder and jacking up the hull to permit access to the lower portions of the cracks. The latter operation was carried out immediately, with an efficiency which did not in the least surprise the hidden watcher. After all, he had hired the men.

Every few minutes, to Cunningham's annoyance, one of the men would carefully examine the landscape; first on the side on which he was working, and then walking around the ship to repeat the performance. Even in the low gravity, Cunningham knew he could not cross the half mile that lay between him and that inviting air lock, between two of those examinations; and even if he could, his leaping figure, clad in the gleaming metal suit, would be sure to catch even an eye not directed at it. It would not do to make the attempt unless success were certain; for his unshielded suit would heat in a minute or two to an unbearable temperature, and the only place in which it was possible either to remove or cool it was on board the ship. He finally decided, to his annoyance, that the watch would not slacken so long as the air lock of the ship remained open. It would be necessary to find some means to distract or—an unpleasant alternative for a civilized man—disable the opposition while Cunningham got aboard, locked the others out, and located a weapon or other factor which would put him in a position to give them orders. At that, he reflected, a weapon would scarcely be necessary; there was a perfectly good medium transmitter on board, if the men had not destroyed or discharged it, and he need merely call for help and keep the men outside until it arrived.

This, of course, presupposed some solution to the problem of getting aboard unaccompanied. He would, he decided, have to examine the ship more closely after sunset. He knew the vessel as well as his own home—he had spent more time on her than in any other home—and knew that there was no means of entry except through the two main locks forward of the control room, and the two smaller, emergency locks near the stern, one of which he had employed on his departure. All these could be dogged shut from within; and offhand he was unable to conceive a plan for forcing any of the normal entrances. The view ports were too small to admit a man in a spacesuit, even if the panes could be broken; and there was literally no other way into the ship so long as the hull remained intact. Malmeson would not have talked so glibly of welding them sufficiently well to stand flight, if any of the cracks incurred on the landing had been big enough to admit a human body—or even that of a respectably healthy garter snake.

Cunningham gave a mental shrug of the shoulders as these thoughts crossed his mind, and reiterated his decision to take a scouting sortie after dark. For the rest of the day he divided his attention between the working men and the equally busy life forms that scuttled here and there in front of his cave; and he would have been the first to admit that he found the latter more interesting.

He still hoped that one would approach the cave closely enough to permit a really good examination, but for a long time he remained unsatisfied. Once, one of the creatures came within a dozen yards and stood "on tiptoe"—rising more than a foot from the ground on its slender legs, while a pair of antennae terminating in knobs the size of human eyeballs extended themselves several inches from the black carapace and waved slowly in all directions. Cunningham thought that the knobs probably did serve as eyes, though from his distance he could see only a featureless black sphere. The antennae eventually waved in his direction, and after a few seconds spent, apparently in assimilating the presence of the cave mouth, the creature settled back to its former low-swung carriage and scuttled away. Cunningham wondered if it had been frightened at his presence; but he felt reasonably sure that no eye adapted to Denebian daylight could see past the darkness of his threshold, and he had remained motionless while the creature was conducting its inspection. More probably it had some reason to fear caves, or merely darkness.

That it had reason to fear something was shown when another creature, also of crustacean aspect but considerably larger than those Cunningham had seen to date, appeared from among the dunes and attacked one of the latter. The fight took place too far from the cave for Cunningham to make out many details, but the larger animal quickly overcame its victim. It then apparently dismembered the vanquished, and either devoured the softer flesh inside the black integument or sucked the body fluids from it. Then the carnivore disappeared again, presumably in search of new victims. It had scarcely gone when another being, designed along the lines of a centipede and fully forty feet in length, appeared on the scene with the graceful flowing motion of its terrestrial counterpart.

For a few moments the newcomer nosed around the remains of the carnivore's feast, and devoured the larger fragments. Then it appeared to look around as though for more, evidently saw the cave, and came rippling toward it, to Cunningham's pardonable alarm. He was totally unarmed, and while the centipede had just showed itself not to be above eating carrion, it looked quite able to kill its own food if necessary. It stopped, as the other investigator had, a dozen yards from the cave mouth; and like the other, elevated itself as though to get a better look. The baseball-sized black "eyes" seemed for several seconds to stare into Cunningham's more orthodox optics; then, like its predecessor, and to the man's intense relief, it doubled back along its own length and glided swiftly out of sight. Cunningham again wondered whether it had detected his presence, or whether caves or darkness in general spelled danger to these odd life forms.

It suddenly occurred to him that, if the latter were not the case, there might be some traces of previous occupants of the cave; and he set about examining the place more closely, after a last glance which showed him the two men still at work jacking up the hull.

There was drifted dust even here, he discovered, particularly close to the walls and in the corners. The place was bright enough, owing to the light reflected from outside objects, to permit a good examination—shadows on airless worlds are not so black as many people believe—and almost at once Cunningham found marks in the dust that could easily have been made by some of the creatures he had seen. There were enough of them to suggest that the cave was a well-frequented neighborhood; and it began to look as though the animals were staying away now because of the man's presence.

Near the rear wall he found the empty integument that had once covered a four-jointed leg. It was light, and he saw that the flesh had either been eaten or decayed out, though it seemed odd to think of decay in an airless environment suffering such extremes of temperature—though the cave was less subject to this effect than the outer world. Cunningham wondered whether the leg had been carried in by its rightful owner, or as a separate item on the menu of something else. If the former, there might be more relics about.

There were. A few minutes' excavation in the deeper layers of dust produced the complete exoskeleton of one of the smaller crablike creatures; and Cunningham carried the remains over to the cave mouth, so as to examine them and watch the ship at the same time.

The knobs he had taken for eyes were his first concern. A close examination of their surfaces revealed nothing, so he carefully tried to detach one from its stem. It finally cracked raggedly away, and proved, as he had expected, to be hollow. There was no trace of a retina inside, but there was no flesh in any of the other pieces of shell, so that proved nothing. As a sudden thought struck him, Cunningham held the front part of the delicate black bit of shell in front of his eyes; and sure enough, when he looked in the direction of the brightly gleaming hull of the spaceship, a spark of light showed through an almost microscopic hole. The sphere *was* an eye, constructed on the pinhole principle—quite an adequate design on a world furnished with such an overwhelming luminary. It would be useless at night, of course, but so would most other visual organs here; and Cunningham was once again faced with the problem of how any of the creatures had detected his presence in the cave—his original belief, that no eye adjusted to meet Deneb's glare could look into its relatively total darkness, seemed to be sound.

He pondered the question, as he examined the rest of the skeleton in a half-hearted fashion. Sight seemed to be out, as a result of his examination; smell and hearing were ruled out by the lack of atmosphere; taste and touch could not even be considered under the circumstances. He hated to fall back on such a time-honored refuge for ignorance as "extrasensory perception," but he was unable to see any way around it.

It may seem unbelievable that a man in the position Laird Cunningham occupied could let his mind become so utterly absorbed in a problem unconnected with his personal survival. Such individuals do exist, however; most people know someone who has shown some trace of such a trait; and Cunningham was a well-developed example. He had a single-track mind, and had intentionally shelved his personal problem for the moment.

His musings were interrupted, before he finished dissecting his specimen, by the appearance of one of the carnivorous creatures at what appeared to constitute a marked distance—a dozen yards from his cave mouth, where it rose up on the ends of its thin legs and goggled around at the landscape. Cunningham, half in humor and half in honest curiosity, tossed one of the dismembered legs from the skeleton in his hands at the creature. It obviously saw the flying limb; but it made no effort to pursue or devour it. Instead, it turned its eyes in Cunningham's direction, and proceeded with great haste to put one of the drifts between it and what it evidently considered a dangerous neighborhood.

It seemed to have no memory to speak of, however; for a minute or two later Cunningham saw it creep into view again, stalking one of the smaller creatures which still swarmed everywhere, nibbling at the plants. He was able to get a better view of the fight and the feast that followed than on the previous occasion, for they took place much nearer to his position; but this time there was a rather different ending. The giant centipede, or another of its kind, appeared on the scene while the carnivore was still at its meal, and came flowing at a truly surprising rate over the dunes to fall on victor and vanquished alike. The former had no inkling of its approach until much too late; and both black bodies disappeared into the maw of the creature Cunningham had hoped was merely a scavenger.

What made the whole episode of interest to the man was the fact that in its charge, the centipede loped unheeding almost directly through a group of the plant-eaters; and these, by common consent, broke and ran at top speed directly toward the cave. At first he thought they would swerve aside when they saw what lay ahead; but evidently he was the lesser of two evils, for they scuttled past and even over him as he lay in the cave mouth, and began to bury themselves in the deepest dust they could find. Cunningham watched with pleasure, as an excellent group of specimens thus collected themselves for his convenience.

As the last of them disappeared under the dust, he turned back to the scene outside. The centipede was just finishing its meal. This time, instead of immediately wandering out of sight, it oozed quickly to the top of one of the larger dunes, in full sight of the cave, and deposited its length in the form of a watch spring, with the head resting above the coils. Cunningham realized that it was able, in this position, to look in nearly all directions and, owing to the height of its position, to a considerable distance.

With the centipede apparently settled for a time, and the men still working in full view, Cunningham determined to inspect one of his specimens. Going to the nearest wall, he bent down and groped cautiously in the dust. He encountered a subject almost at once, and dragged a squirming black crab into the light. He found that if he held it upside down on one hand, none of its legs could get a purchase on anything; and he was able to examine the underparts in detail in spite of the wildly thrashing limbs. The jaws, now opening and closing futilely on a vacuum, were equipped with a set of crushers that suggested curious things about the plants on which it fed; they looked capable of flattening the metal finger of Cunningham's spacesuit, and he kept his hand well out of their reach.

He became curious as to the internal mechanism that permitted it to exist without air, and was faced with the problem of killing the thing without doing it too much mechanical damage. It was obviously able to survive a good many hours without the direct radiation of Deneb, which was the most obvious source of energy, although its body temperature was high enough to be causing the man some discomfort through the glove of his suit; so "drowning" in darkness was impractical. There might, however, be some part of its body on which a blow would either stun or kill it; and he looked around for a suitable weapon.

There were several deep cracks in the stone at the cave mouth, caused presumably by thermal expansion and contraction; and with a little effort he was able to break loose a pointed, fairly heavy fragment. With this in his right hand, he laid the creature on its back on the ground, and hoped it had something corresponding to a solar plexus.

It was too quick for him. The legs, which had been unable to reach his hand when it was in the center of the creature's carapace, proved supple enough to get a purchase on the ground; and before he could strike, it was right side up and departing with a haste that put to shame its previous efforts to escape from the centipede.

Cunningham shrugged, and dug out another specimen. This time he held it in his hand while he drove the point of his rock against its plastron. There was no apparent effect; he had not dared to strike too hard, for fear of crushing the shell. He struck several more times, with identical results and increasing impatience; and at last there occurred the result he had feared. The black armor gave way, and the point penetrated deeply enough to insure the damage of most of the interior organs. The legs gave a final twitch or two, and ceased moving, and Cunningham gave an exclamation of annoyance.

On hope, he removed the broken bits of shell, for a moment looked in surprise at the liquid which seemed to have filled the body cavities. It was silvery, even metallic in color; it might have been mercury, except that it wet the organs bathed in it and was probably at a temperature above the boiling point of that metal. Cunningham had just grasped this fact when he was violently bowled over, and the dead creature snatched from his grasp. He made a complete somersault, bringing up against the rear wall of the cave; and as he came upright he saw to his horror that the assailant was none other than the giant centipede.

It was disposing with great thoroughness of his specimen, leaving at last only a few fragments of shell that had formed the extreme tips of the legs; and as the last of these fell to the ground, it raised the fore part of its body from the ground, as the man had seen it do before, and turned the invisible pinpoints of its pupils on the space-suited human figure.

Cunningham drew a deep breath, and took a firm hold of his pointed rock, though he had little hope of overcoming the creature. The jaws he had just seen at work had seemed even more efficient than those of the plant-eater, and they were large enough to take in a human leg.

For perhaps five seconds both beings faced each other without motion; then, to the man's inexpressible relief, the centipede reached the same conclusion to which its previous examination of humanity had led it, and departed in evident haste. This time it did not remain in sight, but was still moving rapidly when it reached the limit of Cunningham's vision.

The naturalist returned somewhat shakily to the cave mouth, seated himself where he could watch his ship, and began to ponder deeply. A number of points seemed interesting on first thought, and on further cerebration became positively fascinating. The centipede had not seen, or at least had not pursued, the plant-eater that had escaped from Cunningham and run from the cave. Looking back, he realized that the only times he had seen the creature attack was after "blood" had been already shed—twice by one of the carnivorous animals, the third time by Cunningham himself. It had apparently made no difference where the victims had been—two in full sunlight, one in the darkness of the cave. More proof, if any were needed, that the creatures could see in both grades of illumination. It was not strictly a carrion eater, however; Cunningham remembered that carnivore that had accompanied its victim into the centipede's jaws. It was obviously capable of overcoming the man, but had twice retreated precipitately when it had excellent opportunities to attack him. What was it, then, that drew the creature to scenes of combat and bloodshed, but frightened it away from a man; that frightened, indeed, all of these creatures?

On any planet that had a respectable atmosphere, Cunningham would have taken one answer for granted—scent. In his mind, however, organs of smell were associated with breathing apparatus, which these creatures obviously lacked.

Don't ask why he took so long. You may think that the terrific adaptability evidenced by those strange eyes would be clue enough; or perhaps you may be in a mood to excuse him. Columbus probably excused those of his friends who failed to solve the egg problem.

Of course, he got it at last, and was properly annoyed with himself for taking so long about it. An eye, to us, is an organ for forming images of the source of such radiation as may fall on it; and a nose is a gadget that tells its owner of the presence of molecules. He needs his imagination to picture the source of the latter. But what would you call an organ that forms a picture of the source of smell?

For that was just what those "eyes" did. In the nearly perfect vacuum of this little world's surface, gases diffused at high speed—and their molecules traveled in practically straight lines. There was nothing wrong with the idea of a pinhole camera eye, whose retina was composed of olfactory nerve endings rather than the rods and cones of photosensitive organs.

That seemed to account for everything. Of course the creatures were indifferent to the amount of light reflected from the object they examined. The glare of the open spaces under Deneb's rays, and the relative blackness of a cave, were all one to them—provided something were diffusing molecules in the neighborhood. And what doesn't? Every substance, solid or liquid, has its vapor pressure; under Deneb's rays even some rather unlikely materials probably evaporated enough to affect the organs of these life forms—metals, particularly. The life fluid of the creatures was obviously metal—probably lead, tin, bismuth, or some similar metals, or still more probably, several of them in a mixture that carried the substances vital to the life of their body cells. Probably much of the make-up of those cells was in the form of colloidal metals.

But that was the business of the biochemists. Cunningham amused himself for a time by imagining the analogy between smell and color which must exist here; light gases, such as oxygen and nitrogen, must be rare, and the tiny quantities that leaked from his suit would be absolutely new to the creatures that intercepted them. He must have affected their nervous systems the way fire did those of terrestrial wild animals. No wonder even the centipede had thought discretion the better part of valor!

With his less essential problem solved for the nonce, Cunningham turned his attention to that of his own survival; and he had not pondered many moments when he realized that this, as well, might be solved. He began slowly to smile, as the discrete fragments of an idea began to sort themselves out and fit properly together in his mind—an idea that involved the vapor pressure of metallic blood, the leaking qualities of the utility suits worn by his erstwhile assistants, and the blood-thirstiness of his many-legged acquaintances of the day; and he had few doubts about any of those qualities. The plan became complete, to his satisfaction; and with a smile on his face, he settled himself to watch until sunset.

Deneb had already crossed a considerable arc of the sky. Cunningham did not know just how long he had, as he lacked a watch; and it was soon borne in on him that time passes much more slowly when there is nothing to occupy it. As the afternoon drew on, he was forced away from the cave mouth; for the descending star was beginning to shine in. Just before sunset, he was crowded against one side; for Deneb's fierce rays shone straight through the entrance and onto the opposite wall, leaving very little space not directly illuminated. Cunningham drew a sigh of relief for more reasons than one when the upper limb of the deadly luminary finally disappeared.

His specimens had long since recovered from their fright, and left the cavern; he had not tried to stop them. Now, however, he emerged from the low entryway and went directly to the nearest dust dune, which was barely visible in the starlight. A few moments' search was rewarded with one of the squirming plant-eaters, which he carried back into the shelter; then, illuminating the scene carefully with the small torch that was clipped to the waist of his suit, he made a fair-sized pile of dust, gouged a long groove in the top with his toe, with the aid of the same stone he had used before, he killed the plant-eater and poured its "blood" into the dust mold.

The fluid was metallic, all right; it cooled quickly, and in two or three minutes Cunningham had a silvery rod about as thick as a pencil and five or six inches long. He had been a little worried about the centipede at first; but the creature was either not in line to "see" into the cave, or had dug in for the night like its victims.

Cunningham took the rod, which was about as pliable as a strip of solder of the same dimensions, and, extinguishing the torch, made his way in a series of short, careful leaps to the stranded spaceship. There was no sign of the men, and they had taken their welding equipment inside with them—that is, if they had ever had it out; Cunningham had not been able to watch them for the last hour of daylight. The hull was still jacked up, however; and the naturalist eased himself under it and began to examine the damage, once more using the torch. It was about as he had deduced from the conversation of the men; and with a smile, he took the little metal stick and went to work. He was busy for some time under the hull, and once he emerged, found another plant-eater, and went back underneath. After he had finished, he walked once around the ship, checking each of the air locks and finding them sealed, as he had expected.

He showed neither surprise nor disappointment at this; and without further ceremony he made his way back to the cave, which he had a little trouble finding in the star-light. He made a large pile of the dust, for insulation rather than bedding, lay down on it, and tried to sleep. He had very little success, as he might have expected.

Night, in consequence, seemed unbearably long; and he almost regretted his star study of the previous darkness, for now he was able to see that sunrise was still distant, rather than bolster his morale with the hope that Deneb would be in the sky the next time he opened his eyes. The time finally came, however, when the hilltops across the valley leaped one by one into brilliance as the sunlight caught them; and Cunningham rose and stretched himself. He was stiff and cramped, for a spacesuit makes a poor sleeping costume even on a better bed than a stone floor.

As the light reached the spaceship and turned it into a blazing silvery spindle, the air lock opened. Cunningham had been sure that the men were in a hurry to finish their task, and were probably awaiting the sun almost as eagerly as he in order to work efficiently; he had planned on this basis.

Malmeson was the first to leap to the ground, judging by their conversation, which came clearly through Cunning-ham's phones. He turned back, and his companion handed down to him the bulky diode welder and a stack of filler rods. Then both men made their way forward to the dent where they were to work. Apparently they failed to notice the bits of loose metal lying on the scene—perhaps they had done some filing themselves the day before. At any rate, there was no mention of it as Malmeson lay down and slid under the hull, and the other began handing equipment in to him.

Plant-eaters were beginning to struggle out of their dust beds as the connections were completed, and the torch started to flame. Cunningham nodded in pleasure as he noted this; things could scarcely have been timed better had the men been consciously co-operating. He actually emerged from the cave, keeping in the shadow of the hillock, to increase his field of view; but for several min-utes nothing but plant-eaters could be seen moving.

He was beginning to fear that his invited guests were too distant to receive their call, when his eye caught a glimpse of a long, black body slipping silently over the dunes toward the ship. He smiled in satisfaction; and then his eyebrows suddenly rose as he saw a second snaky form following the tracks of the first.

He looked quickly across his full field of view, and was rewarded by the sight of four more of the monsters—all heading at breakneck speed straight for the spaceship. The beacon he had lighted had reached more eyes than he had expected. He was sure that the men were armed, and had never intended that they actually be overcome by the creatures; he had counted on a temporary distraction that would let him reach the air lock unopposed.

He stood up, and braced himself for the dash, as Malmeson's helper saw the first of the charging centipedes and called the welder from his work. Malmeson barely had time to gain his feet when the first pair of attackers reached them; and at the same instant Cunningham emerged into the sunlight, putting every ounce of his strength into the leaps that were carrying him toward the only shelter that now existed for him.

He could feel the ardor of Deneb's rays the instant they struck him; and before he had covered a third of the distance the back of his suit was painfully hot. Things were hot for his ex-crew as well; fully ten of the black monsters had reacted to the burst of—to them—overpoweringly attractive odor—or gorgeous color?—that had resulted when Malmeson had turned his welder on the metal where Cunningham had applied the frozen blood of their natural prey; and more of the same substance was now vaporizing under Deneb's influence as Malmeson, who had been lying in fragments of it stood fighting off the attackers. He had a flame pistol, but it was slow to take effect on creatures whose very blood was molten metal; and his companion, wielding the diode unit on those who got too close, was no better off. They were practically swamped under wriggling bodies as they worked their way toward the air lock; and neither man saw Cunningham as, staggering even under the feeble gravity that was present, and fumbling with eye shield misted with sweat, he reached the same goal and disappeared within.

Being a humane person, he left the outer door open; but he closed and dogged the inner one before proceeding with a more even step to the control room. Here he unhurriedly removed his spacesuit, stopping only to open the switch of the power socket that was feeding the diode unit as he heard the outer lock door close. The flame pistol would make no impression on the alloy of the hull, and he felt no qualms about the security of the inner door. The men were safe, from every point of view.

With the welder removed from the list of active menaces, he finished removing his suit, turned to the medium transmitter, and coolly broadcast a call for help and his position in space. Then he turned on a radio transmitter, so that the rescuers could find him on the planet; and only then did he contact the prisoners on the small set that was tuned to the suit radios, and tell them what he had done.

"I didn't mean to do you any harm," Malmeson's voice came back. "I just wanted the ship. I know you paid us pretty good, but when I thought of the money that could be made on some of those worlds if we looked for something besides crazy animals and plants, I couldn't help myself. You can let us out now; I swear we won't try anything more—the ship won't fly, and you say a Guard flyer is on the way. How about that?"

"I'm sorry you don't like my hobby," said Cunningham. "I find it entertaining; and there have been times when it was even useful, though I won't hurt your feelings by telling you about the last one. I think I shall feel happier if the two of you stay right there in the air lock; the rescue ship should be here before many hours, and you're fools if you haven't food and water in your suits."

"I guess you win, in that case," said Malmeson.

"I think so, too," replied Cunningham, and switched off.

"TROJAN FALL"

A galaxy should be a perfect hiding place. A hundred billion suns and a hundred thousand light-years form an appallingly large haystack in which to seek any such submicroscopic needle as a man, or even a planet. A photograph of the Milky Way, or, better, a projection of such a photograph, can give some idea of the sense of confusion which is experienced by anyone faced with the task of combing such a maze.

That was La Roque's first impression, and his views of the galaxy had not been confined to photographs. Admittedly, he was used to interplanetary rather than interstellar flight; but it is almost as easy to get lost inside solar systems as between them. So, when it became a matter of expedience for him to disappear from sight for a time, he decided quite abruptly that Sol's little family was too crowded.

Getting a ship, even legally, was not too difficult; flight between Sol and the nearer stars was fairly common, and only the usual customs restrictions applied to private journeys. La Roque intended that his journey should be more private than usual.

He purchased a craft; the event which made departure so urgent had left him with plenty of funds. She was about as small as a second-order flyer could be: a metal egg about seventy feet long and thirty in diameter at the widest point. She had the required two second-order converters, either capable of holding the ship and six hundred tons of additional mass in the necessary condition for interstellar flight above light-speed. Her actual capacity for freight was nowhere near that figure, of course. The converters consumed mercury, but could be modified to take any reasonably dense metal of low melting point.

La Roque preferred the concealment of crowds, and for that reason chose to make his departure from the ever-busy Allahabad port. It was a little before midnight, on a July evening, that a pilot beam guided his ship beyond the Earth's atmosphere; by 1 A.M. he had switched free, pointed the blunt nose of his ship at the center of the Milk Dipper's bowl, checked his personal equalizer, and shunted into second-order flight. The universe around him remained visible after a fashion, but aberration altered its appearance vastly. Every star swung forward; and at four hundred times the speed of light, they were all contained in a circular area, centered on his line of flight and a little over eight minutes of arc in radius. Sol was dead ahead, apparently, and prevented any possible view of his goal which might have been furnished by a telescope.

La Roque was not a navigator, and knew no more astronomy than the average educated person of his time. Although the beacon stars Rigel, Deneb, and Canopus would all be visible in any part of the galaxy his ship was likely to reach, they were useless to him. His only hope of eventual return to the Earth lay in the device which, every hour, automatically cut the second-order fields for a split second and simultaneously photographed the heavens dead astern. Even that was likely to be useless if he crossed a region of low star density, where there would be no nearby, recognizable objects on the films to guide his return. He had had sense enough to realize this, and consequently had headed in the general direction of the galactic center. He was reasonably certain of finding a habitable planet; the star that lacked worlds was the exception rather than the rule. Earth-type worlds were rarer, but frequent enough to have forced the enactment of several regulations against unrestricted colonization.

Having made the first step in his getaway, he settled down to figuring out the probable line of action of the law. It would, with luck, be a full month before his means of escape would be deduced, for it was known that he was not trained in cosmic navigation, and his ship would not be missed until sufficient time had elapsed for it to make a round trip to Tau Ceti, which he had indicated at Allahabad as his destination. It would take another day or two to compute his actual direction of departure, from the recording at the observatories which had presumably picked up his "wake." From then on, time would be short; any League cruiser of reasonable size could cover in two or three days any distance he could hope to put behind him in that month. It is an unescapable fact that the speed obtainable from a second-order unit is directly dependent on its size.

Therefore, it was essential that a hiding place be found. A planet, where the ship could be buried or otherwise concealed, would present an impossible search problem to a hundred League ships—*if* there were no inhabitants to hold inconvenient memories of his landing. He might find such a world by random search, but the distance he could travel in his month of grace was limited; and, he realized, very few suns lay within that distance. He got out a set of heliocentric charts and began his search on paper.

There is no excuse for him. His destination should have been planned before he left the ground—planned not only as to planet, but to location on the planet. He had always planned his "deals" with meticulous care; and had sneered at less careful colleagues whose failure to do so had resulted in more or less lengthy retirement to League reform institutions. It is impossible to say why he didn't see that the same principle might apply to interstellar flight. But he didn't.

The reference volume that accompanied the charts was most helpful. Stellar systems were listed by right ascension, declination, and distance; so that he merely had to find the appropriate pages to find in a single group all the systems near his line of flight.

There were twelve suns, in seven systems, lying with a light-year of his course, within the distance measured by a month's flight. Such a number was most surprising; chance alone would not insist on even one star within a cylinder of space two light-years in diameter and thirty-five long. Most of them, of course, were "dead" stars, detectable at only the closest range. Six of them had planetary systems; but the planets, without exception, possessed surface temperatures below the freezing point of mercury.

That was unfortunate. To remain alive on any of these worlds would demand that he stay in the ship, and use power, for heat and light. Even such slight radiation as that would cause meant a virtual certainty of detection by even a cursory sweep of the planet on the part of a League cruiser. He had to find a place where the ship would remain at least habitably warm without aid from its own converters. He could do without light, he thought.

The problem would not have bothered a pilot of even

moderate experience, of course. The ship could easily be set in a circular orbit of any desired radius about one of the stars. Unfortunately, there is a definite relation between the mass of a star, the radius of the desired orbit, and the amount of initial tangential velocity required; and this simple relation was unknown to La Roque. Trial and error would be very unsatisfactory; the error might be unnoticeably small to start with, and become large enough to require correction when searchers were around. A worried frown began to add creases above La Roque's black brows as the little flyer raced on.

The spot of light in the front vision plate grew paler as Sol, who provided most of its radiance, faded astern. Within a day, he was merely a bright star; in a week, dozens of others outshone him whenever La Roque cut the drive fields. Space, the runaway began to realize, was a terrifying lonely environment. Earth was beginning, in his memory, to assume a less forbidding aspect.

Two days out, he passed the first of the seven systems. It was not visible, at half a light-year, even when the fields were off; the chart reference described it as a binary, both stars cool enough to have clouds of solid and liquid particles in their atmospheres, and neither emitting any visible radiation to speak of. The relative orbit was of almost cometary eccentricity, with a period of about seventy years. The suns had passed periastron about a dozen years before, without anyone's being greatly concerned.

It was a dry collection of data, but it jogged La Roque's mind into recalling something. He had been picturing the result of an error in establishing an orbit, as being a spiral drop into the star he had chosen. Now he recalled that he would merely find himself in a slightly eccentric, rather than a circular, orbit; and if the eccentricity were not great enough to bring his periastron point actually within the star's atmosphere, it would be perfectly stable.

The idea attracted him for a moment; even he could set up a passable concealment orbit. The possibility of being alternately too warm and too cold was unpleasant, but not forbidding. The system he was passing would not do, of course; he took it for granted that the perturbations produced by the companion star would nullify his attempts. However, four single suns were among those he had looked up along his course, and were within easy reach.

It remained to choose one of the four. Any reasonable

and normal person would have without hesitation laid a
course for the nearest; La Roque, under the elemental
motivation that sent an incognito Hitler to Borneo rather
than Switzerland, chose the farthest. Perhaps his gambling
spirit had something to do with the choice; for there was
actually some doubt that he would reach the star before a
League cruiser would come nosing along his wake into
detection range.

From where he was, the runaway could not lay a direct
course for his chosen hideout. His knowledge of solid
geometry and trigonometry was so small that all he could
do was to continue on his present course until the proper
heliocentric distance was attained, then stop, put Sol exactly on his beam, hold it there while he turned in the
proper direction, and again run in second-order flight for
a certain length of time—dead reckoning pure and very
simple. By thus reducing his goal position to a known plane
—or near plane; actually the surface of a sphere centered
on Sol—he could get the course of his second leg by simply
measuring, on a plane chart, the angle whose vertex was
the point in the sky toward which he had been driving, and
whose sides were determined, respectively, by some beacon
star such as Rigel or Deneb, and the star of his destination. He dragged out a heliocentric chart and protractor,
and set to work.

Time crawled on. The nearer stars, on the trail photographs, drifted sluggishly toward Sol. La Roque found a
photometer, and managed to obtain with its aid a check on
his distance from the Solar System. He spent much of his
time sleeping. There was nothing to read except the charts,
astrographical and planetographical references, and the
numbers on the currency leaves whose gathering had ne-
cessitated his departure from Earth. The latter kept up his
morale for a while.

Second-order pilotage is not difficult; it depends chiefly
on proper aiming of the ship before cutting in of the
converters. There is practically no tendency to drift from
the original heading; in fact, it is impossible to turn without cutting the fields and re-aligning the vessel's axis.
Actually, the ship will follow the arc of a circle whose
radius depends to some extent on the power of the generators, but in any case is so enormous that a "local" interstellar flight may be considered rectilinear. La Roque's in-

tended flight path was so short that his ignorance of short-order field technology made no difference. An experienced navigator, planning a flight across the galaxy, or to one of the exterior systems, would have to forecast and allow for the "drift" caused by generators of any given make and power.

One by one, the star systems La Roque had rejected dropped behind. Each time he fought the temptation to turn aside and seek refuge. Days turned into weeks, three of them, from the time he had chosen his destination. By the most generous estimate, his margin of clearance from the law was growing narrow, when he cut the fields at—according to his reckoning—twenty-eight point seven seven four seven light-years from the Solar System.

He snapped on plate after plate, looking around in every direction. A fifth-magnitude star on the cross wires of the rear plate was, of course, Sol. He looked for Deneb, but Cygnus was too badly distorted by a parallactic variation of nine parsecs to permit him to identify its alpha star with certainty. Orion was recognizable, since he had been moving more or less directly away from it and all its principal stars were extremely distant; so he decided to use Rigel to control his direction.

He zeroed the cross wires of one of the side plates and, using the gyros, swung the ship until Sol was centered on that plate. Rigel was, conveniently, visible on the same plate; so he snapped a switch which projected a protractor onto it, and swung the ship again until Rigel was on the proper—according to his measures—radius. Using the plate's highest power, he placed the two stars to four decimals of accuracy, released the gyro clutches, and cut in the second-order fields before friction at the gyro bearings could throw off his heading.

His arithmetic said he had eight hours and thirty minutes of flight to his destination. Experience would have told him that his chances of stopping within detection range of his goal were less than one in a hundred thousand; as it was, the chief worry that actually disturbed him was whether or not there was risk of collision. Not too surprising! In dead reckoning, the novice navigator makes a tiny point and says, "Here we are." The junior makes a small circle and says the same. The experienced navigator lays the palm of his hand on the chart and says, "We ought to be here." And La Roque's was the deadest of dead reckoning.

He cut the fields five seconds early, and looked expectantly at the forward plate. There should have been a crimson, glowing coal half a billion miles ahead of him. Of course there wasn't.

For a moment he was completely bewildered; but, as he was a reasonable creature, it was only for a moment. He had evidently made a mistake; not necessarily a very large one. He had already obtained the spectrobolometric curve of the star, and fitted the appropriate templets into the detectors. There would be no confusion; no sun having anything like that energy curve could be picked up by those instruments at more than a few billion miles. The galaxy is crowded with such expiring stars, it is true; but a "crowded" star system still contains a vast amount of empty space.

La Roque "sat down"—strapped himself into a seat, since he was weightless—and planned again. He would have to sweep out the space around him, stopping at least every ten billion miles—every two minutes—for at least the ten seconds the instruments would require to sweep the celestial sphere. A volume of space that could be covered in a reasonable time would have to be decided on, and the decision adhered to. If he started a random search, he might as well open the ports.

The results of some more arithmetic bothered him. A really appalling number of five-billion-mile cubes could be packed into an area that looked very small on the chart. He finally worked the other way—allowing himself one hundred hours for the search. He decided he could cover a cube roughly one hundred and forty billion miles on a side, in that time. He realized sadly that his dead reckoning error could easily be several times that.

He was no quitter, however. He was beginning to realize the chances against him—not merely against his escape, but against his survival; he had long since realized his error in tackling a job about which he knew next to nothing; but having decided on his course of action, he embarked on it without hesitation. He started the sweep.

His patience lasted admirably for the first hour. It stood up fairly well for the second. By the end of the third, the smooth routine of flight—cut-wait-and-watch-flight was growing ragged. When the clock and radiometer dials began to blur, and the urge to break something grew almost irresistible, he called it a day and slept two or three hours. After the second period, he couldn't sleep either.

Really, he was undeservedly lucky. One of the radiometers reacted after only eighteen hours of blind search. His near hysteria vanished instantly, washed away in a flood of relief; and with hands once more reasonably steady he swung the little ship until the emanations registered on the bow meter. He noted the strength of the reading, cut in the second-order fields for five seconds, and read the dial again. He knew the inverse square law, at least; he figured for a moment, then drove forward again for eleven more seconds, and cut the fields between twenty and thirty million miles from the source of the radiation.

It was visible to the naked eye at that range, which, in a way, was unfortunate. Had it not been, La Roque would have had a few more happy minutes. As things were, he took one look at the forward plate, and for the next ninety seconds used language which should really have been recorded for the benefit of future sailors. He had some excuse. The star was listed in the chart reference as single; La Roque had chosen it for that reason. However, plainly visible on the plate, revolving evidently almost in contact, were two smoky red suns—a close binary system.

Of course, no one would normally be greatly interested. The Astrographic Survey vessel which had covered the section had probably swept past fifty billion miles out, and noted the system's existence casually as its radiometers flickered. Size? Mass? Companions, if any? Planets? Who cared!

La Roque, of course.

The stars were red dwarfs, small and dense. They would have been seen to be irregular variables, if anyone had looked long enough; for their surface temperatures were so low that "cirrus" clouds of solid carbon particles formed and dispersed at random in their atmospheres. The larger sun was perhaps a hundred thousand miles in diameter, the other only slightly smaller. Their centers were roughly half a million miles apart, and the period of revolution about eight hours. In spite of their relatively high density, there were very noticeable tidal bulges on both.

All these facts would have been of absorbing interest to an astronomer seeking data on the internal structure of red dwarf stars; La Roque didn't know any of them, and at first didn't give a darn. He was wondering how a stable orbit could be established close enough to this system to keep him from freezing without using ship's power. The near-circular one he had planned was out; it would have had to be less than a million miles from a single sun of such late type, and the doubling of the heat source wasn't much help.

. He thought of doubling back to one of the other systems which the chart had said to be single; but the nerve-racking search and disappointment he had suffered the first time made him hesitate. It was while he hesitated that memory came to his aid.

There had been an episode in his experiences which had occurred on Hector, one of the Trojan asteroids. Circumstances had caused him to remain there for some time, and a friendly jailer had explained to him just where Hector was and why it stayed there. It was in the stability point at the third corner of an equilateral triangle whose other corners were Sol and Jupiter; and though it could—and did—wobble millions of miles from the actual point, gravitational forces always brought it back.

La Roque looked out at the twin suns. Could his ship stand the temperature at the Trojan points of this system? More important, could he stand it?

He could. His instruments gave the energy distribution curve of the suns; one of the reference charts contained a table that turned the curves into surface temperatures. He was able to measure the distance between the centers of the suns, from the scale lines on the plate and his distance, which he knew roughly. Half a million miles from the surface of a star whose radius was fifty thousand miles and whose effective radiating temperature was a thousand degrees absolute, the black-body temperature was, according to his figures, about thirty degrees Centigrade. The presence of two stars made it decidedly warmer, but his ship was well insulated and the surface highly polished. It would eventually reach an equilibrium temperature considerably above that of an ideal black body, but it would take a long time doing so.

It seemed, then, that the Trojan point was the best place for him. He could find it easily enough; getting the centers of the stars sixty degrees apart would put him at the right distance. He could find the proper plane by moving around until the two suns appeared to move across each other in straight lines. It would not take long; by varying his distance from the system he could, in a few minutes, observe it through half a revolution.

It took him, in fact, less than an hour to find the orbital plane of the suns. It took him five and a half hours of first-order acceleration at one gravity to get rid of the hundred and twenty mile per second velocity difference between Sol and this system—fortunately, the chart had mentioned the high relative velocity, or La Roque would never have thought of such a thing. In a way, he didn't mind the necessity; it was good to have weight for the first time in nearly a month. He was, of course, a little worried at the amount of time consumed; he wished he had not wasted so much of the commodity in putting Sol so far behind.

He cut the first-order drive the instant his clock told him the speeds should be equal, headed for the twin suns, and hopped for his Trojan point. Since moving bodies were involved, he had to make five legs out of the short trip—he failed to allow for the short period of the system and the fact that he started the first leg several light-hours from his goal.

He got there eventually, however. He suddenly realized that he would have to use first-order power again, to give his ship something like the proper orbital velocity; but even he was able to understand the proper magnitude and direction of this new vector; the only unjustified assumption he had to make was that the suns were of equal masses, and this happened to be nearly the case. He wasn't too worried; he understood that in a Trojan orbit such small variations are opposed, not helped, by the gravity of the primary bodies. He was quite right.

He cut all his power except the detector relay currents, which did not radiate appreciably. To these he connected an alarm, and set them to synchronize with the low-frequency waves which form the "wake" of a vessel cruising at second-order speeds. Then, abruptly feeling the reaction of the past days, he drifted over to a "bunk," moored himself, and was instantly asleep.

It is impossible to say just how long he slept; he was exhausted mentally and emotionally, and when weightless the human body can approach a condition near to suspended animation, if given the chance. It couldn't have been for very many hours, but the alarm rang for minutes before its sound penetrated to his consciousness. When it did, he had to wait several moments before he could move a muscle.

Recovered at last, he unmoored himself and kicked his body across the narrow cabin to the instrument board, and cut the alarm, cursing. He had forgotten that the bell would radiate, and was not sure that the hull would shield its waves. The detectors were reacting violently, the needles wobbling rapidly from positive to negative limits. He knew that a ship had driven past in second-order flight, but that was as far as he could interpret the readings. It would have required an expert to compute the speed, type, and distance of the ship creating the disturbance.

After a few minutes, the needles quieted. La Roque remained at the board, judging that the ship had not left for good. He was right. The disturbances started again half an hour later, and kept up for hours thereafter—sometimes so feeble as to cause a barely visible quiver of the needles, sometimes slamming them against the stop pins with audible clicks. La Roque was incapable of reading any meaning except changing distance into this phenomenon.

The "wake" of a ship in straight-line, second-order flight consists of a few low-frequency electromagnetic waves, the wave-front being, as can easily be seen, coneshaped, with the ship at the apex. The cone expands radially at the speed of light, and its tip moves forward with the ship—in the case of a military craft, at anywhere up to something like a million light velocities.

If the ship is not in straight-line flight, but cutting its fields and changing direction every few minutes or seconds, the shape of the wave front becomes rather complex. A standard search path spirals around the surface of a torus, and after a few hours the traces of such a flight would be the despair of a competent mathematician, let alone an amateur at a comparatively fixed observation post. The space for billions of miles around that binary sun was quivering with crisscrossing wave fronts. Each set the needles of La Roque's detectors quivering in tune as it passed him, and each quiver brought beads of sweat to the runaway's brow. His own ship, he realized, had left similar fronts; and he had shaved his margin of escape much too fine. Had they been given a week, or even three or four days, for expansion at the speed of light, he could have ceased to worry about their being used to trail him.

He wondered just what the searchers would do. They must have trailed him directly to this system, as he had expected. They might try to find an inactive ship in space, but La Roque doubted that such a search would be practical unless there existed detection instruments unknown to the general public.

He wondered if the system contained any planets, to add to the searchers' difficulties. He himself had seen none, and none was listed on the chart; but they would have been nearly invisible in the dim light of the twin suns, and La Roque's faith in the chart had dropped a long way. If there were any, they would be a real help; they would have to be searched mile by square mile.

But the question of prime importance was, how long would the pursuers stay? Certainly, if they had the patience they could outwait him, for their food supply would outlast his; but for all they knew he might have met with a fatal accident, or encountered an organized outlaw base—either could easily happen. If he refrained from radiating long enough, they might decide further search futile. He could do that; the darkness didn't bother him particularly, and the ship was warm enough—a little too warm, in fact. Evidently his figures had not been exact.

Eventually the detectors stopped reacting, and La Roque started waiting. He was still perspiring, less from worry now than from actual warmth. The ship *was* becoming uncomfortable. He removed his outer clothing and felt better for a while.

Time crawled on—rapidly decelerating, in La Roque's opinion. He had nothing to do except notice his own discomfort, which was on the increase. He cursed the ship's builders for failure to insulate it properly, and the men who had computed the tables he had used to obtain the probable temperature at this distance from the suns. He didn't bother to curse his own arithmetic.

Once he was almost on the point of driving farther out, hoping the pursuing ship had gone; but a flicker from one of the detectors made him change his mind. He hung and sweated; and the temperature mounted.

It must have been a hundred and fifty degrees Fahrenheit when he finally gave in. He could have stood more in

the open—anyone could—but the air-conditioning apparatus had been stopped along with everything else, and the
air in the ship was approaching saturation. With that fact
considered, he held out remarkably well; but eventually his
will power gave out. He kicked his way feebly back to the
board and snapped on the vision plates.

He lacked the energy to curse. For moments he could
only stare in shocked horror at the plates—and realize
how misdirected his previous denunciations had been.
There was nothing wrong with his ship's insulation; the
wonder was that it had held out so well. One of the
suns—he never knew which—completely filled the front,
top, and port plates with a blaze of sooty crimson; he must
have been within thirty or forty thousand miles of its
surface. His hand darted toward the activating switch of
the second-order drivers, and was as quickly checked.
They would only send him straight forward, into the in-
ferno revealed by the front plate. The ship must be
turned.

He started the gyros, careless now of any radiation that
might result. The control knobs were hot to the touch; and
a smell of burning oil reached his nostrils as the gyros
wound up to speed. The ship abruptly shuddered and
began to gyrate slowly, as one of them seized in its bearings. He watched tensely as the vessel went through a full
rotation, his hand hovering over the board; but not once
was the glow in the forward plate replaced by the friendly
darkness of space. The ship was spinning on its longitudinal
axis.

The other gyros were working. He tried to turn the
vessel with them. The result was to shift the axis of spin
about thirty degrees—and increase its rate tenfold as another of the heavy wheels, spinning at full speed, jammed
abruptly. Centrifugal force snatched him away from the
board and against one wall; he shrieked as his flesh
touched hot metal, and kicked violently. His body shot
across the room, reaching the other side at about the
same time his previous point of contact was carried
around by the ship's rotation.

The specks of carbon cirrus on the front plate were
describing circles now—circles whose size was visibly increasing. For part of each turn the nose was now pointing
into space; La Roque tried to fight his way back to the
board to take advantage of one of those moments.

He might have made it, in spite of the agony of his burns, but the overstrained insulation had done its best. It failed; and failed, of all places, over the water tanks that lined part of the hull. The tanks themselves offered only token resistance as steam pressure suddenly built up in them. La Roque never knew when scalding water shorted the control board, for a jet of superheated steam had caught him just before he reached it.

On the enforcement cruiser, a man straightened up from a plotting board.

"That does it, I think," he said. "He was using heavy current for a while, probably trying to turn out with his gyros; then there was a flash of S.H.F., and everything stopped. That must have taken out his second-order, and he'd have had to use about sixty gravities of first-order to pull out of that spot. I wonder what he was doing so close to those suns."

"Could have been hiding," suggested a second pilot. "He might have thought the suns would mask most of his radiation. I wonder how he expected to stay there any length of time, though."

"I know what I'd have done in his place," replied the first man. "I'd have put my ship into a Trojan position and waited the business out. He could have lasted indefinitely there. I wonder why he didn't try that."

"He probably did." The speaker was a navigator, who had kept silent up to this point. "If a smart man like you would do it, a fellow like that couldn't be expected to know any better. Have you *ever* seen a planet in the Trojan points of any double sun? I'll bet you haven't. That Trojan solution works fine for Sol and Jupiter—Sol is a thousand times the more massive. It would work for Earth and Luna, since one has about eighty times the mass of the other. But I have never seen a binary star where the mass ratio was anywhere near twenty-five to one; and if it's less, the Trojan solution to the three-body problem doesn't work. Don't ask me why; I couldn't show you the math; but I know it's true—the stability function breaks, with surprising sharpness, right about the twenty-five-to-one mass ratio. Our elusive friend didn't know that, any more than you did, and parked his ship right in the path of a rapidly moving sun." He shrugged his shoulders, and turned away. "Live and learn, they say," he finished, "but the difficulty seems to lie in living while you learn."

Hart waited a full hour after the last sounds had died away before cautiously opening the cover of his refuge. Even then he did not feel secure for some minutes, until he had made a thorough search of the storage chamber; then a smile of contempt curled his lips.

"The fools!" he muttered. "They do not examine their shipments at all. How do they expect to maintain their zone controls with such incompetents in charge?" He glanced at the analyzers in the forearm of his spacesuit, and revised his opinion a trifle—the air in the chamber was pure carbon dioxide; any man attempting to come as Hart had, but without his own air supply, would not have survived the experiment. Still, the agent felt, they should have searched.

There was, however, no real time for analyzing the actions of others. He had a job to do, and not too long in which to do it. However slack the organization of this launching station might be, there was no chance whatever of reaching any of its vital parts unchallenged; and after the first challenge, success and death would be running a frightfully close race.

He glided back to the crate which had barely contained his doubled-up body, carefully replaced and resealed the cover, and then rearranged the contents of the chamber to minimize the chance of that crate's being opened first. The containers were bulky, but nothing in the free-falling station had any weight, and the job did not take long even for a man unaccustomed to a total lack of apparent gravity. Satisfied with these precautions, Hart approached the door of the storeroom; but before opening it, he stopped to review his plan.

He must, of course, be near the outer shell of the station. Central Intelligence had been unable to obtain plans of this launcher—a fact which should have given him food for thought—but there was no doubt about its general design. Storage and living quarters would be just inside the surface of the sphere; then would come a level of machine shops and control systems; and at the heart, within the shielding that represented most of the station's mass, would be the "hot" section—the chambers containing the fission piles and power plants, the extractors and the remote-controlled machinery that loaded the war heads of the torpedoes which were the main reason for the station's existence.

There were many of these structures circling Earth; every nation on the globe maintained at least one, and usually several. Hart had visited one of those belonging to his own country, partly for technical familiarity and partly to accustom himself to weightlessness. He had studied its plans with care, and scientists had carefully explained to him the functions of each part, and the ways in which the launchers of the Western Alliance were likely to differ. Most important, they had described to him several ways by which such structures might be destroyed. Hart's smile was wolfish as he thought of that; these people who preferred the pleasures of personal liberty to those of efficiency would see what efficiency could do.

But this delay was not efficient. He had made his plans long before, and it was more than time to set about their execution. He must be reasonably near a store of rocket fuel; and some at least of the air in this station must contain a breathable percentage of oxygen. Without further deliberation, he opened the door and floated out into the corridor.

He did not go blindly. Tiny detectors built into the wrists of his suit reacted to the infrared radiations, the water vapor and carbon dioxide and even the breathing sounds that would herald the approach of a human being —unless he were wearing a nonmetallic suit similar to Hart's own. Apparently the personnel of the base did not normally wear these, however, for twice in the first ten minutes the saboteur was warned into shelter by the indications of the tiny instruments. In that ten minutes he covered a good deal of the outer zone.

He learned quickly that the area in which a carbon dioxide atmosphere was maintained was quite limited in extent, and probably constituted either a quarantine zone for newly arrived supplies, or a food storage area. It was surrounded by an uninterrupted corridor lined on one side with airtight doors leading into the CO_2 rooms, and on the other by flimsier portals closing off other storage spaces. Hart wondered briefly at the reason for such a vast amount of storage room; then his attention was taken by another matter. He had been about to launch himself in another long, weightless glide down the corridor in search of branch passages which might lead to the rocket fuel stores, when a tiny spot on one wall caught his eye.

He instantly went to examine it more closely, and as quickly recognized a photoelectric eye. There appeared to be no lens, which suggested a beam-interruption unit; but the beam itself was not visible, nor could he find any projector. That meant a rather interesting and vital problem lay in avoiding the ray. He stopped to think.

In the scanning room on the second level, Dr. Bruce Mayhew chuckled aloud.

"It's wonderful what a superiority complex can do. He's stopped for the first time—didn't seem to have any doubts of his safety until he spotted that eye. The old oil about 'decadent democracies' seems to have taken deep hold somewhere, at least. He must be a military agent rather than a scientist."

Warren Floyd nodded. "Let's not pull the same boner, though," he suggested. "Scientist or not, no stupid man would have been chosen for such a job. Do you think he's carrying explosives? One man could hardly have chemicals enough to make a significant number of breaches in the outer shell."

"He may be hoping to get into the core, to set off a war head," replied the older man, "though I don't for the life of me see how he expects to do it. There's a rocket fuel in his neighborhood, of course, but it's just n.v. for the torpedoes—harmless, as far as we're concerned."

"A fire could be quite embarrassing, even if it weren't an explosion," pointed out his assistant, "particularly since the whole joint is nearly pure magnesium. I know it's sinfully expensive to transport mass away from Earth, but I wish they had built this place out of something a little less responsive to heat and oxygen."

"I shouldn't worry about that," replied Mayhew. "He won't get a fire started."

Floyd glanced at the flanking screens which showed armored men keeping pace with the agent in parallel corridors, and nodded. "I suppose not—provided Ben and his crew aren't too slow closing in when we give the signal."

"You mean when *I* give the signal," returned the other man. "I have reasons for wanting him free as long as possible. The longer he's free, the lower the opinion he'll have of us; when we do take him, he'll be less ready to commit suicide, and the sudden letdown of his self-confidence will make interrogation easier."

Floyd privately hoped nothing would happen to deflate his superior's own self-confidence, but wisely said nothing; and both men watched Hart's progress almost silently for some minutes. Floyd occasionally transmitted a word or two to the action party to keep them apprised of their quarry's whereabouts, but no other sound interrupted the vigil.

Hart had finally found a corridor which branched away from the one he had been following, and he proceeded cautiously along it. He had learned the intervals at which the photocells were spotted, and now avoided them almost automatically. It did not occur to him that, while the sight of a spacesuited man in the outer corridors might not surprise an observer, the presence of such a man who failed consistently to break the beams of the photocell spotters would be bound to attract attention. The lenses of the scanners were too small and too well hidden for Hart to find easily, and he actually believed that the photocells were the only traps. With his continued ease in avoiding them, his self-confidence and contempt for the Westerners were mounting as Mayhew had foretold.

Several times he encountered air breaks—sliding bulkheads actuated by automatic pressure-controlled switches, designed to cut off any section with a bad air leak. His action at each of these was the same; from an outer pocket of his armor he would take a small wedge of steel and skillfully jam the door. It was this action which convinced Mayhew that the agent was not a scientist—he was displaying the skill of an experienced burglar or spy. He was apparently well supplied with the wedges, for in the hour before he found what he was seeking he jammed more than twenty of the air breaks. Mayhew and Floyd did not bother to have them cleared at the time, since no one was in the outer level without a spacesuit.

Nearly half of the outer level was thus unified when Hart reached a section of corridor bearing valve handles and hose connections instead of doors, and knew there must be liquids behind the walls. There were code indexes stenciled over the valves, which meant nothing to the spy; but he carefully manipulated one of the two handles to let a little fluid into the corridor, and sniffed at it cautiously through the gingerly cracked face plate of his helmet. He was satisfied with the results; the liquid was one of the low-volatility hydrocarbons used with liquid oxygen as a fuel to provide the moderate acceleration demanded by space launched torpedoes. They were cheap, fairly dense, and their low-vapor pressure simplified the storage problem in open-space stations.

All that Hart really knew about it was that the stuff would burn as long as there was oxygen. Well—he grinned again at the thought—there would be oxygen for a while; until the compressed, blazing combustion gases blew the heat-softened metal of the outer wall into space. After that there would be none, except perhaps in the central core, where the heavy concentration of radioactive matter made it certain there would be no one to breathe it.

At present, of course, the second level and any other intermediate ones were still sealed; but that could and would be remedied. In any case, the blast of the liberated fuel would probably take care of the relatively flimsy inner walls. He did not at the time realize that these were of magnesium, or he would have felt even more sure of the results.

He looked along the corridor. As far as the curvature of the outer shell permitted him to see, the valves projected from the wall at intervals of a few yards. Each valve had a small electric pump, designed to force air into the tank behind it to drive the liquid out by pressure, since there was no gravity. Hart did not consider this point at all; a brief test showed him that the liquid did flow when the valve was on, and that was enough for him. Hanging poised beside the first handle, he took an object from still another pocket of his spacesuit, and checked it carefully, finally clipping it to an outside belt where it could easily be reached.

At the sight of this item of apparatus, Floyd almost suffered a stroke.

"That's an incendiary bomb!" he gasped aloud. "We can't possibly take him in time to stop his setting it off—

which he'll do the instant he sees our men! And he already has free fuel in the corridor!"

He was perfectly correct; the agent was proceeding from valve to valve in long glides, pausing at each just long enough to turn it full on and to scatter the balloon-like mass of escaping liquid with a sweep of his arm. Gobbets and droplets of the inflammable stuff sailed lazily hither and yon through the air in his wake.

Mayhew calmly lighted a cigarette, unmindful of the weird appearance of the match flame driven toward his feet by the draft from the ceiling ventilators, and declined to move otherwise. "Decidedly, no physicist," he murmured. "I suppose that's just as well—it's the military information the army likes anyway. They certainly wouldn't have risked a researcher on this sort of job, so I never really did have a chance to get anything I wanted from him."

"But what are we going to do?" Floyd was almost frantic. "There's enough available energy loose in that corridor now to blast the whole outer shell off—and gallons more coming every second. I know you've been here a lot longer than I, but unless you can tell me how you expect to keep him from lighting that stuff up, I'm getting into a suit right now!"

"If it blows, a suit won't help you," pointed out the older man.

"I know that!" almost screamed Floyd, "but what other chance is there? Why did you let him get so far?"

"There is still no danger," Mayhew said flatly, "whether you believe it or not. However, the fuel does cost money, and there'll be some work recovering it, so I don't see why he should be allowed to empty all the torpedo tanks. He's excited enough now, anyway." He turned languidly to the appropriate microphone and gave the word to the action squad. "Take him now. He seems to be without hand weapons, but don't count on it. He certainly has at least one incendiary bomb." As an afterthought, he reached for another switch, and made sure the ventilators in the outer level were not operating; then he relaxed again and gave his attention to the scanner that showed the agent's activity. Floyd had switched to another pickup that covered a longer section of corridor, and the watchers saw the space-suited attackers almost as soon as did Hart himself.

The European reacted to the sight at once—too rapidly, in fact, for the shift in his attention caused him to miss his grasp on the valve handle he sought and flounder helplessly through the air until he reached the next. Once anchored, however, he acted as he had planned, ignoring with commendable self-control the four armored figures converging on him. A sharp twist turned the fuel valve full on, sending a stream of oil mushrooming into the corridor; his left hand flashed to his belt, seized the tiny cylinder he had snapped there, jammed its end hard against the adjacent wall, and tossed the bomb gently back down the corridor. In one way his lack of weightless experience betrayed him; he allowed for a gravity pull that was not there. The bomb, in consequence, struck the "ceiling" a few yards from his hand, and rebounded with a popping noise and a shower of sparks. It drifted on down the corridor toward the floating globules of hydrocarbon, and the glow of the sparks was suddenly replaced by the eye-hurting radiance of thermite.

Floyd winced at the sight, and expected the attacking men to make futile plunges after the blazing thing; but though all were within reach of walls, not one swerved from his course. Hart made no effort to escape or fight; he watched the course of the drifting bomb with satisfaction, and, like Floyd, expected in the next few seconds to be engulfed in a sea of flame that would remove the most powerful of the Western torpedo stations from his country's path of conquest. Unlike Floyd, he was calm about it, even when the men seized him firmly and began removing equipment from his pockets. One unclamped and removed the face plate of his helmet; and even to that he made no resistance—just watched in triumph as his missile drifted toward the nearest globes of fuel.

It did not actually strike the first. It did not have to; while the quantity of heat radiated by burning thermite is relatively small, the temperature of the reaction is notoriously high—and the temperature six inches from the bomb was well above the flash point of the rocket fuel, comparatively non-volatile as it was. Floyd saw the flash as its surface ignited, and closed his eyes.

Mayhew gave him four or five seconds before speaking, judging that that was probably about all the suspense the younger man could stand.

"All right, ostrich," he finally said quietly. "I'm not an

angel, in case you were wondering. Why not use your eyes, and the brain behind them?"

Floyd was far too disturbed to take offense at the last remark, but he did cautiously follow Mayhew's advice about looking. He found difficulty, however, in believing what his eyes and the scanner showed him.

The group of five men was unchanged, except for the expression on the captive's now visible face. All were looking down the corridor toward the point where the bomb was still burning; Lang's crew bore expressions of amusement on their faces, while Hart wore a look of utter disbelief. Floyd, seeing what he saw, shared the expression.

The bomb had by now passed close to several of the floating spheres. Each had caught fire, as Floyd had seen —for a moment only. Now each was surrounded by a spherical, nearly opaque layer of some grayish substance that looked like a mixture of smoke and kerosene vapor; a layer that could not have been half an inch thick, as Floyd recalled the sizes of the original spheres. None was burning; each had effectively smothered itself out, and the young observer slowly realized just how and why as the bomb at last made a direct hit on a drop of fuel fully a foot in diameter.

Like the others, the globe flamed momentarily, and went out; but this time the sphere that appeared and grew around it was lighter in color, and continued to grow for several seconds. Then there was a little, sputtering explosion, and a number of fragments of still burning thermite emerged from the surface of the sphere in several directions, traveled a few feet and went out. All activity died down, except in the faces of Hart and Floyd.

The saboteur was utterly at a loss, and seemed likely to remain that way; but in the watch room Floyd was already kicking himself mentally for his needless worry. Mayhew, watching the expression on his assistant's face, chuckled quietly.

"Of course you get it now," he said at last.

"I do *now*, certainly," replied Floyd. "I should have seen it earlier—I've certainly noticed you light enough cigarettes, and watched the behavior of the match flame. Apparently our friend is not yet enlightened, though," he nodded toward the screen as he spoke.

He was right; Hart was certainly not enlightened. He

belonged to a service in which unpleasant surprises were
neither unexpected nor unusual, but he had never in his
life been so completely disorganized. The stuff looked like
fuel; it smelled like fuel; it had even started to burn—but it
refused to carry on with the process. Hart simply relaxed
in the grip of the guards, and tried to find something in the
situation to serve as an anchor for his whirling thoughts.
A spaceman would have understood the situation without
thinking, a high school student of reasonable intelligence
could probably have worked the matter out in time; but
Hart's education had been that of a spy, in a country
which considered general education a waste of time. He
simply did not have the background to cope with his present environment.

That, at least, was the idea Mayhew acquired after a
careful questioning of the prisoner. Not much was learned
about his intended mission, though there was little doubt
about it under the circumstances. The presence of an alien
agent aboard any of the free-floating torpedo launchers of
the various national governments bore only one interpretation; and since the destruction of one such station would
do little good to anyone, Mayhew at once radioed all other
launchers to be on the alert for similar intruders—all
others, regardless of nationality. Knowledge by Hart's superiors of his capture might prevent their acting on the
assumption that he had succeeded, which would inevitably
lead to some highly regrettable incidents. Mayhew's business was to prevent a war, not win one. Hart had not
actually admitted the identity of his superiors, but his
accent left the matter in little doubt; and since no action
was intended, Mayhew did not need proof.

There remained, of course, the problem of what to do
with Hart. The structure had no ready-made prison, and it
was unlikely that the Western government would indulge
in the gesture of a special rocket to take the man off.
Personal watch would be tedious, but it was unthinkable
merely to deprive a man with the training Hart must have
received of his equipment, and then assume he would not
have to be watched every second.

The solution, finally suggested by one of the guards, was
a small storeroom in the outer shell. It had no locks, but
there were welding torches in the machine shops. There
was no ventilator either, but an alga tank would take care

of that. After consideration, Mayhew decided that this was
the best plan, and it was promptly put into effect.

Hart was thoroughly searched, even his clothing replaced as a precautionary measure. He asked for his cigarettes and lighter, with a half smile. Mayhew supplied the
man with some of his own, and marked those of the spy
for special investigation. Hart said nothing more after
that, and was incarcerated without further ceremony.
Mayhew was chuckling once more as the guards disappeared with their charge.

"I hope he gets more good than I out of that lighter," he
remarked. "It's a wick-type my kid sent me as a present,
and the ventilator draft doesn't usually keep it going.
Maybe our friend will learn something, if he fools with it
long enough. He has a pint of lighter fluid to experiment
with—the kid had large ideas."

"I was a little surprised—I thought for a moment you
were giving him a pocket flask," laughed Floyd. "I suppose
that's why you always use matches—they're easier to wave
than that thing. I guess I save myself a lot of trouble not
smoking at all. I suppose you have to put potassium nitrate
in your cigarettes to keep 'em going when you're not
pulling on them." Floyd ducked as he spoke, but Mayhew
didn't throw anything. Hart, of course, was out of hearing
by this time, and would not have profited from the remark
in any case.

He probably, in fact, would not have paid much attention. He knew, of course, that the sciences of physics and
chemistry are important; but he thought of them in connection with great laboratories and factories. The idea that
knowledge of either could be of immediate use to anyone
not a chemist or physicist would have been fantastic to
him. While his current plans for escape were based largely
on chemistry, the connection did not occur to him. The
only link between those plans and Mayhew's words or
actions gave the spy some grim amusement; it was the fact
that he did not smoke.

The cell, when he finally reached it, was perfectly satisfactory; there were no peepholes which could serve as
shotholes, no way in which the door could be unsealed
quickly—as Mayhew had said, not even a ventilator. Once
he was in, Hart would not be interrupted without plenty of

notice. Since the place was a storeroom, there was no
reason to expect even a scanner, though, he told himself,
there was no reason to assume there was none, either. He
simply disregarded that possibility, and went to work the
moment he heard the torch start to seal his door.

His first idea did not get far. He spent half an hour
trying to make Mayhew's lighter work, without noticeable
success. Each spin of the "flint" brought a satisfactory
shower of sparks, and about every fourth or fifth try
produced a faint "pop" and a flash of blue fire; but he was
completely unable to make a flame last. He closed the
cover at last, and for the first time made an honest effort
to think. The situation had got beyond the scope of his
training.

He dismissed almost at once the matter of the rocket
fuel that had not been ignited by his bomb. Evidently the
Westerners stored it with some inhibiting chemical, probably as a precaution more against accident than sabotage.
Such a chemical would have to be easily removable, but he
had no means of knowing the method, and that line of
attack would have to be abandoned.

But why wouldn't the lighter fuel burn? The more he
thought the matter out, the more Hart felt that Mayhew
must have doctored it deliberately, as a gesture of contempt. Such an act he could easily understand; and the
thought of it roused again the wolfish hate that was such a
prominent part of his personality. He would show that
smart Westerner! There was certainly some way!

Powerful hands, and a fingernail deliberately hardened
long since to act as a passable screw-driver blade, had the
lighter disassembled in the space of a few minutes. The
parts were disappointingly small in number and variety;
but Hart considered each at length.

The fuel, already evaporating as it was, appeared useless
—he was no chemist, and had satisfied himself the stuff
was incombustible. The case was of magnalium, apparently;
and might be useful as a heat source if it could be lighted;
its use in a cigarette lighter did not encourage pursuit of
that thought. The wick might be combustible, if thoroughly
dried. The flint and wheel mechanism was promising—at
least one part would be hard enough to cut or wear most
metals, and the spring might be decidedly useful.

Elsewhere in the room there was very little. The light
was a gas tube, and, since the chamber had no opening

whatever, would probably be most useful as a light. The alga tank, of course, had a minute motor and pump which forced air through its liquid, and an ingenious valve and trap system which recovered the air even in the present weightless situation; but Hart, considering the small size of the room, decided that any attempt to dismantle his only source of fresh air would have to be very much of a last resort.

After much thought, and with a grimace of distaste, he took the tiny striker of the lighter and began slowly to abrade a circular area around the latch of the door, using the inside handle for anchorage.

He did not, of course, have any expectation of final escape; he was not in the least worried about his chances of recovering his spacesuit. He expected only to get out of the cell and complete his mission; and if he succeeded, no possible armor would do him any good.

As it happened, there was a scanner in his compartment; but Mayhew had long since grown tired of watching the spy try to ignite the lighter fuel, and had turned his attention elsewhere, so that Hart's actions were unobserved for some time. The door metal was thin and not particularly hard; and he was able without interference and with no worse trouble than severe finger cramp to work out a hole large enough to show him another obstacle—instead of welding the door frame itself, his captors had placed a rectangular steel bar across the portal and fastened it at points well to each side of the frame, out of the prisoner's reach. Hart stopped scraping as soon as he realized the extent of this barrier, and gave his mind to the new situation.

He might, conceivably, work a large enough hole through the door to pass his body without actually opening the portal; but his fingers were already stiff and cramped from the use made of the tiny striker, and it was beyond reason to expect that he would be left alone long enough to accomplish any such feat. Presumably they intended to feed him occasionally.

There was another reason for haste, as well, though he was forgetting it as his nose became accustomed to the taint in the air. The fluid, which he had permitted to escape while disassembling the lighter, was evaporating with fair speed, as it was far more volatile than the rocket fuel; and

it was diffusing through the air of the little room. The alga
tank removed only carbon dioxide, so that the air of the
cell was acquiring an ever-greater concentration of hydrocarbon molecules. Prolonged breathing of such vapors is
far from healthy, as Hart well knew; and escape from the
room was literally the only way to avoid breathing the
stuff.

What would eliminate a metal door—quickly? Brute
force? He hadn't enough of it. Chemicals? He had none.
Heat? The thought was intriguing and discouraging at the
same time, after his recent experience with heat sources.
Still, even if liquid fuels would not burn perhaps other
things would: there was the wicking from the lighter; a
little floating cloud of metal particles around the scene of
his work on the magnesium door; and the striking mechanism of the lighter.

He plucked the wicking out of the air where it had been
floating, and began to unravel it—without fuel, as he realized, it would need every advantage in catching the sparks
of the striker.

Then he wadded as much of the metallic dust as he could
collect—which was not too much—into the wick, concen-
trating it heavily at one end and letting it thin out toward
the more completely raveled part.

Then he inspected the edges of the hole he had ground
in the door, and with the striker roughened them even
more on one side, so that a few more shavings of metal
projected. To these he pressed the fuse, wedging it between
the door and the steel bar just outside the hole, with the
"lighting" end projecting into the room. He inspected the
work carefully, nodded in satisfaction, and began to reas-
semble the striker mechanism.

He did not, of course, expect that the steel bar would be
melted or seriously weakened by an ounce or so of magnesium, but he did hope that the thin metal of the door itself
would ignite.

Hart had the spark mechanism almost ready when his
attention was distracted abruptly. Since the hole had been
made, a very gentle current of air had been set up in the
cell by the corridor ventilators beyond—a current in the
nature of an eddy which tended to carry loose objects
quite close to the hole. One of the loose objects in the room
was a sphere comprised of the remaining lighter fluid,

which had not yet evaporated. When Hart noticed the shimmering globe, it was scarcely a foot from his fuse, and drifting steadily nearer.

To him, that sphere of liquid was death to his plan; it would not burn itself, it probably would not let anything else burn either. If it touched and soaked his fuse, he would have to wait until it evaporated; and there might not be time for that. He released the striker with a curse, and swung his open hand at the drop, trying to drive it to one side. He succeeded only partly. It spattered on his hand, breaking up into scores of smaller drops, some of which moved obediently away, while others just drifted, and still others vanished in vapor. None drifted far; and the gentle current had them in control almost at once, and began to bear many of them back toward the hole—and Hart's fuse.

For just a moment the saboteur hung there in agonized indecision, and then his training reasserted itself. With another curse he snatched at the striker, made sure it was ready for action, and turned to the hole in the door. It was at this moment that Mayhew chose to take another look at his captive.

As it happened, the lens of his scanner was so located that Hart's body covered the hole in the door; and since the spy's back was toward him, the watcher could not tell precisely what he was doing. The air of purposefulness about the captive was so outstanding and so impressive, however, that Mayhew was reaching for a microphone to order a direct check on the cell when Hart spun the striker wheel.

Mayhew could not, of course, see just what the man had done, but the consequences were plain enough. The saboteur's body was flung away from the door and toward the scanner lens like a rag doll kicked by a mule. An orange blossom of flame outlined him for an instant; and in practically the same instant the screen went blank as a heavy shock wave shattered its pickup lens.

Mayhew, accustomed as he was to weightless maneuvering, never in his life traveled so rapidly as he did then. Floyd and several other crewmen, who saw him on the way, tried to follow; but he outstripped them all, and when they reached the sight of Hart's prison Mayhew was hanging poised outside, staring at the door.

There was no need of removing the welded bar. The

thin metal of the door had been split and curled outward
fantastically; an opening quite large enough for any man's
body yawned in it, though there was nothing more certain
than the fact that Hart had not made use of this avenue of
escape. His body was still in the cell, against the far wall;
and even now the relatively strong currents from the hall
ventilators did not move it. Floyd had a pretty good idea
of what held it there, and did not care to look closely. He
might be right.

Mayhew's voice broke the prolonged silence.

"He never did figure it out."

"Just what let go, anyway?" asked Floyd.

"Well, the only combustible we know of in the cell was
the lighter fluid. To blast like that, though, it must have
been almost completely vaporized, and mixed with just the
right amount of air—possible, I suppose, in a room like
this. I don't understand why he let it all out, though."

"He seems to have been using pieces of the lighter,"
Floyd pointed out. "The loose fuel was probably just a
by-product of his activities. He was even duller than I,
though. It took me long enough to realize that a fire needs
air to burn—and can't set up convection currents to keep
itself supplied with oxygen, when there is no gravity."

"More accurately, when there is no *weight*," interjected
Mayhew. "We are well within Earth's gravity field, but in
free fall. Convection currents occur because the heated
gas is *lighter* per unit volume than the rest, and rises. With
no weight, and no 'up' such currents are impossible."

"In any case, he must have decided we were fooling him
with noncombustible liquids."

Mayhew replied slowly: "People are born and brought
up in a steady gravity field, and come to take all its manifes-
tations for granted. It's extremely hard to foresee *all* the
consequences which will arise when you dispense with it.
I've been here for years, practically constantly, and still
get caught sometimes when I'm tired or just waking up."

"They should have sent a spaceman to do this fellow's
job, I should think."

"How would he have entered the station? A man is
either a spy or a spaceman—to be both would mean he
was too old for action at all, I should say. Both professions
demand years of rigorous training, since habits rather
than knowledge are required—habits like the one of al-

ways stopping within reach of a wall or other massive object." There was a suspicion of the old chuckle in his voice as Mayhew spoke the final sentence, and it was followed by a roar of laughter from the other men. Floyd looked around, and blushed furiously.

He was, as he had suspected from the older man's humor, suspended helplessly in midair out of reach of every source of traction. Had there been anything solid around, he would probably have used it for concealment instead, anyway. He managed at last to join that laughter; but at its end he glanced once more into Hart's cell, and remarked, "If this is the worst danger that inexperience lands on my head, I don't think I'll complain. Bruce, I want to go with you on your next leave to Earth; I simply must see you in a gravity field. I bet you won't wait for the ladder when we step off the rocket—though I guess it would be more fun to see you drop a dictionary on your toe. As you implied, habits are hard to break."

"You disappoint me," the class superintendent said with some feeling. "I have a personal as well as a professional dislike of wastefully run farms, and you seem to have furnished a prime example." He paused briefly, watching in silence as the spheroidal forcing beds drifted smoothly about their central radiator. "Of course, I would be much more sympathetic with *you* if your own ill-advised actions were not so largely responsible for this situation." He checked his young listener's half-uttered protest. "Oh, I realize that youngsters have to learn, and experiment is the only source of knowledge; but why not use the results of other people's experiments? This sort of thing has happened before, I think you'll find."

"I didn't know." The answer was sullen despite the grudging respect. "How was I supposed to?"

"Did you get an education or not?" There was some heat in the query. "I can't imagine what the primary teachers do these days. Even though you are so young, I understood that you had some qualifications and even a bit of promise in agriculture. That's why I thought you could be trusted without supervision for a few years. Am I to assume that you became dissatisfied with the yield of this farm?"

"Of course. Why else study agriculture?"

"Until you can answer that for yourself, I won't try to. Tell me in detail what you did. Did you try to step up the output of the central radiator?"

"What do you think I am?" The younger being's indignation flared abruptly.

The other remained calm and exhibited faint traces of amusement, permitting the feeling to show in his answer rather more plainly than was strictly tactful.

"Don't boil your crust off. You might not be able to spare it next time you go in to harvest. People still do try the stunt I mentioned, you know. Every now and then it works for someone after a fashion, so the rest feel it's still worth trying. If it wasn't that, just what did you do?

You're missing a culture unit, if I remember this solar system correctly."

The student took a moment to find just the right words. "One of the lots seemed to be practically ideal. When it first solidified, it was just far enough from the radiator and just large enough to retain a thin surface film of light elements; and it responded beautifully to culturing with water-base growths. On the colder ones, by the way, I had good luck with ammonia cultures."

"Quite possible, in that sort of bed. I noticed a couple of them were bare, though. Was that another result of this experiment of yours?"

"Indirectly, yes." The young farmer looked a trifle apprehensive. "There was another plot, a good deal farther out and colder than my ideal one. But it was too hot for ammonia growths and too small to furnish the pressure they seem to need—at least the ones I'm familiar with." The addition was made hastily.

"I judged that it should have a good supply of food elements, cooling where it did; and since it wasn't doing well where it was, I thought it would be a good idea to move it farther in."

The listener's manner lost some of its amused aspect.

"Just how did you decide to go about that? The energy involved would have demanded several times the mass of your own body, even with total conversion—which I can't believe you've mastered."

"I don't suppose I have. It seemed to me that the unit itself could furnish the mass without serious loss, though."

"I see." The comment was grim. "Go on."

"Well, I went in and set up a conversion reaction. I touched it off as well as I could on the forward side of the unit, though that was a little hard to arrange—the thing was spinning like mad, as most of them do. Maybe that was the reason I let a little too much mass get involved, or maybe the globe wasn't as massive as I had thought."

"You mean you were uncertain of its mass? Is something wrong with your perceptive faculties as well as your judgment? Just how old are you, anyway?"

"Fifteen." The sullenness, which had begun to depart from the youngster's tone as he warmed to his narrative, returned in full strength. The questioner noted it and realized that he was not being as tactful as he might be; but under the circumstances he felt entitled to a little emotion.

"Fifteen years on what scale?"

"Local—this furnace, around the mass-center of the system."

"Hmph. Continue."

"Most of the sphere was volatilized, and most of what wasn't was blown completely out of the system's gravitational influence. The rest—well, it's still circling the furnace in quite a wide variety of orbits but it's not much good to anyone."

There was a pause while the nearly useless outermost unit swung beneath the two speakers, then on to the far side of the glowing sphere of gas that held it with unbreakable fingers of gravity. The supervisor was not actually boiling—that would be difficult even for a body composed largely of methane, oxygen, and similar solids when it is at a temperature of about half a degree absolute—but his temper was simmering. After a moment he spoke again.

"Let me get this straight. You sent a slave with a message that your farm had gotten out of hand and that you would like advice. Am I to understand that you spent so much time ruining one of your units that some of the others developed culture variations whose taste didn't appeal to you? I'm afraid my sympathy grows rapidly less."

"It's not that I don't like the stuff; it's that I can't eat it." The youngster must have been angry, too; there was no other imaginable reason why he should have made a statement at once so true in fact and so misleading in implication. The superintendent, swallowing the implication whole, permitted the remains of his temper to evaporate completely.

"You can't eat it? That is really too bad. Pardon me while I go to sample some of this repulsive chemical—or perhaps you would like to come along and show me what you *have* been eating. There is hardly enough drift in this area to support you, particularly with a decent-sized crew of slaves. What have you been feeding them? Perhaps you ought to let someone else take over this farm and get yourself a research job out in one of the drift clouds, soaking up your nourishment from a haze of free atoms ten parsecs across for a few years. You youngsters!"

"I've been eating from the ammonia units. So have the slaves."

"Very well, then I shall look over your water culture, which by elimination must be the one that's been giving trouble. On second thought, you needn't come along. It's the third plot from the furnace. I can find my way." He moved off abruptly, not even waiting for an answer.

And the student, with no slightest shadow of an excuse, simply because of his own childish loss of temper, let him go without a word of warning.

It might, of course, have made no difference if he had spoken. The superintendent was annoyed, too, and might understandably have chosen to ignore his junior. His attention, as he permitted himself to fall toward the central radiator, was divided between his own irritation and the condition of the various plots. Only gradually did the latter feeling predominate.

He had to admit the outermost was too cold for much chemical action except actual life processes which were too slow to be useful. The fact that the youngster he had left above had induced anything at all to grow there was at least one point to his credit. It swung past only once while he was falling by its orbit. Though his gravity-given speed was slow, its speed was slower—and it had farther to go.

The next two he had noted earlier were bare of useful growths. He remembered now that the student had admitted this fact to be an indirect result of his experiment. The superintendent could not see the connection. The plots themselves, on closer inspection, seemed physically undamaged, and the student himself could not possibly have eaten them both clean, no matter what his hunger. Of course, a crowd of slaves might—but he was not going to accuse anybody *yet* of letting slaves get that far out from under control. They were not even allowed to approach a culture plot in person, being fed from its produce by their master.

The plots themselves were large bodies, though not the largest in the system, with their solid bulks veiled under mile after mile of hydrogen compounds. The superintendent's senses probed in vain for the enormously complex compounds that were the preferred food of his kind. Several much smaller bodies were gravitating about each of these plots, but none was large enough to hold the light elements in the liquid or gaseous form necessary for food culture.

The next unit had the merit of interesting appearance, if nothing else. In addition to the more or less standard quota of bodies circling it, it possessed a regular halo of minute particles traveling in a solidly interwoven maze of orbits just outside the atmosphere. On the surface, and even in the atmosphere itself, its cultures were flourishing. The superintendent paused to take a sample, and had to admit that once again the youngster had not done too badly.

His temper cooling, he rode the farm plot most of the way around its orbit, taking an occasional taste and growing calmer by the moment. By the time he left the limits of his atmosphere, he was almost his normal self.

This, however, did not last long enough even for him to get rid of the globe's orbital speed, to say nothing of resuming his drop toward the Sun. He had slanted some distance inward and fallen well behind the ringed sphere when his attention was drawn to another, much smaller object well to one side of his line of flight.

Physically, there was little remarkable about it. It was less massive even than his own body, though a short period of observation disclosed that it was in an orbit about the central furnace, just as the farm plots were. Sometimes its outline was clear, at others it blurred oddly. Its brightness flickered in an apparently meaningless pattern. Merely on its physical description, there was nothing remarkable about it, but it seized and held the superintendent's puzzled attention. Off his planned course though it was, he swung toward it, wondering. The student had mentioned no friends or co-workers—

Gradually, details grew clearer and the superintendent's feelings grew grimmer. He did not like to believe what he saw, but the evidence was crowding in.

"Help! Please help! Master!"

The bubble of horror burst, and one of anger grew in its place. Not one of his own kind, injured or dying and an object of terror and revulsion thereby; this thing was a slave. A slave, moreover, well within the limits of the farm, where it had no business to be without supervision; a slave who dared call on him for help!

"What are you doing here?" The superintendent sent the question crackling along a tight beam toward the apparently helpless creature. "Did you enter this region without orders?"

"No, Master. I was . . . ordered."

"By whom? What happened to you? Speak more clearly!"

"By—I cannot, Master. Help me!" The irregular flickering of the slave's auroral halo brightened fitfully with the effort of radiating speech.

Unsympathetic as the superintendent normally was to such beings, he realized that help must be given if he were to learn anything. Conquering a distinct feeling of repugnance, he moved up beside the slave to investigate its injuries. He expected, naturally, to find the visible results of a thorough ion-lashing, that being the principal occupational hazard faced by the slaves; but what he actually saw almost made him forget his anger.

The unfortunate creature's outer crust was *pitted*—dotted and cratered with a pattern of circular holes which resembled nothing the superintendent had ever encountered. He knew the long, shallow scars of an ion-lashing and the broad, smoothed areas which showed on the crust of one of his people when close exposure to a sun had boiled away portions of his mass. These marks, however, looked almost as though the slave had been exposed to a pelting by granules of solid *matter!*

A ridiculous thought, of course. The stupidest slave could detect and avoid the occasional bits of rock and metal which were encountered in the interstellar void. After all, they had the same sensory equipment and physical powers as the masters. An unprejudiced judge might even have said they were of the same species as the masters.

Whatever had caused the creature's injury, there was little that could be done for it. Grudgingly, inspired far more by curiosity than by sympathy, the superintendent did that little, supplying hydrocarbons and other organic matter lately skimmed from the ringed planet.

Food, however, was not enough. Bits of extraneous metal were imbedded in its body, altering the precise pattern of charged metal nodes that spelled life to these beings. Some of its own field nodes had apparently been chipped or blown away, and others were discharged. The creature's body was only a fraction of its normal size—the

regular reserve of "food" compounds that ordinarily
made up so much of even a slave's bulk had long since
been consumed or had evaporated.

There was no doubt that it was dying. But there was
some chance that it might gain strength enough to impart
information if it were fed. It was—sparingly, of course.

"No sense wasting food on a slave that's about to die,"
the superintendent explained without brutality.

"Certainly not, Master," the slave agreed without re-
sentment.

"What happened to you?" the superintendent repeated.
The slave was in no condition to be coherent; but a lifetime
of conditioning brought some order to its agony-dazed
mind, and it answered.

"I was ordered to the inner plots—to harvest." The
word-symbols came haltingly, but with sufficient clarity to
be unmistakable, shocking as their implication was.

So the student had trusted slaves near a food supply!
Perhaps that accounted for the two stripped planets.

"You went to harvest when a young fool like this orders
it?"

"He was a master, and he gave the order. Many of us
went; many of us have been going for years—and seldom
returning. We did not wish it, Master, but he ordered it.
What could we do?"

"You could have asked the first superintendent who
came here whether it was better to disobey a Prime Order
or a young master."

"You are the first to come, Master, as far as I know.
And the young master said we were not to speak of this
order to anyone. It is only because you command me to
speak that I do so now—that and the fact that there is little
more that he could do to me, anyway."

The overseer ignored the pointed closing sentence. "You
say many of you have been ordered to do this, but few
have returned from the errand? What happened to them?
What happened to you?"

"They die. I did not know how; now I suppose it must
be—this way."

There was a pause, and the supervisor was moved to
sarcasm. "I suppose they are struck by meteoric particles,
as you seem to have been. Do slaves absorb personal

characteristics such as stupidity from their masters? Could
you not dodge the meteors?"

"No, not all of them. The region near the central furnace has more of such matter than any other place I have
ever seen. Some pieces are iron, some are of other matter;
but they cannot be avoided. They strike too hard. They
cannot be absorbed in normal fashion, but simply boil off
one's body material into space. The shock is so tremendous
that I, at least, could do nothing toward recovering the
material until it had dissipated beyond hope of salvage.
That is the reason so much of my mass is gone; it was not
merely starvation.

"Some of the other slaves did better than I—as I said,
some of them have survived—but others did much worse.
They would dive in toward the furnace, and their bodies
would come falling back out in just about the shape I am."

"And still he sends his slaves in to harvest?"

"Yes. We did not do too badly, actually, on the largest
plots; but then he got interested in the others farther in.
After all, they're hotter. He ventured in himself almost to
the orbit of the plot that was destroyed—did you know
that?—but came out very quickly and sent us on all such
journeys thereafter.

"We—or, rather, those who preceded me—cleaned off
the next inner plot, the fourth from the central furnace,
fairly well, though the loss of slaves was high. Then he
wanted to start on the third. I was one of the first to work
on this project.

"I did not expect to live, of course, after what I had
heard from the others; but the order came, and I let
myself fall toward the sun. My orbit passed close to the
greatest of the plots, which the master has been harvesting
himself, and I hoped to strengthen myself with a little food
from it as I passed."

That confession showed how certain the slave felt of his
own imminent death, as well as the state of demoralization
into which the student's activities had permitted his servi-
tors to fall.

"But I did not dare take any food when the time came,"
the slave went on feebly. "As I passed through the region
where the destroyed plot had been, drifting particles began
to grow more numerous. At first there would be an occa-

sional bit of stone or iron, which I could dodge easily.
Then they came in twos and threes, and sometimes I would
have to change an escape curve in mid-maneuver. Then
they came in dozens and clusters, and at last I could avoid
them no longer. I was struck several times in rapid succession.

"For a moment I almost turned back—I had never
dreamed that anything could feel like that—and then I
remembered the order and went on. And I was struck
again, and again, and each time the order faded in my
mind. I reached the orbit of the fourth planet, crossed
it—and turned out again. It didn't seem to help; I was still
being pelted. For a time I must have almost lost orientation; but at last I won out to a place near the orbit of the
giant planet. That was where I remembered the order
again.

"I had never disobeyed a master before, and I didn't
know what to do, or say, or think. I'd start back toward
the Sun, and remember what had happened, and come
back out. Then I'd remember the master, and head in
again. I didn't dare go out in the cold where he would be
waiting. I didn't dare dive back into that storm of rock
and metal from the old fifth planet. But I had to do
something. I couldn't float by the orbit of the Giant Planet
forever. He would find me there sooner or later, and that
would be worse than if I had come out to him. I had to
think."

That word struck the superintendent like a shock. The
very idea of a slave's thinking—making a decision for
himself concerning an action he was to perform—was
repugnant to a member of the dominant race. They preferred to think of their slaves as mindless creatures relying on their masters for the necessities of existence—a
comforting fiction that had been maintained for so many
rotations of the Galaxy that its originators had come to
believe it themselves. He had suspected that this particular
slave must be an unusual specimen in many ways; now he
was sure of it.

It was this that kept him silent while the creature
paused, visibly collected its waning energies, and resumed
the tale.

"I found what I thought was the answer at last. Since the
tremendous number of particles must have come from the
farm that had been blown up, it seemed likely that their

orbits would be more or less controlled by that and would have at least a slight family resemblance. If I were to take up a powered, nearly elliptical path through that region, matching velocities with most of them instead of falling in a practically parabolic orbit across their path, I should be able to avoid the worst of the blows."

Weakly, the shattered creature shuddered and paused, mustering strength to continue.

"I had about made up my mind to try this when I detected another slave inbound," it went on, "and it occurred to me that two would be better than one. If one died, at least the other could learn from what had happened. I caught him easily since he was in free fall and explained the idea. He seemed willing to follow any suggestion, not thinking for himself at all, so he went with me.

"For a while it worked. We got inside the orbit of the fourth planet without being hit more than a few times each —that was harder on me than on him, because I'd already been hurt quite a lot on the first trip. Into that level, a great deal of the wreckage is formed of quite large particles, anyway; it's easy to see and avoid. Farther in, though, where most of the heavy stuff either never went or was cleared out by collision with the inner planets in a few million of their revolutions, there was much more extremely fine stuff. It actually seems to increase in concentration near the sun. Maybe radiation pressure has something to do with it.

"Anyway, we began to take a bad beating again. It was a little better than before. My idea must have had something to it, but it still wasn't good. The other slave wasn't used to it, either, and lost control of himself just as I had. We were almost to the third farm plot then, but he must have gone completely blind from pain. He apparently never sensed the food so near by—that plot is incredibly rich.

"He went blundering squarely into another, useless plot that accompanies the third one in its orbit; an object too small to hold culture material in that temperature range, though still several hundred times the diameter of my body or his. He rammed it hard, and the energy involved in matching velocities was more than enough to volatilize his mass completely. The object was pretty well scarred with impact craters, but he made one of the neatest.

"I was close enough then to the third planet to start

harvesting—at least, I would have been under normal circumstances. I tried, but couldn't concentrate on one course of action long enough. The bombardment was endless. There are simply no words to describe what it was like. I was not twenty of its own diameters from the most amazingly rich farm plot I have ever seen, and was not able to touch a *bit* of it!

"It had been so long since it was harvested that substances completely strange to me had developed in its surface layers. There were carbohydrates, of course, and light-element oxides and carbonates which anyone would expect; but there were proteins more fantastically complex than anyone could well imagine. Their emanations nearly drove me wild. They must have been building up and breaking down at incredible speed at that temperature—I had quite an atmosphere out, as a result of boiling off surface matter to use up incoming radiant energy—and they had evolved to an unheard-of degree. And I couldn't get a taste!

"I could sense them, though, and in spite of the pain of the meteor bombardment, I stayed near the planet, vacillating as I had done before, for a couple of hundred of its trips around the Sun. That may seem like a short time, but it was long enough to ruin my body past saving. It was only when my senses began to fail that I was able to turn away from it and fight my way out this far. I just managed to get into a stable orbit that would keep me clear of that hellish halo of planet fragments, and every now and then I succeeded in mustering enough energy to call for help, but I knew it was useless. Even had you come much sooner, it would still have been too late for me.

"I live to warn you, however. *Do not go within the orbit of the old fifth planet!* Do not even look within it, for if you sense what lies on that unharvested third world, you will be drawn to your doom as surely as I was ordered to mine!"

The slave fell silent, and the superintendent pondered its tale as they drifted on about the Sun. He could not, offhand, think of any adequate punishment for the student whose recklessness had brought about this state of affairs. The mere cruelty of ordering endless crowds of slaves to nearly certain death did not affect him particularly; but the waste of it did, very much. To him the thought of hundreds of lifeless bodies drifting endlessly about the Sun, boiling off a little more of their masses with each perihelion passage until nothing was left but a loose collection of high melting-point pebbles, was a painful picture of economic loss. The fact that the best farm plot in the system had apparently become unattainable was also to be considered, and the driving of at least one slave to the extreme of thinking for himself was not to be ignored.

Of course, everything should be checked before confronting the student with such charges. Only the last, after all, could be considered as yet a matter of objective knowledge.

The overseer moved abruptly away from the slave—sunward. The dying creature, seeing him depart, called once more for aid, and was silenced instantly and permanently by a slashing beam of ions. For an instant the overseer regretted the impulsive act—not from gratitude for the warning, to which he attached little weight and which was part of a slave's duty, but simply because it *was* impulsive rather than reasoned. But then he reflected that the creature could probably not have told much more anyway, even if it had survived until his return.

He was in no hurry. He let the gravity of the central furnace draw him in to the orbit of the Giant Planet, his senses covering the half-billion-mile sphere of space ahead where death was reputed to lurk.

At this range, all seemed innocuous. He watched the inner planets circling rapidly in their paths—even the giant one made most of a revolution during his fall—and noted that the slave had spoken the truth about a companion body to the third planet. But space seemed otherwise empty.

He did not completely abandon caution, however. What had proven fatal to slaves might be inconvenient or even dangerous to a master.

He stopped at the fifth planet's orbit and began a more minute examination of that suspicious volume of space.

The small bodies were there, all right. Thousands of them, even though he was not trying to detect anything less than a twentieth of his own diameter. They did show a rather vague preference for the orbit of the old fifth planet, as the slave had said. The greater number circled between the present fourth and fifth orbits, at any rate,

There seemed no reason why he could not match velocities well enough to keep out of trouble. Why, chance alone could be trusted to protect him from collision with a few thousand asteroids, when they were scattered through something like ten-to-the-twenty-fourth-power cubic miles of space!

Still, there was little wisdom in going into possible danger without a very sound reason. It would be well to judge from his present position if such reason existed. His finer senses could easily operate at the half billion miles that separated him from the farthest point of the third planet's orbit. So, holding his position, he focused his attention on the elusive farm plot in question.

Being so close to the central furnace, it revolved rapidly. He faced somewhat the same problem in examining it that a man would have trying to recognize a friend on a merry-go-round—assuming that the friend were spinning in his seat like a top at the same time.

It took the superintendent only a few revolutions of the body to adjust to this situation, however, and as details registered more and more clearly on his consciousness, he began to admit grudgingly that the slave had not exaggerated.

The plot was fabulous!

Substances for which he had no name abounded, impressing themselves on the analytical sense that was his equivalent of both taste and smell. Strange as they were, he could tell easily that they were foods—packed with available energy and carrying fascinating taste potentialities, organized to a completely unheard-of degree. They were growths of a type and complexity which simply never had a chance to evolve on the regularly harvested worlds of the Galaxy.

The overseer wondered whether it might not be worth while to let other plots run wild for a few years. His principal vice, by the standards of his people, was gluttony; but the most ascetic of his species would have been tempted uncontrollably by that planet.

He almost regretted the few tons of food he had taken on from the ringed planet—though he had, he told himself quickly, sacrificed much of that in helping the slave and would lose still more if he decided actually to penetrate into the high-temperature zones near the Sun.

Huge as his mass was, his normal temperature was so

low that life processes went on at an incredibly slow pace. To him, a chemical reaction requiring only a few millennia to go to completion was like a dynamite explosion. A few pounds of organic compounds would feed his miles-thick bulk for many human lifetimes of high activity.

In short, the slave had been quite right.

Almost involuntarily, rationalizing his appetite as he went, the superintendent permitted himself to drift into the asteroid zone. With only the smallest part of his attention, he assumed a parabolic, free-fall orbit in the general plane of the system, with its perihelion point approximately tangent to the orbit of the third planet. At this distance from the Sun, the difference between parabolic and circular velocities was not too great to permit him to detect even the tiniest particles in time to avoid them. That fact, of course, changed as he fell sunward.

Perhaps he had been counting on a will power naturally superior to that of the slave who had warned him. If so, he had forgotten the effects of an equally superior imagination. The pull of the third planet was correspondingly stronger and, watching the spinning globe, he was jarred out of an almost hypnotic trance by the first collision. It awakened him to the fact that his natural superiority to the slave race might not be sufficient to keep him out of serious trouble.

The space around him—he was now well inside the orbit of the fourth planet—was literally crowded with grain-of-dust meteors, each, as he had seen on the slave's crust, able to blast out a crater many times its own volume in a living body. Individually, they were insignificant; collectively, they were deadly.

His attention abruptly wrenched back to immediate problems of existence, the superintendent started to check his fall and veer once more toward the safe, frozen emptiness of interstellar space. But the spell of the gourmet's paradise he had been watching was not that easily thrown off. For long moments, while the planet circled its primary once and again, he hung poised, with gluttony and physical anguish alternately gaining the upper hand in a struggle for possession of his will. Probably he would have lost, alone; but his student did have a conscience.

"Sir!" The voice came faintly but clearly to his mind. "Don't stay! You mustn't! I should never have let you come—but I was angry! I know I was a fool; I should have told you everything!"

"I learned. It was my own fault." The superintendent found it curiously difficult to speak. "I came of my own free will and I still think that plot is worth investigation."

"No! It's not your own free will—no will could remain free after seeing what that planet has to offer. I knew it and expected you to die—but I couldn't go through with it. Come, and quickly. I will help."

The student was in an orbit almost identical with that of the superintendent, though still a good deal farther out. Perhaps it was the act of looking at him, which took his attention momentarily from the alluring object below, that made the older being waver. Whatever it was, the student perceived the break and profited by it.

"Don't even look at it again, sir. Look at me, and follow —or if you'd rather not look at me, look at *that!*"

He indicated the direction plainly, and the dazed listener looked almost involuntarily.

The thing he saw was recognizable enough. It consisted of a small nucleus which his senses automatically analyzed. It consisted of methane and other hydrocarbons, some free oxygen, a few other light-element compounds, and had nuggets of heavier elements scattered through it like raisins in a plum pudding. Around it for thousands of miles there extended a tenuous halo of the more volatile of its constituent compounds. The thing was moving away from the Sun in an elliptical orbit, showing no sign of intelligent control. A portion of its gaseous envelope was driven on ahead by the pressure of sunlight from below.

It was a dead slave, but it could as easily have been a dead master.

A dead slave was nothing; *but the thing that had killed it could do the same to him.*

It was the first time in his incredibly long life that the *personal* possibility of death had struck home to him; and probably nothing less than that fear could have saved his life.

With the student close beside, he followed the weirdly glowing corpse out to the farthest point of its orbit; and as it started to fall back into the halo of death girdling that harmless-looking star, he pressed on out into the friendly darkness.

Perhaps some day that third planet would be harvested; but it would not be by one of his kind—not, at least, until that guarding haze had been swept up by the planets that drifted through its protecting veil.

It was not a very good group, Wright reflected. That always seemed to be the case. When he had luck with observing weather, he had no one around to appreciate the things that could be seen. He cast a regretful glance toward the dome of the sixty-inch telescope, where a fellow candidate was taking another plate of his series, and wondered whether there were not some better way than part-time instructing to pay the expenses of a doctorate program.

Still, the night *was* good. Most of the time in the latitude—

"Mr. Wright! Is that a cloud or the Aurora?"

"If you will stop to consider the present position of the Sun below the horizon," he answered indirectly, "you will discover that the patch of light you are indicating is directly opposite that point. It lies along the path of the Earth's shadow, though, of course, well beyond it. It is called the *Gegenschein* and, like the Zodiacal Light, is not too commonly visible at this latitude. We did see the Light some time ago, if you remember, on an evening when we started observing earlier. Actually, the *Gegenschein* is a continuation of the luminous band we call the Zodiacal Light. The latter can sometimes be traced all the way around the sky to the point we are now watching."

"What causes them?"

"The most reasonable assumption is that they are light reflected from small, solid particles—meteors. Apparently a cloud of such matter extends outward for some distance past the Earth's orbit, though just how far, it is hard to say. It grows fainter with distance from the Sun, as would be expected, except for the patch we call the *Gegenschein*."

"Why the exception?"

"I think one of you can answer that."

"Would it be for the same reason that the full Moon is so much more than twice as bright as either quarter? Simply because the particles are rough, and appear dark in most positions because of the shadows of irregularities on their own surfaces—shadows which disappear when the light is behind the observer?"

"I think you will agree that that would account for it," Wright said. "Evidently the meteors are there, are large compared to wavelengths of visible light, and form a definite part of the Solar System. I believe it was once estimated that if the space inside the Earth's orbit contained particles one millimeter in diameter and five miles apart, they would reflect enough light to account for what we are observing. They might, of course, be smaller and more numerous. Only that amount of reflecting surface is necessary."

"You had me worried," another voice broke in. "I'd been hearing for years that there would be little reason to fear collision with meteors when we finally get a rocket out of the atmosphere. For a moment, I thought a cloud such as you were working up to would riddle anything that got into space. One pinhead every five miles isn't so bad, though."

"There is a fairly good chance of collision, I would say," returned Wright, "but just what damage particles of that size would do, I am not sure. It seems rather likely that they would be volatilized by impact. How the hull of a rocket would react, we will have to find out by experience. I wouldn't mind taking the risk myself. I think we can sum up the greatest possibilities by saying that the meteoric content of the Solar System has and will have nothing but nuisance value to the human race, whether or not we ever leave our own planet."

A streak of white fire arced silently across the sky, putting a fitting period to the subject.

Wright wondered whether it would appear on his friend's photographic plate.

THE FOUNDLING STARS

"All right—perfect. You're the most nearly motionless thing in the universe."

Hoey's words were figurative, of course; whether they were accurate or not depended entirely on point of view. Rocco Luisi and his *Ymyrgar* were indeed at rest with respect to Hoey and the *Anfforddus,* after more than four hours of maddening effort, but neither machine was motionless with respect to much else. Both were travelling at about four kilometers a second, roughly galactic northward, with respect to their home port on Rhyddid, seventy-five parsecs away. They were moving at a much greater velocity with respect to the far more distant Solar System. With respect to each other, however, velocity had been whittled down to somewhat less than five centimeters a year.

How long this would last was problematical. An automatic tracker was now on duty in Hoey's ship, trying to hold steady the fringe pattern produced by combining two ultraviolet laser beams, one originating in his own vessel and the other in Luisi's in one of the most precise interferometers ever made. Since the crafts were about a lighthour apart, however, corrections tended to be late in time and, in spite of a computer's best efforts, erratic in amount and direction.

"Nineteen decimals" had been a proverbial standard of accuracy for well over a century; but achieving it on any but the atomic size and time scale was not yet standard art.

"That seems to be it," Hoey repeated. "That means that you and I stay strapped in our seats, with no more motion than we can help, for the next four hours or so. If either of the instrument platforms on our ships moves more than half a micron with respect to the other, a lot of time and money go down the drain."

"I know—I've had it hammered into me as often and as hard as you have." Luisi's voice was undistorted, and the responses instant, on the medium communicator.

"Sure you have," retorted Hoey, "only a lot of people wonder whether you really believe it."

"Well, it depends on what you mean by believe. I can figure as well as anyone where the center of mass of my ship would go if I stood up; I—"

"I know you can. Your trouble is that you can't believe it would make as much trouble as they say. Just remember that they were even concerned about tidal forces from Cinder over there—" he gestured, rather uselessly, at the grossly misnamed 06e star glaring at them from half a parsec away—"and even went to the trouble of finding a part of this neighborhood where the wind was steady—"

"Right there I break connection. Space is space. You only worry about wind when you're close to a sun, and then it's only a hard-radiation problem."

"True enough, as a rule. The trouble is that the usual run of stellar winds involves a mass density of around ten atoms to the cubic centimeter; here it's a couple of thousand. It turned out that even that much mass wouldn't accelerate the ships seriously unless the relative velocity were very high indeed, but it was something the planners had to check on. You see what I mean; so stay put. Let's cut the chatter. The sooner the folks in 'Big Boy' can get to work, the sooner we can breathe comfortably. I'll call 'em."

Hoey's fingers tensed on a button, replacing the microscopic crystal in the activity field of his communicator with another, whose twin was aboard "Big Boy"—more formally, the *Holiad*. He spoke without preamble, knowing that someone would be listening.

"We're in position, and my tracker says we're holding. Get the job going while the going's good."

"Right." The answer was terse, but not casual. The speaker, a heavy-set, middle-aged man with an almost fanatically intense stare in his blue eyes, leaned forward over the console in front of him and began punching buttons in an intricate sequence. He paused every second or two to interpret the patterns of light which winked at him from the board. After half a minute or so the pattern became fixed, and he leaned back, more relaxed.

"Program A is running." A younger man, seated at a similar console a few yards away, nodded at the words. At first he did not answer aloud; then he decided to speak, though for several seconds he was obviously trying to make up his mind what to say. It was easy to make the wrong remark to Elvin Toner.

"D'you think we'll get full time out of it?" he ventured at last. "Those pilots are good, but I still wish it had been possible to use robotships for the key stations. A man can't hold still forever."

"So do I." Toner answered without obvious irritation, and his eyes remained fixed on his console, to the younger man's relief. "I also wish," the director went on, "that it were possible to use the medium communicator system directly for automatic control of such things as distance, so as to get away from light-lag. But until some genius in your generation works out a way to measure the frequency, wavelength, and propagation velocity of medium waves—or at least, furnishes some evidence that a wave phenomenon is involved—we'll have to stick with electromagnetic radiation and, at times, with human beings. You may not like it, but by the time you reach my age you'll have learned to put up with it."

"I hope not," Ledermann couldn't help replying.

"Eh? Why not?" Toner's eyes almost flicked away from his instruments for a moment, but didn't quite.

"I mean that if I learn to put up with inconveniences, it'll be because I haven't been able to figure out anything else to do about them. Who wants to admit that?"

Toner grinned. "Nobody wants to, I suppose, but the honest people do anyway. Hold up; here comes the end of the first minute; any irregularities on your board?"

"Not so far. I don't know what that proves, though; all we are measuring is what's going into the generators. We can't touch what's coming out without changing it—"

"Of course." The older man made a gesture of impatience. "It's some relief, though, to know that things are going in right. I don't know about you, Dick, but Program A is going to be the second longest couple of hours in my life."

"I know," replied Ledermann. It was the first time Toner had ever been so frank about his feelings—even though they were usually quite obvious from other evidence—and certainly the first time the assistant had felt much real sympathy for the director. Since the younger

man was not a fast thinker, the remark left him once more
unsure of what to say.

As a matter of fact, there was probably nothing to say
which would have been just right. Toner, like most middle-aged men, had developed a pretty firm personal philos-
ophy and a rather rigid set of fundamental beliefs. The
present experiment involved very heavily one of those
beliefs—one which Ledermann did not share.

Although, the assistant thought as he glanced through
one of the *Holiad*'s great view ports, this was a place
where it was hard to feel sure and right about anything
fundamental.

Space was not dark, though the nebular material which
abounds in the Orion spur of the Milky Way system is
never very bright even when no planetary atmosphere
dims it. Getting closer to an extended light source, of
course, doesn't make each square degree look any brighter; it merely increases the number of square degrees.
From the *Holiad*'s position, most of the sky is nebula-
bright; and to a spaceman, anything resembling a cloud
looks wrong in space. In some directions the stars blaze
steadily, as they do from Earth's moon; other directions
are blacked out by light-years of dust. Some of the dust
itself is bright, for 41 Orionis, named "Cinder" by some
humorist who had explored the region earlier, is only half
a parsec away. Not only does its fierce ultraviolet radiation keep the nebular gases fluorescing, but its visible is
quite enough to light up the dust for immense distances.
Not counting its emission envelope, Cinder is only about
five times the diameter of Sol, which means that it looks
like a point from half a parsec away; but that point illuminated the *Holiad* almost as effectively as the full moon
illuminates the earth. Several other O and B stars flame in
the neighborhood; some look brighter than Venus as seen
from Earth, some reveal themselves only by illuminating
the surrounding dust clouds, some are invisible in the
nebulosity. The Orion Spur is one of the cradles of the
galaxy.

Unfortunately, the occupants of the cradle are foundlings. The general circumstances surrounding a star's
birth are now fairly clear; ships prowling the cloudier
regions of the spiral arms have found them in all stages of
gestation, from gas and dust clouds half a light-year across

and little denser than the interstellar background, through T Tauri variables hot enough to radiate visibly, to the vast population of main-sequence suns whose hydrogen fires are safely alight. Like foundlings, while an entire birth has never been observed in any one case, we know enough to picture the circumstances with some confidence.

Also like foundlings, however, the precise details of a star's conception are somewhat obscure. It has been widely supposed for several decades that random variations in the density of the interstellar medium are the key factor—that the law of chance is the father. Dick Ledermann, young and conservative, had no trouble accepting this view. To him, it was obvious that the random "winds" of space must at times produce a gas concentration so dense that its gravity would override the disruptive tidal force of the rest of the galaxy—override it enough to produce a local potential well able to trap at least the lower energy particles of the cloud.

Elvin Toner, nearly twenty years older, had strong reservations about the potency of unaided statistics. Like anyone with even a modest grounding in physical science, he realized the basically statistical nature of many of the universe's laws; he admitted that a star *could* come into existence by the concatenations of chance which most people took for granted; but he doubted seriously that the random motions of interstellar gas could set up the appropriate conditions often enough to account for the number of observed stars, even allowing for the fairly impressive lifetime of a star. He felt sure—it was as much an article of faith as the normal scientific belief that there is a natural reason for everything—that some specific, widespread, underlying process was operating to improve the chance of protostar formation.

He was able to prove that some such process was needed to account for the observed star density. Ledermann was able to prove that it was not. Both "proofs" were statistical, using the same "laws" of chance. They differed, of course, in the basic conditions which were assumed. Both sets of conditions were reasonable; the two hypotheses continued to survive because neither could be checked adequately. Elvin Toner had spent nearly thirty years acquiring a professional reputation impressive enough to interest a sufficiently wealthy foundation in doing the checking. And now he had the chance.

It had taken wealth—or its equivalent—and a vast amount of human effort.

The basic check required detailed measurement of the positions, velocities and accelerations of all the particles, as exactly as Heisenberg allowed and as nearly simultaneously as possible, along a range of more than five astronomical units. Since electromagnetic energy had to be used, this meant that the best part of two hours would be needed merely to set up the web of standing waves which was to serve as the "framework" of the battery of measuring instruments, which were themselves force fields.

The basic design of the experiment was standard—even unimaginative. After setting up the wave pattern, a period would be spent measuring the initial vector quantities of the particles along the range. Fundamentally, the measuring process would be practically instantaneous, but scanning and recording would use up an hour as the chain of reading impulses travelled from the *Ymyrgar* along the wave web to the *Anfforddus,* from which the readings would be transferred by medium crystal to the mother ship.

This was "Program A" which was now in progress. Electromagnetic waves of almost five hundred different frequencies, ranging from the blue part of the visible spectrum to the output of a huge electromagnet fed by an alternating current source with a three-hundred-second period, were propagating away from the *Ymyrgar,* groping their way through the not-quite-empty billion kilometers or so which separated the little tender from her sister. Some of the frequencies had been selected for their ability to interact with the atoms and ions known to occupy the space, some for the fact that they would not. Some would be absorbed and analyzed by the apparatus aboard the *Anfforddus,* some would be reflected back toward their source to create the standing-wave patterns needed for Program B. All would represent a waste of energy if the two tiny ships changed their relative positions by one part in ten billion billion.

Lights on the control consoles aboard the *Holiad* recorded the behavior, microsecond by microsecond, of each separate frequency generator; but the one which Toner never let out of his sight was that which kept track of the interferometer on the *Anfforddus.* This light shone yellow as long as the original pattern of fringes remained

unchanged; a one-fringe shift one way would carry it into
the red; a similar change in the other would turn it violet.
So far, while there had been at times a suspicion of green
or orange in its tint, it had held within the English language limits of yellow.

"I think you can relax a little," remarked Ledermann.
"All the general run of disturbances should have had their
licks by now; A has been cooking for over half an hour.
Unless Hoey or Luisi has a fit, their ships can hardly move
enough to make trouble."

"They both had EEG checks before they were hired."
Toner was not joining in any levity, yet. "I'm not worried
about that possibility."

"Then why not take it easy? Surely you're not worrying
about a meteor."

"Well—comet nuclei are found pretty far from suns,
but I really wasn't thinking of anything specific. It's just
that so little need go wrong to wreck the whole works.
Program A isn't so bad, in spite of the precision we need;
but when B gets going it will really mean something. I can't
keep my mind off that."

Ledermann nodded. Program B was the experiment
itself—the check on the Toner hypothesis. In assuming that
non-statistical forces existed which tended to start interstellar matter drawing together into protostars, the astronomer had not fallen back on mysticism. He had computed
many combinations of electric and magnetic fields which
should have such an effect, and which might reasonably—
or at least conceivably—exist along the arms of the Milky
Way. The wave patterns of Program B had been designed
from these computations. Naturally, phenomena as
complex as, say, the human nervous system or even the
circuitry of a television set or the measuring patterns of
Program A would be no improvement on pure chance as
an explanation for star formation; such things were too
improbable by any standards. Toner's fields were simple
enough so that, in his opinion, they were more probable
than random gas and dust concentrations. They were also
complex and extensive enough so that looking around for
examples of them already in existence seemed impractical
—so far. Of course, if Program B showed that such fields
would, or could, produce the results Toner expected, he
would have little trouble financing such a search.

If the program failed to give the results Toner hoped for, Ledermann was both unsure and uneasy about what to expect. Few men can abandon a favorite hypothesis abruptly and completely, and the need to do so can have painful effects.

Actually, Toner would not be forced to such an extreme at first; many more variations on the original theme would have to fail before the whole idea would have to be abandoned. What bothered Ledermann was the doubt that the foundation would go along with any such extension of the project and how Toner would react if it refused.

Actually he needn't have worried. The director was philosophical enough to take such a problem in his stride. Since the younger man had no way of knowing this, he watched his console with even more anxiety than his director—in spite of what they had both been saying.

But the green lights stared unwinkingly back at them, as the waves spread across space. No news, with the proverbial implication. The clock was the only instrument which showed change; the clock, that is, and two human nervous systems.

"Stuff coming in from Hoey's receivers," Ledermann reported abruptly. Toner nodded.

"On time," was his only answer. Neither bothered to ask, or to say, what sort of stuff was coming in; the data was no more meaningful to human senses than were the photons which carried the first Mariner pictures from Mars. The main thing was that news was coming in; it was being recorded; it could, in due time, be decoded; and—Program B was due to start.

Both men sat up a little straighter and stared more tensely at their consoles as the light patterns began to change.

Simultaneously—the word was as nearly truthful as it had ever been in human history—sets of electromagnetic fields began to grow around both the *Ymyrgar* and the *Anfforddus*.

Neither set was complete by itself, but their interference would produce something which Ledermann thought of as a huge lens. The analogy was a poor one geometrically, but has some excuse from a functional viewpoint. Drifting slowly with respect to the surrounding gases, many of whose atoms were ionized, it should—if Toner were right

—tend to deflect their relative motions toward its own "optical axis." To that extent, Toner's idea was a simple one. The precise pattern of fields which should have the desired effect was somewhat less so, as any engineer who has been involved with an electron microscope would expect.

Each "lens" of the series making up the program was to be followed by a set of reading patterns similar to those of Program A, so that its individual effect on the motion of the nebular particles could be measured. In principle, the whole thing was easy . . .

"Intervals seem to be right." Ledermann dredged a little good news out of his light pattern. "Four seconds, plus or minus ten to the minus tenth. Interlens distances are within tolerance, I'd say."

"If we haven't been too grossly off in computing the refractive index of the nebula—"

"Which is handled automatically by the original A measures, as I understood the plan. Calm down, Boss."

"All right. You're talking a little louder than usual yourself. I still wish you'd invent a method for using the communicator medium for direct viewing; we could *see* whether these things are building right, instead of having to infer from generator behavior—"

"*Maybe* we could. I'm a conservative; I still buy the Uncertainty Principle. Even if we could do anything with the medium which would make it react to something besides a communicator crystal, I bet it would affect the thing we were trying to measure."

"It doesn't affect the crystals—just the space around them."

"Not measurably. Has anyone tried to check on them, to within fifteen figures of what we're doing now?"

"Not as far as I know. I—Dick! What happened then?"

Ledermann didn't know either. At least, he didn't know in the sense that Toner wanted to. Like the director, he had seen every light on his console except the one indicating tender separation turn a solemn red for a full second, and then switch back to green. If they had been looking away for that second, the men would not have known that anything had ever been wrong; after the event, the lights stared back at them, apparently unchanged.

The first thought to occur to both men was that something had happened to the console circuits; the second, that something had happened to their own nervous systems. Three seconds of checking with test switches seemed to dispose of the first possibility; and since they had both seen the same thing, the second was very low on the probability list.

Toner frowned, and spoke very slowly.

"If that is to be taken at face value, everything in both tenders which was putting out program radiation stopped for about a second and then started up again—all together. That would cause a gap of about three hundred thousand kilometers in the wave pattern—at each end—with the gaps due to meet in half an hour; let's see—what would that do to the lenses?"

"If you can work that out in your head, especially with only estimated time data, you didn't need to set up this experiment at all. You must have put the universe together in the first place," retorted Ledermann. "There's no more chance of telling that than of telling which of my next half million coin tosses is going to be heads."

"True." For a man whose work was taking such a blow, Toner seemed remarkably detached. "That would suggest that we should cut off our generators, let the present set of patterns radiate out of the area, and start over."

"We'd have to do more than that. The gas in the area has probably been affected by the part of B which has already gone out. We'd have to move the tenders to a different area altogether and set up the whole works again. Wouldn't it be better to let this program run itself through? We don't really know that the generators did stop; test circuits or no test circuits, I find it easier to believe that something messed up the indicators than that the whole set of generators went out and came back on again at once. If we let things run, the worst that can happen will be the loss of a couple of hours—and we *might* not have to start over, if this run is really all right."

"You're partly right. Letting it run won't cost us much time. But we will have to do it over anyway; we won't be able to tell if the first run was really okay until we get the data reduced, which we can't do here. We'll just have to do the whole thing twice."

And Ledermann slowly nodded his head.

Hoey's reaction, some hours later, was more impressive. He and Luisi were celebrating their release, to the accompaniment of an improvised song whose burden was the supreme difficulty of doing nothing at all, when Toner broke the news as gently as possible that the whole thing would have to be done over.

He wrapped the information in flattery, lubricated it with all the soft soap he could bring himself to use, and sweetened it with a respectable bonus offer; but neither pilot accepted the word at all philosophically. They were still visibly nettled sixty hours later when the tenders once more pulled away from the *Holiad*. This *may* have had something to do with the results.

They did calm down again, just a little, during the setup of the measuring line, however. Earlier practice may have helped, for it took them less than ninety minutes this time to get their little vessels "fixed" relative to each other.

"That's it, Doc!" Hoey's voice was almost jubilant. Toner, who had pretty well convinced himself by this time that the first run had really been all right, was able to answer in similar mood.

"Good going—that was very quick work. I'm starting the A tapes now. About how far are you from where the other run was made?"

"A couple of flight-hours, I'd say; we didn't try to check it exactly. You didn't say it was necessary."

"It isn't. Relax. And I do mean *relax*."

"I know, Boss. We're getting used to it. Let things roll."

"They're rolling."

Even in the calmer atmosphere of the second run, tension built up a little during Program A. Even though this part had gone without a visible hitch the first time, there was no way of knowing whether the unknown interference had a preference for Program B.

Of course, it might have. The programs *were* different —and the word "unknown" certainly was a key one. No one is quite sure, yet.

Toner and Ledermann of course knew to the second just when the Program B interruption, if it had really been one, had occurred; Hoey and Luisi knew almost as well from the physicists' account of the affair. All four were watching clocks; and perhaps it was the tension wound up by the whirling clock hands which caused the trouble; perhaps not. No one was ever sure. Whatever the cause, six seconds before the critical moment, when both scien-

tists were gripping their chair arms and staring frozenly
at their consoles, Hoey sneezed.

It was quite a sneeze, and the fact that Toner heard it
clearly through the medium communicator did not operate
to lessen its effects. The pilot's head had been resting in the
padded support which formed part of his seat—the support in which it was supposed to remain through the experiment. The muscular convulsion of the sneeze snapped that
head some twenty centimeters forward and down.

The *Anfforddus* had, roughly, a million times the mass
of Hoey's head, so its center of mass moved only about a
millionth as far. This amounted to about a fifth of a
micron. The fact that this was within the set tolerances for
the experiment did not at once dawn on Toner—for one
thing, it would have taken him a moment to figure it out
under any circumstances, and for another his reaction was
reflexive rather than rational. He was like a confirmed
anti-vivisectionist reacting to an account of a mechanical
heart's being tested on a dog; he exploded. He jumped—
much farther than Hoey, though fortunately it didn't matter how much the *Holiad* moved. He also began to talk,
though just what he said is uncertain—Ledermann charita-
bly wiped that part of the monitor tape, later. It took the
younger man some thirty seconds to calm his superior
down enough to listen to reason, and perhaps fifteen more
to supply the reason. Another five seconds passed while
Toner actually recovered control of himself, and started
to apologize to Hoey.

But Hoey did not hear the apology—we think.

In the fifty seconds or so since his sneeze, radiation from
his ship travelled some fifteen million kilometers. This is
easy to compute; it is pretty certainly a fact. It may
possibly be a useful one, though no one so far has put it to
any real use.

The trouble is, of course, that there is no way to be sure
whether the sneeze put any significant alteration into the
radiation pattern which the *Anfforddus* was broadcasting.
This, equally of course, is because no one can be sure just
how big a change must be in order to be significant.

Toner had just started to talk in a normal tone when
Ledermann gave an astonished yelp; and the director,
whose attention had shifted entirely to the screen of the
medium communicator, looked back at his console.

Its lights were out. It was blank. So, when he turned back to it, was the medium screen. And so was Ledermann's console.

One hundred seconds later, after repeated calls to the tenders had proven futile, the *Holiad*'s captain snapped her into irrelevance drive. Between four and five seconds later still, a hundredth of a parsec from where she had been lying, the research vessel halted again. Presumably she was within a few tens of thousands of kilometers of Hoey's tender, but no sign of the little ship could be detected by eye or instrument.

Calls continued to go unanswered. Searchers went out with detection and rescue equipment; the former gave no response, the latter went unused. Not a particle of solid matter could be found within light-minutes of either tender's former position; and it was not until much later, when the routine sample-bottles were being checked back on Rhyddid, that the slightly high count of aluminum atoms in that particular volume of space was noticed.

Of course, this may not be a significant fact, either.

"And just who was that?" The query came in the growl which seems to be a distinguishing property of sergeants, whether their linear dimensions be two meters or two hundred astronomical units. It received no immediate answer. "Well? Who was it? It came from just about where you should be, VA741. Was it you?"

"I—I guess so."

"You *guess* so? A soldier lets out a yelp that can be heard half way across the spiral, and he only *guesses* that he did it?"

"I did it, I—I—"

"You did. Never mind the guessing. Why did you do it? You know why we're here?"

"Yes, Sergeant."

"You know what we're doing here?"

"Yes, Sergeant."

"In fact, up to now you've been helping to do it."

"Yes, Sergeant."

"And you know why we've been sweeping this stuff together."

"Yes, Sergeant. To clear a path for—"

"Shut up. How much use will the path be if the Flickers find it before our boys have a chance to come through?"

"Not much, I suppose, Sergeant."

"You suppose. Well, I suppose I should be glad it even occurred to you. Now that you've squealed like a stuck baby, how long do you suppose it will be before Flicker scouts are poking around this cloud?"

"I don't know, Sergeant."

"I don't know either, but I'll be very surprised if we drift a hundredth of the way around the spiral. If it were possible to travel faster than radiation, they'd be spearing you before you cleared another cubic parsec."

"They may show up anyway; we can't tell yet."

"That, soldier—I use the term loosely—is the only reason you're not under formal charges right now. If we're spotted in the next little while—say, before the cloud you're sweeping up right now starts to radiate—I'll assume it wasn't your fault. But if we're found after that, when that squeal of yours has spread out a few hundred parsecs, you're in for it. What I ever did to be saddled with a—"

"But Sergeant, I couldn't help it. Something bit me."

"So something bit you. Let it bite! Since when—"

"But I really couldn't help it. It did something to my muscles, and I twitched so I thought someone might spot me anyway; but I relaxed and even damped out the spot with dope. I know how important it is not to make a disturbance. The sensation quit for a moment, but then it came back stronger than before, and before I could take another tranquilizer I cramped up tight all over. I couldn't help giving a little yelp—"

"Little? It was loud enough to—never mind. I hope you can produce whatever bit you; it may help in court. After all, I suppose anything which can interfere with even a sloppy soldier's self-control might be usable as a weapon. If we could breed more of 'em—that's an idea. See if you can catch it, without making too much noise."

"I'm afraid I didn't think of that in time, Sarge. We'll never catch that one. The whole business was just reflex, and I'm very sorry, but I swatted it without thinking."

In addition to their voice qualities, sergeants are sometimes known for a certain gift of rhetoric. This one, DA6641, of the 44th Company, 6261st Field Engineering Battalion, Army of the Republic of Whilth, was no exception.

If he had not been careful to use only short radiation in his remarks, they would have been audible back in Whilth, in the spiral arm of the Milky Way next outward from Sol's. Even with the short waves, he might possibly have made an impression on the *Holiad*'s instruments; but of course the *Holiad* was no longer there.

Long before he had really made himself clear about just what sort of poor excuse for a soldier the unfortunate VA741 was, both Elvin Toner and Dick Ledermann were dead of old age.

I

"It's not very comfortable footing, but at least you can't fall off."

Even through the helmet phones, Silbert's voice carried an edge that Bresnahan felt sure was amused contempt. The younger man saw no point in trying to hide his fear; he was no veteran of space and knew that it would be silly to pretend otherwise.

"My mind admits that, but my stomach isn't so sure," he replied. "It can't decide whether things will be better when I can't see so far, or whether I should just give up and take a running dive back there."

His metal-clad arm gestured toward the station and its comfortable spin hanging half a mile away. Technically the wheel-shaped structure in its synchronous orbit was above the two men, but it took careful observing to decide which way was really "up."

"You wouldn't make it," Silbert replied. "If you had solid footing for a jump you might get that far, since twenty feet a second would take you away from here permanently. But speed and velocity are two different animals. I wouldn't trust even myself to make such a jump in the right direction—and I know the vectors better than you do by a long shot. Which way would you jump? Right at the station? Or ahead of it, or behind it? And which is ahead and which is behind? Do you know?"

"I know which is ahead, since I can see it move against the star background, but I wouldn't know which way to jump. I *think* it should be ahead, since the rotation of this overgrown raindrop gives us less linear speed than the station's orbit; but I wouldn't know how far ahead," Silbert said.

"Good for you." Bresnahan noted what he hoped was approval in the spaceman's tone as well as in his words. "You're right as far as you committed yourself, and I wouldn't dare go any farther myself. In any case, jumping off this stuff is a losing game."

"I can believe that. Just walking on it makes me feel as though I were usurping a Biblical prerogative."

The computerman's arm waved again, this time at the surface underfoot, and he tried to stamp on it at the same moment. The latter gesture produced odd results. The material, which looked a little like clear jelly, gave under the boot but bulged upward all around it. The bulge moved outward very slowly in all directions, the star patterns reflected in the surface writhing as it passed. As the bulge's radius increased its height lessened, as with a ripple spreading on a pond. It might have been an ultra-slow motion picture of such a ripple, except that it did not travel far enough. It died out less than two yards from Bresnahan's foot, though it took well over a minute to get that far.

"Yeah, I know what you mean. Walking on water was kind of a divine gift, wasn't it? Well, you can always remember we're not right on the water. There's the pressure film, even if you can't see it."

"That's so. Well, let's get on to the lock. Being inside this thing can't be much worse than walking around on its surface, and I have a report to make up." Silbert started walking again at this request, though the jelly-like response of the water to his footfalls made the resulting gait rather odd. He kept talking as he led the way.

"How come that friend of yours can't come down from the station and look things over for himself? Why should you have to give the dope to him second-hand? Can't he take weightlessness?"

"Better than I can, I suspect," replied Bresnahan, "but he's not my friend. He's my boss, and pays the bills. Mine not to reason why, mine but to act or fry. He already knows as much as most people do about Raindrop, here. What more he expects to get from me I'm not sure. I just hope that what I can find to tell him makes him happy. I take it this is the lock."

They had reached a disk of metal some thirty feet in diameter, projecting about two feet from the surface of the satellite. It continued below the surface for a distance which refraction made hard to estimate.

Its water line was marked by a ring of black, rubbery-looking material where the pressure film adhered to it. The men had been quite close to it when they landed on

Raindrop's surface a few minutes before, but it is hard to
make out landscape details on a water surface under a
black, starfilled sky; the reflection underfoot is not very
different from the original above. A five-mile radius of
curvature puts the reflected images far enough down so
that human depth perception is no help.

Waves betrayed themselves, of course, and might have
shown the lock's location—but under a gravitational acceleration of about a tenth of an inch per second squared,
the surface waves raised by spacesuit boots traveled much
more slowly than the men who wore them. And with their
high internal energy losses they didn't get far enough to be
useful.

As a result, Bresnahan had not realized that the lock
was at hand until they were almost upon it. Even Silbert,
who had known about where they would land and could
orient himself with Raindrop's rotation axis by celestial
reference features, did not actually see it until it was only
a few yards away.

"This is the place, all right," he acknowledged. "That
little plate near the edge is the control panel. We'll use the
manhole; no need to open the main hatch as we do when
it's a matter of cargo."

He bent over—slowly enough to keep his feet on the
metal—and punched one of the buttons on the panel he
had pointed out. A tiny light promptly flashed green, and
he punched a second button.

A yard-square trap opened inward, revealing the top of
a ladder. Silbert seized the highest rung and pulled himself through the opening head first—when a man weighs
less than an ounce in full space panoply it makes little real
difference when he elects to traverse a ladder head downward. Bresnahan followed and found himself in a cylindrical chamber which took up most of the inside of the lock
structure. It could now be seen that this must extend some
forty feet into the body of Raindrop.

At the inner end of the compartment, where curved and
flat walls met, a smaller chamber was partitioned off.
Silbert dove in this direction.

"This is a personnel lock," he remarked. "We'll use it; it
saves flooding the whole chamber."

"We can use ordinary spacesuits?"

"Might as well. If we were going to stay long enough for

real work, we'd change—there is local equipment in those cabinets along the wall. Spacesuits are safe enough, but pretty clumsy when it comes to fine manipulation."

"For me, they're clumsy for anything at all."

"Well, we can change if you want; but I understood that this was to be a fairly quick visit, and that you were to get a report back pronto. Or did I misread the tone your friend Weisanen was using?"

"I guess you didn't, at that. We'll go as we are. It still sounds queer to go swimming in a spacesuit."

"No queerer than walking on water. Come on, the little lock will hold both of us."

The spaceman opened the door manually—there seemed to be no power controls involved—and the two entered a room some five feet square and seven high. Operation of the lock seemed simple; Silbert closed the door they had just used and turned a latch to secure it, then opened another manual valve on the other side of the chamber. A jet of water squirted in and filled the space in half a minute. Then he simply opened a door in the same wall with the valve, and the spacesuited figures swam out.

This was not as bad as walking on what had seemed like nothingness. Bresnahan was a good swimmer and experienced free diver, and was used to being suspended in a medium where one couldn't see very far.

The water was clear, though not as clear as that sometimes found in Earth's tropical seas. There was no easy way to tell just how far vision could reach, since nothing familiar and of known size was in view except for the lock they had just quitted. There were no fishes—Raindrop's owners were still debating the advisability of establishing them there—and none of the plant life was familiar, at least to Bresnahan. He knew that the big sphere of water had been seeded by "artificial" life forms—algae and bacteria whose genetic patterns had been altered to let them live in a "sea" so different from Earth's.

II

Raindrop was composed of the nuclei of several small comets, or rather what was left of those nuclei after some of their mass had been used in reaction motors to put them into orbit about the earth. They had been encased in a polymer film sprayed on to form a pressure seal, and then melted by solar energy, concentrated by giant foil mirrors.

Traces of the original wrapping were still around, but its function had been replaced by one of the first tailored life forms to be established after the mass was liquid. This was a modification of one of the gelatin-capsule algae, which now encased all of Raindrop in a microscopically thin film able to heal itself after small meteoroid punctures, and strong enough to maintain about a quarter of an atmosphere's pressure on the contents. The biological engineer who had done that tailoring job still regarded it as his professional masterpiece.

The methane present in the original comet material had been oxidized by other bacteria to water and carbon dioxide, the oxygen of course coming from normal photosynthesis. A good deal of the ammonia was still present, and furnished the principal reason why genetic tailoring was still necessary on life forms being transplanted to the weightless aquarium.

The men were drifting very slowly away from the lock, though they had stopped swimming, and the younger one asked,

"How do we find our way back here if we get out of sight?"

"The best trick is not to get out of sight. Unless you want to examine the core, which I've never done, you'll see everything there is to see right here. There is sonic and magnetic gear—homing equipment—in your suit if you need it, though I haven't checked you out on its use. You'd better stay with me. I can probably show you what's needed. Just what points do you think Weisanen wants covered?"

"Well, he knows the general physical setup—temperature, rotation, general current pattern, the nature of the skin. He knows what's been planted here at various times; but it's hard to keep up to date on what's evolved since. These tailored life forms aren't very stable toward mutation influences, and a new-stocked aquarium isn't a very stable ecological environment. He'll want to know what's here now in the way of usable plants, I suppose. You know the Agency sold Raindrop to a private concern after the last election. The new owners seem willing to grant the importance of basic research, but they would sort of like a profit to report to the stockholders as well."

"Amen. I'm a stockholder."

"Oh? Well, it does cost something to keep supply ships coming up here, and—"

"True enough. Then this Weisanen character represents the new owners? I wonder if I should think of him as my boss or my employee."

"I think he is one of them."

"Hmph. No wonder."

"No wonder what?"

"He and his wife are the first people I ever knew to treat a space flight like a run in a private yacht. I suppose that someone who could buy Raindrop wouldn't be bothered by a little expense like a private Phoenix rocket."

"I suppose not. Of course, it isn't as bad as it was in the days of chemical motors, when it took a big commercial concern or a fair-sized government to launch a manned spaceship."

"Maybe not; but with fourteen billion people living on Earth, it's a little unusual to find a really rich individual, in the old Ford-Carnegie tradition. Most big concerns are owned by several million people like me."

"Well, I guess Weisanen owns a bigger piece of Raindrop than you do. Anyway, he's my boss, whether he's yours or not, and he wants a report from me, and I can't see much to report on. What life is there in this place besides the stuff forming the surface skin?"

"Oh, lots. You just aren't looking carefully enough. A lot of it is microscopic, of course; there are fairly ordinary varieties of pond-scum drifting all around us. They're the main reason we can see only a couple of hundred yards, and they carry on most of the photosynthesis. There are lots of non-photosynthetic organisms— bacteria—producing carbon dioxide just as in any balanced ecology on Earth, though this place is a long way from being balanced. Sometimes the algae get so thick you can't see twenty feet, sometimes the bacteria get the upper hand. The balance keeps hunting around even when no new forms are appearing or being introduced. We probably brought a few new bacteria in with us on our suits just now; whether any of them can survive with the ammonia content of Raindrop this high I don't know, but if so the ecology will get another nudge.

"There are lots of larger plants, too—mostly modifications of the big seaweeds of Earth's oceans. The lock behind us is overgrown with them, as you can see—you can look more closely as we go back—and a lot of them grow in contact with the outer skin, where the light is best. Quite a few are free-floating, but of course selection works fast on those. There are slow convection currents, because of Raindrop's size and rotation, which exchange water between the illuminated outer regions and the darkness inside. Free-floating weeds either adapt to long periods of darkness or die out fast. Since there is a good deal of hard radiation near the surface, there is also quite a lot of unplanned mutation over and above the regular gene-tailoring products we are constantly adding to the pot. And since most of the organisms here have short life spans, evolution goes on rapidly."

"Weisanen knows all that perfectly well," replied Bresnahan. "What he seems to want is a snapshot—a report on just what the present spectrum of life forms is like."

"I've summed it up. Anything more detailed would be wrong next week. You can look at the stuff around us— there. Those filaments which just tangled themselves on your equipment clip are a good example, and there are some bigger ones if you want *there*—just in reach. It would take microscopic study to show how they differ from the ones you'd have gotten a week ago or a year ago, but they're different. There will be no spectacular change unless so much growth builds up inside the surface film that the sunlight is cut down seriously. Then the selection factors will change and a radically new batch—probably of scavenger fungi—will develop and spread. It's happened before. We've gone through at least four cycles of that sort in the three years I've worked here."

Bresnahan frowned thoughtfully, though the facial gesture was not very meaningful inside a space helmet.

"I can see where this isn't going to be much of a report," he remarked.

"It would have made more sense if you'd brought a plankton net and some vacuum jars and brought up specimens for him to look over himself," replied Silbert. "Or wouldn't they mean anything to him? Is he a biologist or just a manager?"

"I couldn't say."

"How come? How can you work for him and not know that much?"

"Working for him is something new. I've worked for Raindrop ever since I started working, but I didn't meet Weisanen until three weeks ago. I haven't been with him more than two or three hours' total time since. I haven't talked with him during those hours; I've listened while he told me what to do."

"You mean he's one of those high-handed types? What's your job, anyway?"

"There's nothing tough or unpleasant about him; he's just the boss. I'm a computer specialist—programming and maintenance, or was until he picked me to come up here to Raindrop with him and his wife. What my job here will be, you'll have to get from him. There are computers in the station, I noticed, but nothing calling for full-time work from anyone. Why he picked me I can't guess. I should think though, that he'd have asked you rather than me to make this report, since whatever I am I'm no biologist."

"Well, neither am I. I just work here."

Bresnahan stared in astonishment.

"Not a biologist? But aren't you in charge of this place? Haven't you been the local director for three years, in charge of planting the new life forms that were sent up, and reporting what happened to them, and how Raindrop was holding together, and all—?"

"All is right. I'm the bo's'un tight and the midshipmite and the crew of the captain's gig. I'm the boss because I'm the only one here full time; but that doesn't make me a biologist. I got this job because I have a decently high zero-gee tolerance and had had experience in space. I was a space-station handyman before I came here."

"Then what sort of flumdiddle is going on? Isn't there a professional anywhere in this organization? I've heard stories of the army using biochemists for painters and brick-layers for clerks, but I never really believed them. Besides, Raindrop doesn't belong to an army—it isn't even a government outfit any more. It's being run by a private outfit which I assumed was hoping to make a profit out of it. Why in blazes is there no biologist at what has always been supposed to be a biological research station, devoted

to finding new ways of making fourteen billion people like
what little there is to eat?"

Silbert's shrug was just discernible from outside his suit.
"No one ever confided in me," he replied. "I was given a
pretty good briefing on the job when I first took it over,
but that didn't include an extension course in biology or
biophysics. As far as I can tell they've been satisfied with
what I've done. Whatever they wanted out of Raindrop
doesn't seem to call for high-caliber professionals on the
spot. I inspect to make sure no leaks too big for the algae
to handle show up, I plant any new life forms they send up
to be established here, and I collect regularly and send
back to Earth the samples of what life there is. The last
general sampling was nearly a month ago, and another is
due in a few days. Maybe your boss could make do with
that data—or if you like I can offer to make the regular
sampling run right away instead of at the scheduled time.
After all, he may be my boss too instead of the other way
around, so I should be reporting to him."

Bresnahan thought for a moment.

"All right," he said. "I'm in no position to make either a
decent collection or a decent report, as things stand. Let's
go back to the station, tell him what's what, and let him
decide what he does want. Maybe it's just a case of a new
boss not knowing the ropes and trying to find out."

"I'd question that, somehow, but can't think of anything
better to do. Come on."

Silbert swam back toward the lock from which they had
emerged only a few minutes before. They had drifted far
enough from it in that time so that its details had faded to
a greenish blur, but there was no trouble locating the big
cylinder. The door they had used was still open.

Silbert pulled himself through, lent Bresnahan a hand in
doing likewise, closed the portal, and started a small pump.
The pressure head was only the quarter atmosphere maintained by the tension of the alga skin, and emptying the
chamber of water did not take long. The principal delay
was caused by Bresnahan's failure to stand perfectly still;
with gravity only a little over one five-thousandths Earth
normal, it didn't take much disturbance to slosh some
water away from the bottom of the lock where the pump
intake was located.

Silbert waited for some of it to settle, but lacked the
patience to wait for it all. When he opened the door into

the larger lock chamber the men were accompanied through it by several large globules of boiling liquid.

"Wasteful, but helps a bit," remarked the spaceman as he opened the outside portal and the two were wafted through it by the escaping vapor. "Watch out—hang on there. You don't have escape velocity, but you'd be quite a while getting back to the surface if you let yourself blow away." He seized a convenient limb of Bresnahan's space armor as the younger man drifted by, and since he was well anchored himself to the top rung of the ladder was able to arrest the other's flight. Carefully they stepped away from the hatch, Silbert touching the closing button with one toe as he passed it, and looked for the orbiting station.

This, of course, was directly overhead. The same temptation which Bresnahan had felt earlier to make a jump for it came back with some force; but Silbert had a safer technique.

He took a small tube equipped with peep-sights from the equipment clip at his side and aimed it very carefully at the projecting hub of the wheel-shaped station—the only part of the hub visible, since the station's equator was parallel to that of Raindrop and the structure was therefore edge-on to them. A bright yellow glow from the target produced a grunt of satisfaction from Silbert, and he fingered a button on the tube. The laser beam, invisible in the surrounding vacuum, flicked on and off in a precisely timed signal pattern which was reported faithfully by the source-return mirror at the target. Another response was almost as quick.

III

A faintly glowing object emerged from the hub and drifted rapidly toward Raindrop, though not quite toward the men. Its details were not clear at first, but as it approached it began to look more and more like a luminous cobweb.

"Just a lattice of thin rods, doped with luminous paint for spotting and launched from the station by a spring gun," explained Silbert. "The line connecting it with the station isn't painted, and is just long enough to stop the grid about fifty feet from the water. It's launched with a small backward component relative to the station's orbit, and when the line stops it it will drift toward us. Jump for it when I give the word; you can't miss."

Bresnahan was not as certain about the last statement as his companion seemed to be, but braced himself anyway. As the glowing spiderweb approached, however, he saw it was over a hundred feet across and realized that even he could jump straight enough to make contact. When Silbert gave the word, he sprang without hesitation.

He had the usual moment of nausea and disorientation as he crossed the few yards to his target. Lacking experience, he had not "balanced" his jump perfectly and as a result made a couple of somersaults en route. This caused him to lose track of his visual reference points, and with gravity already lacking he suffered the moment of near-panic which so many student pilots had experienced before him. Contact with one of the thin rods restored him, however; he gripped it frantically and was himself again.

Silbert arrived a split second later and took charge of the remaining maneuvers. These consisted of collapsing the "spiderweb"—a matter of half a minute, in spite of its apparent complexity, because of the ingenuity of its jointing—and then starting his companion hand-over-hand along the nearly invisible cord leading back to the station. The climb called for more coordination than was at first evident; the spaceman had to catch his less experienced companion twice as the latter missed his grip for the line.

Had Silbert been going first the situation might have been serious. As it was, an extra tug on the rope enabled him to catch up each time with the helpless victim of basic physics. After the second accident, the guide spoke.

"All right, don't climb any more. We're going a little too fast as it is. Just hold onto the rope now and to me when I give the word. The closing maneuver is a bit tricky, and it wouldn't be practical to try to teach you the tricks on the spot and first time around."

Silbert did have quite a problem. The initial velocities of the two men in their jumps for the spiderweb had not, of course, been the correct ones to intercept the station—if it had been practical to count on their being so, the web would have been superfluous. The web's own mass was less than fifty pounds, which had not done much to the sum of those vectors as it absorbed its share of the men's momentum. Consequently, the men had an angular velocity with respect to the station, and they were *approaching* the latter.

To a seventeenth century mathematician, conservation of angular momentum may have been an abstract concept, but to Silbert it was an item of very real, practical, everyday experience—just as the orbit of a comet is little more than a set of numbers to an astronomer while the orbit of a baseball is something quite different to an outfielder. The problem this time was even worse than usual, partly because of Bresnahan's mass and still more because of his inexperience.

As the two approached the station their sidewise motion became evident even to Bresnahan. He judged that they would strike near the rim of the spinning structure, if they hit it at all, but Silbert had other ideas.

Changing the direction of the spin axis by landing at the hub was one thing—a very minor one. Changing the *rate* of spin by meeting the edge could be a major nuisance, since much of the apparatus inside was built on and for Earth and had Earth's gravity taken for granted in its operation. Silbert therefore had no intention of making contact anywhere but at one of the "poles" of station. He was rather in the situation of a yo-yo whose string is winding up on the operator's finger; but he could exercise a little control by climbing as rapidly as possible "up" the cord toward the structure or allowing himself to slide "down" away from it.

He had had plenty of experience, but he was several minutes playing them into a final collision with the entry valve, so close to the center of mass of the station that the impact could produce only a tiny precession effect. Most of its result was a change in the wheel's orbit about Raindrop, and the whole maneuver had taken such a small fraction of an orbital period that this effect nearly offset that produced when they had started up the rope.

"Every so often," remarked the spaceman as he opened the air lock, "we have to make a small correction in the station orbit; the disturbances set up by entering and leaving get it out of step with Raindrop's rotation. Sometimes I wonder whether it's worth the trouble to keep the two synchronized."

"If the station drifted very far from the lock below,

you'd have to jump from the liquid surface, which might
be awkward," pointed out the younger man as the closing
hatch cut off the starlight.

"That's true," admitted the other as he snapped a switch
and air started hissing into the small lock chamber. "I
suppose there's something to be said for tradition at that.
There's the safety light"—as a green spot suddenly glowed
on the wall—"so you can open up your suit whenever you
like. Lockers are in the next room. But you arrived
through this lock, didn't you?"

"Right. I know my way from here."

Five minutes later the two men, divested of spacesuits,
had "descended" to the rim of the station where weight
was normal. Most of this part of the structure was devoted
to living space which had never been used, though there
were laboratory and communication rooms as well. The
living space had been explained to Bresnahan, when he
first saw it, why Silbert was willing to spend three quarters of his time alone at a rather boring job a hundred
thousand miles from the nearest company. Earth was
badly crowded; not one man in a million had either as
much space or as much privacy.

Weisanen and his wife had taken over a set of equally
sumptuous rooms on the opposite side of the rim, and had
been in the process of setting up housekeeping when the
two employees had descended to Raindrop's surface a
short time before. This had been less than an hour after
their arrival with Bresnahan on the shuttle from Earth;
Weisanen had wasted no time in issuing his first orders.
The two men were prepared to find every sign of disorder
when the door to the "headquarters" section opened in
response to Silbert's touch on the annunciator, but they
had reckoned without Mrs. Weisanen.

At their employer's invitation, they entered a room
which might have been lived in for a year instead of an
hour. The furniture was good, comfortable, well arranged, and present in quantity which would have meant a
visible bulge in a nation's space research budget just for
the fuel to lift it away from the earth in the chemical fuel
days.

Either the Weisanens felt strongly about maintaining the
home atmosphere even when visiting, or they planned to
stay on the station for quite a while.

The official himself was surprisingly young, according to both Bresnahan's and Silbert's preconceived notions of a magnate. He could hardly have been thirty, and might have been five years younger. He matched Bresnahan's five feet ten of height and looked about the same weight; but while the computerman regarded himself as being in good physical shape, he had to admit the other was far more muscular. Even Silbert's six feet five of height and far from insignificant frame seemed somehow inadequate beside Weisanen's.

"Come in, gentlemen. We felt your return a few minutes ago! I take it you have something to report, Mr. Bresnahan. We did not expect you back quite so soon." Weisanen drew further back from the door and waved the others past him. "What can you tell us?" He closed the door and indicated armchairs. Bresnahan remained on his feet, uneasy at the incompleteness of his report; Silbert sank into the nearest chair. The official also remained standing. "Well, Mr. Bresnahan?"

"I have little—practically nothing—to report, as far as detailed, quantitative information is concerned," the computerman took the plunge.

"We stayed inside the Raindrop only a few minutes, and it was evident that most of the detailed search for life specimens would have to be made with a microscope. I hadn't planned the trip at all effectively. I now understand that there is plankton-collecting apparatus here which Mr. Silbert uses regularly and which should have been taken along if I were to get anything worth showing to you."

Weisanen's face showed no change in its expression of courteous interest. "That is quite all right," he said. "I should have made clear that I wanted, not a detailed biological report, but a physical description by a non-specialist of what it is like subjectively down there. I should imagine that you received an adequate impression even during your short stay. Can you give such a description?"

Bresnahan's worried expression disappeared, and he nodded affirmatively.

"Yes, sir. I'm not a literary expert, but I can tell what I saw."

"Good. One moment, please," Weisanen turned toward another door and raised his voice. "Brenda, will you come in here, please? You should hear this."

Silbert got to his feet just as the woman entered, and both men acknowledged her greeting.

Brenda Weisanen was a full head shorter than her husband. She was wearing a robe of the sort which might have been seen on any housewife expecting company; neither man was competent to guess whether it was worth fifty dollars or ten times that. The garment tended to focus attention on her face, which would have received it anyway. Her hair and eyebrows were jet black, the eyes themselves gray, and rounded cheeks and chin made the features look almost childish, though she was actually little younger than her husband. She seated herself promptly, saying no more than convention demanded, and the men followed suit.

"Please go on, Mr. Bresnahan," Weisanen said. "My wife and I are both greatly interested, for reasons which will be clear shortly."

Bresnahan had a good visual memory, and it was easy for him to comply. He gave a good verbal picture of the greenish, sunlit haze that had surrounded him—sunlight differing from that seen under an Earthly lake, which ripples and dances as the waves above refract it. He spoke of the silence, which had moved him to keep talking because it was the "quietest" silence he had known, and "didn't sound right."

He was interrupted by Silbert at this point; the spaceman explained that Raindrop was not always that quiet. Even a grain-of-dust meteoroid striking the skin set up a shock wave audible throughout the great sphere; and if one were close enough to the site of collision, the hiss of water boiling out through the hole for the minute or two needed for the skin to heal could also be heard. It was rather unusual to be able to spend even the short time they had just had inside the satellite without hearing either of these sounds.

Bresnahan nodded thanks as the other fell silent, and took up the thread of his own description once more. He closed with the only real feature he had seen to describe —the weed-grown cylinder of the water-to-space lock, hanging in greenish emptiness above the dead-black void which reached down to Raindrop's core. He was almost poetical in spots.

The Weisanens listened in flattering silence until he had done, and remained silent for some seconds thereafter. Then the man spoke.

"Thank you, Mr. Bresnahan. That was just what we wanted." He turned to his wife. "How does that sound to you, dear?"

The dark head nodded slowly, its gray eyes fastened on some point far beyond the metal walls.

"It's fascinating," she said slowly. "Not just the way we pictured it, of course, and there will be changes anyway, but certainly worth seeing. Of course they didn't go down to the core, and wouldn't have seen much if they had. I suppose there is no life, and certainly no natural light, down there."

"There is life," replied Silbert. "Non-photosynthetic, of course, but bacteria and larger fungi which live on organic matter swept there from the sunlit parts. I don't know whether anything is actually growing *on* the core, since I've never gone in that far, but free-floating varieties get carried up to my nets. A good many of those have gone to Earth, along with their descriptions, in my regular reports."

"I know. I've read those reports very carefully, Mr. Silbert," replied Weisanen.

"Just the same, one of our first jobs must be to survey that core," his wife said thoughtfully. "Much of what has to be done will depend on conditions down there."

"Right." Her husband stood up. "We thank you gentlemen for your word pictures; they have helped a lot. I'm not yet sure of the relation between your station time and that of the Terrestrial time zones, but I have the impression that it's quite late in the working day. Tomorrow we will all visit Raindrop and make a very thorough and more technical examination—my wife and I doing the work, Mr. Bresnahan assisting us, and Mr. Silbert guiding. Until then—it has been a pleasure, gentlemen."

Bresnahan took the hint and got to his feet, but Silbert hesitated. There was a troubled expression on his face, but he seemed unable or unwilling to speak. Weisanen noticed it.

"What's the matter, Mr. Silbert? Is there some reason why Raindrop's owners, or their representatives, shouldn't look it over closely? I realize that you are virtually the only person to visit it in the last three years, but I assure you that your job is in no danger."

Silbert's face cleared a trifle.

"It isn't that," he said slowly. "I know you're the boss, and I wasn't worried about my job anyway. There's just one point—of course you may know all about it, but I'd rather be safe, and embarrassed, than responsible for something unfortunate later on. I don't mean to butt into anyone's private business, but Raindrop is essentially weightless."

"I know that."

"Do you also know that unless you are quite certain that Mrs. Weisanen is not pregnant, she should not expose herself to weightlessness for more than a few minutes at a time?"

Both Weisanens smiled.

"We know, thank you, Mr. Silbert. We will see you tomorrow, in spacesuits, at the big cargo lock. There is much equipment to be taken down to Raindrop."

IV

That closing remark proved to be no exaggeration.

As the four began moving articles through the lock the next morning, Silbert decided at first that the Weisanen's furniture had been a very minor item in the load brought up from Earth the day before, and wondered why it had been brought into the station at all if it were to be transferred to Raindrop so soon. Then he began to realize that most of the material he was moving had been around much longer. It had come up bit by bit on the regular supply shuttle over a period of several months. Evidently whatever was going on represented long and careful planning—and furthermore, whatever was going on represented a major change from the original plans for Raindrop.

This worried him, since Silbert had become firmly attached to the notion that the Raindrop plan was an essential step to keeping the human race fed, and he had as good an appetite as anyone.

He knew, as did any reasonably objective and well-read adult, how barely the advent of fusion power and gene tailoring had bypassed the first critical point in the human population explosion, by making it literally possible to use the entire surface of the planet either for living space or the production of food. As might have been expected, mankind had expanded to fill even that fairly generous limit in a few generations.

A second critical point was now coming up, obviously enough to those willing to face the fact. Most of Earth's fourteen billion people lived on floating islands of gene-tailored vegetation scattered over the planet's seas, and the number of these islands was reaching the point where the total sunlight reaching the surface was low enough to threaten collapse of the entire food chain. Theoretically, fusion power was adequate to provide synthetic food for all; but it had been learned the hard way that man's selfishness could be raised to the violence point almost as easily by a threat to his "right" to eat natural—and tasty—food as by a threat to his "right" to reproduce without limit. As a matter of fact, the people whom Silbert regarded as more civilized tended to react more stongly to the first danger.

Raindrop had been the proposed answer. As soon as useful, edible life forms could be tailored to live in its environment it was to be broken up into a million or so smaller units which could receive sunlight throughout their bulks, and use these as "farms."

But power units, lights, and what looked like prefabricated living quarters sufficient for many families did not fit with the idea of breaking Raindrop up. In fact, they did not fit with any sensible idea at all.

No one could live on Raindrop, or in it, permanently; there was not enough weight to keep human metabolism balanced. Silbert was very conscious of that factor. He never spent more than a day at a time on his sampling trips, and after each of these he always remained in the normal-weight part of the station for the full number of days specified on the AGT tables.

It was all very puzzling.

And as the day wore on, and more and more material was taken from the low-weight storage section of the station and netted together for the trip to Raindrop, the spaceman grew more puzzled still. He said nothing, however, since he didn't feel quite ready to question the Weisanens on the subject and it was impossible to speak privately to Bresnahan with all the spacesuit radios on the same frequency.

All the items moved were, of course, marred with their masses, but Silbert made no great effort to keep track of the total tonnage. It was not necessary, since each cargo net was loaded as nearly as possible to an even one thousand pounds and it was easy enough to count the nets when the job was done. There were twenty-two nets.

A more ticklish task was installing on each bundle a five hundred pound-second solid-fuel thrust cartridge, which had to be set so that its axis pointed reasonably close to the center of mass of the loaded net and firmly enough fastened to maintain its orientation during firing. It was not advisable to get rid of the orbital speed of the loads by "pushing off" from the station; the latter's orbit would have been too greatly altered by absorbing the momentum of eleven tons of material. The rockets had to be used.

Silbert, in loading the nets, had made sure that each was spinning slowly on an axis parallel to that of Raindrop. He had also attached each cartridge at the "equator" of its net. As a result, when the time came to fire it was only necessary to wait beside each load until its rocket was pointing "forward" along the station's orbit, and touch off the fuel.

The resulting velocity change did not, in general, exactly offset the orbital speed, but it came close enough for the purpose. The new orbit of each bundle now intersected the surface of Raindrop—a target which was, after all, ten miles in diameter and only half a mile away. It made no great difference if the luggage were scattered along sixty degrees of the satellite's equatorial zone; moving the bundles to the lock by hand would be no great problem where each one weighed about three and a half ounces.

With the last net drifting toward the glistening surface of Raindrop, Weisanen turned to the spaceman.

"What's the best technique to send us after them? Just jump off?"

Silbert frowned, though the expression was not obvious through his face plate.

"The best technique, according to the AGT Safety Tables, is to go back to the rim of the station and spend a couple of days getting our personal chemistry back in balance. We've been weightless for nearly ten hours, with only one short break when we ate."

Weisanen made a gesture of impatience which was much more visible than Silbert's frown.

"Nonsense!" he exclaimed. "People have remained weightless for a couple of weeks at a time without permanent damage."

"Without having their bones actually turn to rubber, I grant. I don't concede there was no more subtle damage done. I'm no biophysicist, I just believe the tables; they were worked out on the basis of knowledge gained the hard way. I admit they have a big safety factor, and if you consider it really necessary I won't object to staying out for four or five days. But you haven't given us any idea so far why this should be considered an emergency situation."

"Hmmm. So I haven't. All right, will you stay out long enough to show Brenda and me how to work the locks below, so we can get the stuff inside?"

"Why—of course—if it's that important we'll stay and do the work too. But I didn't—"

Silbert fell silent as it dawned on him that Weisanen's choice of words meant that he had no intention of explaining just yet what the "emergency" was. Both newcomers must have read the spaceman's mind quite accurately at that point, since even Bresnahan was able to, but neither of them said anything.

Conversation for the next few minutes consisted entirely of Silbert's instructions for shoving off in the proper direction to reach Raindrop, and how to walk on its not-quite-zero-gravity, jelly-like surface after they reached it. The trip itself was made without incident.

Because fast movement on the surface was impossible, several hours were spent collecting the scattered bundles and stacking them by the lock. The material could not be placed inside, as most of it had to be assembled before it could go under water; so for the moment the lesson in lock management was postponed. Weisanen, after some hesitation, agreed to Silbert's second request that they return to the station for food and rest. He and his wife watched with interest the technique of getting back to it.

With four people instead of two, the velocity-matching problem might have been worse, but this turned out not to be the case. Silbert wondered whether it was strictly luck, or whether the Weisanens actually had the skill to plan their jumps properly. He was beginning to suspect that both of them had had previous space experience, and both were certainly well-coordinated physical specimens.

According to the tables which had been guiding Silbert's life, the party should have remained in the high-weight part of the station for at least eighty hours after their session of zero-gee, but his life was now being run by Weisanen rather than the tables. The group was back on the water twelve hours after leaving it.

Bresnahan still had his feeling of discomfort, with star-studded emptiness on one side and its reflection on the other, but he was given little time to brood about it.

The first material to go into the lock consisted of half a dozen yard-wide plastic bubbles of water. Silbert noted with interest that all contained animal life, ranging from barely visible crustacea to herring-sized fish.

"So we're starting animal life here at last," remarked the spaceman. "I thought it was a major bone of contention whether we ever would."

"The question was settled at the first meeting of the new board," replied Weisanen. "Life forms able to live here— or presumably able to live here—have been ready for several years. Please be careful in putting those in the lock —just the odd-numbered ones first, please, first. The evens contain predators, and the others should be given a few hours to scatter before they are turned loose."

"Right. Any special techniques for opening? Or just get the bubbles through the second lock and cut them open?"

"That will do. I assume that a few hours in the currents inside, plus their own swimming abilities, will scatter them through a good part of the drop."

"It should. I suppose they'll tend to stay pretty close to the skin because of the light; I trust they can take a certain amount of hard radiation."

"That matter has been considered. There will be some loss, damage, and genetic change, of course, but we think the cultures will gain in spite of that. If they change, it is no great matter. We expect rapid evolution in an environment like this, of course. It's certainly been happening so far."

Bresnahan helped push the proper spheres into the lock at the vacuum end and out of it at the other, and watched with interest as each was punctured with a knife and squeezed to expel the contents.

"I should have asked about waiting for temperatures to match," remarked Silbert as the cloud of barely visible, jerkily moving specks spread from the last of the containers, "but it doesn't seem to be bothering them."

"The containers were lying on Raindrop's surface all night, and the satellite is in radiative equilibrium," pointed out Bresnahan. "The temperatures shouldn't be very different anyway. Let's get back outside and see what's going on next. Either these water-bugs are all right, or they're beyond our help."

"Right." Silbert followed the suggestion, and the newly released animals were left to their own devices.

Outside, another job was under way. The largest single items of cargo had been a set of curved segments of metal, apparently blue-anodized aluminum. In the few minutes that Silbert and Bresnahan had been inside, the Weisanens had sorted these out from the rest of the material and were now fitting them together.

Each section attached to its neighbor by a set of positive-acting snap fasteners which could be set almost instantly, and within a very few minutes it became evident that they formed a sphere some twenty feet in diameter. A transparent dome of smaller radius was set in one pole, and a cylindrical structure with trap doors in the flat ends marked the other. With the assembly complete, the Weisanens carefully sprayed everything, inside and out, from cylinders which Silbert recognized as containing one of the standard fluorocarbon polymers used for sealing unfindable leaks in space ships.

Then both Weisanens went inside.

Either the metallic appearance of the sphere was deceptive or there were antennae concealed in its structure, because orders came through the wall on the suit-radio frequency without noticeable loss. In response to these, Bresnahan and the spaceman began handing the rest of the equipment in through the cylindrical structure, which had now revealed itself as a minute air lock. As each item was received it was snapped down on a spot evidently prepared to receive it, and in less than two hours almost all the loose gear had vanished from the vicinity of Raindrop's entry lock. The little that was left also found a home as Weisanen emerged once more and fastened it to racks on the sphere's outer surface, clustered around the air lock.

The official went back inside, and, at his orders, Silbert and the computerman lifted the whole sphere onto the top of the cylindrical cargo lock of the satellite. Either could have handled the three-pound weight alone, but its shape and size made it awkward to handle and both men felt that it would be inadvisable to roll it.

"Good. Now open this big hatch and let us settle into the lock chamber," directed Weisanen. "Then close up, and let in the water."

It was the first time Silbert had caught his boss in a slip, and he was disproportionately pleased. The hatch opened outward, and it was necessary to lift the sphere off again before the order could be obeyed.

Once it was open, the two men had no trouble tossing the big globe into the yawning, nearly dark hole—the sun was just rising locally and did not shine into the chamber—but they had to wait over a minute for Raindrop's feeble gravity to drag the machine entirely inside. They could not push it any faster, because it was not possible to get a good grip on sphere and lock edge simultaneously; and pushing down on the sphere without good anchorage would have done much more to the pusher than to the sphere.

However, it was finally possible to close the big trap. After making sure that it was tightly latched—it was seldom used, and Silbert did not trust its mechanism unreservedly—he and Bresnahan entered the lock through the smaller portal.

"Aren't there special suits for use inside Raindrop, a lot more comfortable than this space armor?" asked Weisanen.

"Yes, sir," replied the spaceman, "though the relative comfort is a matter of opinion. There are only three, and two of them haven't been used since I came. They'll need a careful checkout."

"All right. Bring them in here, and then let the water into this lock." Silbert found the suits and handed them to Bresnahan to carry out the first part of the order, while he went to the controls to execute the second.

"All ready?" he asked.

"All set. Both lock doors here are shut, and the three of us are inside. Let the flood descend."

"Wrong verb," muttered Silbert to himself.

He very cautiously cracked the main inner hatch; opening it would have been asking for disaster. Even at a mere quarter atmosphere's pressure the wall of water would have slammed into the evacuated lock violently enough to tear the outer portal away and eject sphere and occupants at a speed well above Raindrop's escape value. There was a small Phoenix rocket in the station for emergency use, but Silbert had no wish to create a genuine excuse for using it. Also, since he was in the lock himself, he would probably be in no condition to get or pilot it.

V

The water sprayed in violently enough through the narrow opening he permitted, bouncing the sphere against the outer hatch and making a deafening clamor even for the spacesuited trio inside. However, nothing gave way, and in a minute it was safe to open the main hatch completely.

Silbert did so. Through the clear dome which formed the sphere's only observation window he could see Weisanen fingering controls inside. Water jets from almost invisible ports in the outer surface came into action, and for the first time it became evident that the sphere was actually a vehicle. It was certainly not built for speed, but showed signs of being one of the most maneuverable ever built.

After watching for a moment as it worked its way out of the lock, Silbert decided that Weisanen had had little chance to practice handling it. But no catastrophe occurred, and finally the globe was hanging in the greenish void outside the weed-grown bulk of the lock. The spaceman closed the big hatch, emerged through the personnel lock himself, and swam over to the vehicle's entrance.

The outer door of the tiny air lock opened manually. Thirty seconds later he was inside the rather crowded sphere removing his helmet—some time during the last few minutes Weisanen had filled the vehicle with air.

The others had already unhelmeted and were examining the "diving" suits which Bresnahan had brought inside. These were simple enough affairs; plastic form-fitting coveralls with an air-cycler on the chest and an outsized, transparent helmet which permitted far more freedom of head movement than most similar gear. Since there was no buoyance in this virtually weight-free environment, the helmet's volume did not create the problem it would have on Earth. Silbert was able to explain everything necessary about the equipment in a minute or two.

Neither of the Weisanens needed to have any point repeated, and if Bresnahan was unsure about anything he failed to admit it.

"All right." Raindrop's owner nodded briskly as the lesson ended. "We seem to be ready. I started us down as soon as Mr. Silbert came aboard, but it will take the best part of an hour to reach the core. When we get there a regular ecological sampling run will be made. You can do that, Mr. Silbert, using your regular equipment and techniques; the former is aboard, whether you noticed it being loaded or not. Brenda and I will make a physical, and physiographical, examination of the core itself, with a view to finding just what will have to be done to set up living quarters there and where will be the best place to build them."

Silbert's reaction to this remark may have been expected; both Weisanens had been watching him with slight smiles on their faces. He did not disappoint them.

"*Living* quarters? That's ridiculous! There's no weight to speak of even at Raindrop's surface, and even less at the core. A person would lose the calcium from his skeleton in a few weeks, and go unbalanced in I don't know how many other chemical ways—"

"Fourteen known so far, Mr. Silbert. We know all about that, or as much as anyone does. It was a shame to tease you, but my husband and I couldn't resist. Also, some of the factors involved are not yet public knowledge, and we have reasons for not wanting them too widely circulated for a while yet." Brenda Weisanen's interruption was saved from rudeness by the smile on her face. "I would invite you to sit down to listen, but sitting means nothing here—I'll get used to that eventually, no doubt."

"The fact you just mentioned about people leaching calcium out of their skeletons after a few days or weeks of weightlessness was learned long ago—even before long manned space flights had been made; the information was gained from flotation experiments. Strictly speaking, it is not an effect of weightlessness *per se,* but a feedback phenomenon involving relative muscular effort—something which might have been predicted, and for all I know may actually have been predicted, from the fact that the ankle bones in a growing child ossify much more rapidly than the wrist bones. A very minor genetic factor is involved; after all, animals as similar to us as dolphins which *do* spend all their time afloat grow perfectly adequate skeletons.

"A much more subtle set of chemical problems were noticed the hard way when manned space stations were set up, as you well know. A lot of work was done on these, as you might expect, and we now are quite sure that all which will produce detectable results in less than five years of continuous weightlessness are known. There are fourteen specific factors—chemical and genetic keys to the log jam, if you like to think of it that way.

"You have the ordinary educated adult's knowledge of gene tailoring, Mr. Silbert. What was the logical thing to do?"

"Since gene tailoring on human beings is flagrantly illegal, for good and sufficient reasons, the logical thing to do was and is to avoid weightlessness," Silbert replied. "With Phoenix rockets, we can make interplanetary flight at a continuous one-gravity acceleration, while space stations can be and are centrifuged."

Brenda Weisanen's smile did not change, but her husband looked annoyed. He took up the discussion.

"Illegal or not, for good or bad reasons, it was perfectly reasonable to consider modifying human genetic patterns so that some people at least could live and work normally and indefinitely in a weightless environment. Whether it shocks you or not, the thing was tried over seventy years ago, and over five hundred people now alive have this modification—and are not, as I suppose you would put it, fully human."

Bresnahan interrupted. "I would *not* put it that way!" he snapped. "As anyone who has taken work in permutation and combination knows perfectly well, there is no such thing as a fully human being if you define the term relative to some precise, specific idealized gene pattern. Mutations are occurring all the time from radiation, thermal effects, and just plain quantum jumping of protons in the genetic molecules. The sort of phenomenon is used as example material in elementary programming courses, and one of the first things you learn when you run such a problem is that no one is completely without such modifications. If, as I suppose you are about to say, you and Mrs. Weisanen are genetically different enough to take weightlessness, I can't see why it makes you less human. I happen to be immune to four varieties of leukemia virus and sixteen of the organisms usually responsible for the common cold, according to one analysis of my own gene pattern. If Bert's had ever been checked we'd find at least as many peculiarities about his—and I refuse to admit that either of us is less human than anyone else we've ever met."

"Thank you, Mr. Bresnahan," Brenda Weisanen took up the thread of the discussion once more. "The usual prejudice against people who are known to be significantly different tends to make some of us a little self-conscious. In any case, my husband and I can stand weightlessness indefinitely, as far as it is now possible to tell, and we plan to stay here permanently. More of us will be coming up later for the same purpose."

"But why? Not that it's any of my business. I like Raindrop, but it's not the most stimulating environment and in any case I'm known to be the sort of oddball who prefers being alone with a collection of books to more other activities."

The woman glanced at her husband before answering. He shrugged.

"You have already touched on the point, Mr. Silbert. Modifying the human genetic pattern involves the same complication which plagued medicine when hormones became available for use in treatment. Any one action is likely to produce several others as an unplanned, and commonly unwanted, by-product. Our own modification is not without its disadvantages. What our various defects may be I would not presume to list in toto—any more than Mr. Bresnahan would care to list his—but one of them strikes very close to home just now. Aino and I are expecting a child, and about nine times out of ten when a woman of our type remains in normal gravity any child she conceives is lost during the fifth or sixth month. The precise cause is not known; it involves the mother's physique rather than the child's, but that leaves a lot still to be learned. Therefore, I am staying here until my baby is born, at the very least. We expect to live here. We did not ask to be modified to fit space, but if it turns out that we can live better here—so be it."

"Then Raindrop is going to be turned into a—a—maternity hospital?"

"I think a fairer term would be 'colony,' Mr. Silbert," interjected Weisanen. "There are a good many of us, and most if not all of us are considering making this place our permanent home."

"Which means that breaking it up according to the original plan to supply farming volume is no longer on the books."

"Precisely."

"How do you expect to get away with that? This whole project was planned and paid for as a new source of food."

"That was when it was a government project. As you know, it became a private concern recently; the government was paid full value for Raindrop, the station, and the shuttle which keeps it supplied. As of course you do not know, over eighty per cent of the stock of that corporation is owned by people like myself. What we propose to do is perfectly legal, however unpopular it may make us with a few people."

"More than a few, I would say. And how can you afford to be really unpopular, living in something as fragile as Raindrop?" queried Bresnahan. "There are lots of spaceships available. Even if no official action were or could be taken, anyone who happened to have access to one and disliked you sufficiently could wreck the skin of this tank so thoroughly in five minutes that you'd have to start all over again even if you yourselves lived through it. All the life you'd established would freeze before repairs could be made complete enough to stop the water from boiling away."

"That is true, and is a problem we haven't entirely solved," admitted the other. "Of course, the nasty laws against the publication of possible mob-rousing statements which were found necessary as Earth's population grew should operate to help us. Nowadays many people react so negatively to any unsupported statement that the word would have trouble getting around. In any case, we don't intend to broadcast the details and comparatively few people know much about the Raindrop project at all. I don't think that many will feel cheated."

Silbert's reaction to the last sentence was the urge to cry

out, "But they *are* being cheated!" However, it was beginning to dawn on him that he was not in the best possible position to argue with Weisanen.

He subsided. He himself had been living with the Raindrop project for three years, had become closely identified with it, and the change of policy bothered him for deeper reasons than his intelligence alone could recognize.

Bresnahan was also bothered, though he was not as deeply in love with the project as the spaceman. He was less impressed by Weisanen's conviction that there would be no trouble; but he had nothing useful to say about the matter. He was developing ideas, but they ran along the line of wondering when he could get to a computer keyboard to set the whole situation up as a problem. His background and training had left him with some doubt of any human being's ability—including his own—to handle all facets of a complex problem.

Neither of the Weisanens seemed to have any more to say, either, so the sphere drifted downward in silence.

VI

They had quickly passed the limit which sunlight could reach, and were surrounded by blackness, which the sphere's own interior lights seemed only to accentuate.

With neither gravity nor outside reference points, the sphere was of course being navigated by instrument. Sonar equipment kept the pilot informed of the distance to the nearest point of the skin, the distance and direction of the lock through which they had entered, and the distance and direction of the core. Interpretation of the echoes was complicated by the fact that Raindrop's outer skin was so sharply curved, but Weisanen seemed to have that problem well in hand as he drove the vehicle downward.

Pressure, of course, did not change significantly with depth. The thirty per cent increase from skin to core meant nothing to healthy people. There was not even an instrument to register this factor, as far as Silbert could see. He was not too happy about that; his spaceman's prejudices made him feel that there should be independent instrumentation to back up the sonar gear.

As they neared the core, however, instruments proved less necessary than expected.

To the mild surprise of the Weisanens and the blank astonishment of Silbert—Bresnahan knew too little to expect anything, either way—the central region of the satellite was not completely dark. The light was so faint that it would not have been noticed if they had not been turning off the sphere's lamps every few minutes, but it was quite bright enough to be seen, when they were a hundred yards or so from the core, without waiting for eyes to become dark-adapted.

"None of your samples ever included luminous bacteria," remarked the official. "I wonder why none of them ever got close enough to the skin for you to pick up."

"I certainly don't know," replied Silbert. "Are you sure it's caused by bacteria?"

"Not exactly by a long shot; it just seems the best starting guess. I'm certain it's not heat or radioactivity, and offhand I can't think of any other possibilities. Can you?"

"No, I can't. But maybe whatever is producing the light is attached to the core—growing on it, if it's alive. So it wouldn't have reached the surface."

"That's possible, though I hope you didn't think I was criticizing your sampling techniques. It was one of my friends who planned them, not you. We'll go on down; we're almost in contact with the core now, according to the fathometer."

Weisanen left the lights off, except for the tiny fluorescent sparks on the controls themselves, so the other three crowded against the bulge of the viewing port to see what was coming. Weightlessness made this easier than it might have been; they didn't have to "stand" at the same spot to have their heads close together.

For a minute or so, nothing was perceptible in the way of motion. There was just the clear, faintly luminous water outside the port. Then a set of slender, tentacular filaments as big around as a human thumb seemed to writhe past the port as the sphere sank by them; and the eyes which followed their length could suddenly see their point of attachment.

"There!" muttered Brenda Weisanen softly. "Slowly, dear—only a few yards."

"There's no other way this thing can travel," pointed out her husband. "Don't worry about our hitting anything too hard."

"I'm not—but look! It's beautiful! Let's get anchored and go outside."

"In good time. It will stay there, and anyway I'm going out before you do—long enough before to, at least, make reasonably certain it's safe."

The wife looked for a moment as though she were about to argue this point, if her facial expression could be read accurately in the faint light, but she said nothing. Bresnahan and Silbert had the intelligence to keep quiet as well; more could be learned by looking than by getting into the middle of a husband-wife disagreement, and now there was plenty to look at.

The core was visible for at least two hundred yards in all directions, as the sphere spun slowly under Weisanen's control. The light definitely came from the life forms which matted its surface.

Presumably these were fungi, since photosynthetic forms could hardly have grown in such an environment, but they were fungi which bore little resemblance to their Terrestrial ancestors. Some were ribbon-like, some feather-like, some snaky—even patches of what looked like smoothly mown lawn were visible. The greenish light was evidently not pure color, since other shades were visible; red, purple, and yellow forms stood out here and there in eye-catching contrast to grays and browns. Some forms were even green, though it seemed unlikely that this was due to chlorophyll. Practically all seemed to emit the vague light which bathed the entire scene—so uniformly that outlines would have been hard to distinguish were it not for a few specimens which were much brighter than the others. These types bore what might have been spore pods; brilliantly luminous knobs ranging from fist to grapefruit size, raised "above" the rest of the surface as much as eight or ten feet on slender stalks. These cast shadows which helped distinguish relief.

The woman was right; weird it might be, but the scene was beautiful.

Weisanen cut off the water jets and waited for a minute or two. The vehicle drifted slowly but perceptibly away from the surface; evidently there was some current.

"We'll have to anchor," he remarked. "Bren, stay inside until we've checked. I'll go out to see what we can fasten ourselves to; there's no information at all on what sort of

surface there may be. A fair-sized stony meteoroid—
really an asteroid—was used as the original core, but the
solids from the comets would be very fine dust. There
could be yards of mud too fine to hold any sort of anchor
surrounding the solid part. You gentlemen will please get
into the other suits and come with me. If nothing has
happened to any of us in half an hour, Bren, you may join
us."

"There are only three suits," his wife pointed out.

"True. Well, your spacesuit will do; or if you prefer,
one of us will use his and let you have the diving gear. In
any case, that problem is low-priority. If you gentlemen
are ready we'll go. I'll start; this is strictly a one-man air
lock."

All three had been climbing out of their spacesuits as
Weisanen was talking. The other garments were easy
enough to get into, though Bresnahan found the huge
helmet unwieldy even with no weight. Weisanen was
through the lock before either of the others was ready to
follow; Silbert was slowed by his space-born habit of
double-checking every bit of the breathing apparatus, and
Bresnahan by his inexperience. They could see their employer through the window as they finished, swimming
slowly and carefully toward the weedy boundary of Raindrop's core.

Both men stayed where they were for the moment, to see
what would happen when he reached it. Brenda Weisanen
watched even more closely; there was no obvious reason to
be afraid, but her breath was coming unevenly and her
fists tightly clenched as her husband approached the plants
and reached out to touch the nearest.

Nothing spectacular happened. It yielded to his touch;
when he seized it and pulled, it broke.

"Either the plants are awfully fragile or there is fairly
firm ground anchoring them," remarked Silbert. "Let's go
outside. You're checked out on the controls of this thing,
aren't you, Mrs. Weisanen?"

"Not in great detail," was the reply, "I know which
switches handle lights and main power for the lock pump,
and which control bank deals with the jets; but I've had no
practice in actually handling it. Aino hadn't, either, until
we started this trip an hour ago. Go ahead, though; I won't
have to do anything anyway. Aino is anchoring us now."

She gestured toward the port. Her husband could now be seen through it carrying something, maybe a harpoon, with a length of fine line attached to it. A couple of yards from the surface he poised himself and hurled the object, javelin style—or as nearly to that style as anyone can manage in water—into the mass of vegetation.

The shaft buried itself completely. Weisanen gave a tug on the line, whose far end was attached to the sphere. He seemed satisfied and turned to look at the vehicle. Seeing the men still inside, he gestured impatiently. Bresnahan followed Silbert through the tiny air lock as rapidly as its cycling time would permit, leaving the woman alone in the sphere.

Outside, Weisanen was several yards away, still beckoning imperiously.

"You can talk, sir," remarked Silbert in ordinary tones. "There's no need for sign language."

"Oh. Thanks; I didn't see any radio equipment in these helmets."

"There isn't any. The helmets themselves aren't just molded plastic; they're a multi-layered arrangement that acts as an impedance matcher between the air inside and the water outside. Sound goes through water well enough; it's the air-water interface that makes conversation difficult. This stuff gets the sound across the boundary."

"All right; good. Let's get to work. If the figures for the size of the original nucleus still mean anything, we have nearly twenty million square feet to check up on. Right now we won't try to do it all; stay in sight of the sphere. Get test rods and plankton gear from that rack by the air lock. Mr. Silbert, use the nets and collectors as you usually do. Mr. Bresnahan, you and I will use the rods; simply poke them into the surface every few yards. The idea is to get general knowledge of the firmness of the underlying surface, and to find the best places to build—or attach—permanent structures. If you should happen to notice any connection between the type of vegetation and the kind of ground it grows on, so much the better; surveying by eye will be a lot faster than by touch. If any sort of trouble comes up, yell. I don't see why there should be any, but I don't want Brenda out here until we're a little more certain."

The men fell to their rather monotonous tasks. The

plant cover, it developed, ranged from an inch or two to over a yard in thickness, not counting the scattered forms which extended their tendrils scores of feet out toward the darkness. At no point was the underlying "ground" visible.

Where the growing cover was pushed or dug away, the core seemed to be made of a stiff, brownish clay, which reached at least as deep as the test prods could be pushed by hand. This rather surprised Silbert, who had expected either solid rock or oozy mud. He was not geochemist enough to guess at the reactions which might have formed what they actually found, and was too sensible to worry about it before actual analyses had been made.

If Weisanen had any opinions, he kept them to himself.

Bresnahan was not worried about the scientific aspect of the situation at all. He simply poked away with his test bar because he had been told to, devoting only a fraction of his attention to the task. His thoughts were elsewhere.

Specifically, he was following through the implications of the information the Weisanens had furnished during the trip down. He admitted to himself that in the other's position he would probably be doing the same thing; but it seemed as though some compromise should be possible which would salvage the original purpose of Raindrop.

Bresnahan did not, of course, expect to eat as well as the average man of mid-twentieth century. He never had, and didn't know what he was missing. He did know, however, that at his present age of twenty-five there was a smaller variety of foodstuffs available than he could remember from his childhood, and he didn't want that process to go any farther. Breaking up Raindrop according to the original plan seemed to him the obvious thing to do. If land and sea farming areas were disappearing under the population flood, the logical answer was farming areas in the sky. This should be as important to the Weisanens as to anyone else.

He felt a little uneasy about bringing the matter up again, however. Somehow, he had a certain awe of Weisanen which he didn't think was entirely due to the fact that the latter was his employer.

Several times their paths came close together as the two plied their test bars, but Bresnahan was unable to wind his courage up to the necessary pitch for some time—not, in fact, until they had been exploring the region uneventfully for over half an hour and Weisanen had finally, with some hesitation, decided that it was safe for his wife to join them.

There was some slight rivalry between Silbert and Bresnahan over who should give up his diving gear to the woman and resume his spacesuit. If Bresnahan had won, a good deal of subsequent trouble might have been avoided; but when all four were finally outside, Silbert was wearing space armor. He had pointed out quite logically that he was the most used to it and would work better than any of the others in its restrictions.

VII

The key to the subsequent trouble was that one of the restrictions involved communication. If Silbert had been able to hear clearly, he might have understood what was developing before it had gone too far; but he couldn't. His space helmet lacked the impedance-matching feature of the diving gear, and the latter equipment had no radios.

Some sound did get through his helmet both from and into the water, but not much; for real conversation he had to bring the helmet into physical contact with that of the other party. He therefore knew little of what went on during the next few minutes. He spent them continuing his ecology sample, and paid little attention to anything else.

With Mrs. Weisanen present, some of Bresnahan's unease in her husband's presence left him, and he brought up at last the point which had occurred to him.

"I've been wondering, sir," he opened, "why it wouldn't be possible to break up Raindrop just as was planned, and still use the smaller drops as homes for people like yourselves. I can't see that it would be very different from your present plan."

Weisanen did not seem annoyed, but answered in a straightforward fashion. "Aside from the fact that we would prefer to be in a single city rather than a lot of detached houses which would require us to visit our neighbors by spaceship, the smaller drops will have the radiation problem. Here we have nearly five miles of water shielding us."

"Hmph. I never thought of that."

"No reason why you should have. It was never your problem."

"But still—what do we do about food? Conditions on

Earth are getting worse all the time. Starting another
Raindrop project would take years. Couldn't you at least
compromise? Permit the small drops to be skimmed off the
surface of this one while you are living here, and while
another Raindrop is set up?"

"I don't like the idea. Can you imagine what it will be
like here with shock waves from exploding steam bubbles
echoing all through the globe every time the skin is opened
for a new farm lot?"

"Why should they break the skin? I should think they'd
want to draw off the water through the lock, or other
locks which might be built, anyway; otherwise there'd be a
lot of waste from boiling. I should think—"

Weisanen's annoyance suddenly boiled over, though no
sign of it had been visible before.

"Mr. Bresnahan, it matters very little what you think
when you forget that Raindrop is now, legally and properly, private property. I dislike to sound selfish and misan-
thropic, but I belong to a group which has gone to a great
deal of thought and labor to get for itself, legally and
without violence, an environment which it needs and which
no one else—including the people responsible for our
existence—was willing to provide. In addition, if you would
think with your brain instead of your stomach you'd realize that the whole original project was pure nonsense. The
only possible way mankind can keep himself adequately fed
is to limit his population. If you'll pardon the pun, the
whole idiotic project was a drop in the bucket. It might
have put the day of reckoning back five years, conceivably
ten or fifteen, but then we'd have been right back where
we started. Even with fusion energy there's a limit to the
number of space farms which could be built in a given
time, and the way Earth's population grows it would soon
be impossible just to make new farms fast enough, let alone
operate them. Cheating people? Nonsense! We're doing
the rest of mankind a favor by forcing them to face facts
while there are a few billion less of them to argue with
each other. One group has had to exercise the same sort of
control the rest of mankind should be using for a good
half century. We didn't *dare* have children except when it
was practicable to keep the mother in orbit for the best
part of a year. Why should we be particularly sympathetic
with the rest of you?"

"I see your point," admitted Bresnahan, "but you've forgotten one other thing. The food problem is yours, too. What will you do as *your* food supply shrinks like everyone else's? Or worse, when people decide not to send any food at all up here, since you won't send any down? Raindrop is a long way yet from being self-supporting, you know."

A grin, clearly visible in the light from a nearby plant knob, appeared on Weisanen's face; but his irritation remained.

"Slight mistake, my young friend. There is another minor modification in our structure; our saliva glands produce an enzyme you lack. We can digest cellulose." He waved his hand at the plants around them.

"How do you know these plants contain cellulose?"

"All plants do; but that's a side issue. The weeds near the surface were analyzed long ago, and proved to contain all the essentials for human life—in form which we can extract with our own digestive apparatus. Raindrop, as it now is, could support all of us there are now and there are likely to be for a couple of generations. Now, please get back to checking this little world of ours. Brenda and I want to decide where to build our house."

Bresnahan was silent, but made no move to get back to work. He floated for a minute or so, thinking furiously; Weisanen made no effort to repeat or enforce his order.

At last the computerman spoke slowly—and made his worst mistake.

"You may be right in your legal standing. You may be right in your opinion about the value of Raindrop and what the rest of the human race should do—personally, I want a family some day. You may even be right about your safety from general attack because the communication laws will keep down the number of people who know about the business. But, right or wrong, if even a single person with access to a spaceship *does* find out, then you —and your wife—and your baby—are all in danger. Doesn't that suggest to you that some sort of compromise is in order?"

Weisanen's expression darkened and his mucles tensed. His wife, looking at him, opened her mouth and made a little gesture of protest even before he started to speak; but if she made a sound it was drowned out.

"It certainly suggests something, young fellow," snapped the official. "I was hoping the matter wouldn't descend to this level, but remember that while we can live here indefinitely, you cannot. A few weeks of weightlessness will do damage which your bodies can never repair. There is no regular food down here. And we control the transportation back to the station and weight."

"Aino—no!" His wife laid a hand on his arm and spoke urgently. "Wait, dear. If you threaten at all, it's too close to a threat of death. I don't want to kill anyone, and don't want to think of your doing so. It wouldn't be worth it."

"You and the little one *are* worth it. Worth anything! I won't listen to argument on that."

"But argument isn't needed. There is time. Mr. Bresnahan and his friend will certainly wait and think before risking the consequences of a mob-raising rumor. He wants a compromise, not—"

"His compromise endangers you and the others. I won't have it. Mr. Bresnahan, I will not ask you for a promise to keep quiet; you might be the idealistic type which can justify breaking its word for what it considers a good cause. Also, I will not endanger your life and health more than I can help. Brenda is right to some extent; I don't want a killing on my conscience either, regardless of the cause. Therefore, you and Mr. Silbert will remain here at the core until Brenda and I have returned to the station and made sure that no communication gear will function without our knowledge and consent. That may be a few days, which may be more than your health should risk. I'm sorry, but I'm balancing that risk to you against one to us."

"Why should it take days? An hour to the surface, a few minutes to the station—"

"And Heaven knows how long to find and take care of all the radios. Neither of us is an expert in that field, and we'll be a long time making sure we have left no loopholes."

"Will you at least stop to find out whether the air renewers in these diving suits are indefinite-time ones, like the spacesuit equipment? And if they aren't, let me change back into my spacesuit?"

"Of course. Change anyway. It will save my trying to get the substance of this conversation across to Mr. Silbert. You can tell him on radio while we are on the way.

Come with me back to the sphere and change. Brenda stay here."

"But, dearest—this isn't right. You know—"

"I know what I'm doing and why I'm doing it. I'm willing to follow your lead in a lot of things, Bren, but this is not one of them."

"But—"

"No buts. Come, Mr. Bresnahan. Follow me."

The wife fell silent, but her gaze was troubled as she watched the two men vanish through the tiny lock. Bresnahan wondered what she would do. It was because he felt sure she would do something that he hadn't simply defied Weisanen.

The woman's face was no happier when the computer-man emerged alone and swam back to a point beside her. Her husband was visible through the port, outsized helmet removed, beckoning to her.

For a moment Bresnahan had the hope that she would refuse to go. This faded as she swam slowly toward the sphere, occasionally looking back, removed the anchor in response to a gesture from the man inside, and disappeared through the lock. The vehicle began to drift upward, vegetation near it swirling in the water jets. Within a minute it had faded from view into the darkness.

"Just what's going on here?" Silbert's voice was clear enough; the suit radios carried for a short distance through water. "Where are they going, and why?"

"You didn't hear any of my talk with Weisanen?"

"No. I was busy, and it's hard to get sound through this helmet anyway. What happened? Did you argue with him?"

"In a way." Bresnahan gave the story as concisely as he could. His friend's whistle sounded eerily in the confines of his helmet.

"This—is—really—something. Just for the record, young pal, we are in a serious jam, I hope you realize."

"I don't think so. His wife is against the idea, and he'll let himself get talked out of it—he's a little afraid of the results already."

"Not the point. It doesn't matter if the whole thing was a practical joke on his part. They're out of sight, in a medium where no current charts exist and the only navigation aids are that sphere's own sonar units. He could find his way back to the core, but how could he find *us?*"

"Aren't we right under the lock and the station? We came straight down."

"Don't bet on that. I told you—there are currents. If we made a straight track on the trip down here I'll be the most surprised man inside Luna's orbit. There are twenty million square feet on this mudball. We'd be visible from a radius of maybe two hundred—visible and recognizable, that is, with our lights on. That means they have something like two hundred search blocks, if my mental arithmetic is right, without even a means of knowing when they cover a given one a second time. There is a chance they'd find us, but not a good one—not a good enough one so that we should bet your chance of dodging a couple of weeks of weightlessness on it. When that nut went out of sight, he disposed of us once and for all."

"I wouldn't call him a nut," Bresnahan said.

"Why not? Anyone who would leave a couple of people to starve or get loaded with zero-gee symptoms on the odd chance that they might blab his favorite scheme to the public—"

"He's a little unbalanced at the moment, but not a real nut. I'm sure he didn't realize he'd passed the point of no return. Make allowances, Bert; I can. Some of my best friends are married, and I've seen 'em when they first learned a kid was on the way. It's just that they don't usually have this good a chance to get other people in trouble; they're all off the beam for a little while."

"You're the most tolerant and civilized character I've met, and you've just convinced me that there can be too much of even the best of things. For my money the guy is a raving nut. More to the point, unless we can get ourselves out of the jam he's dropped us into, we're worse than nuts. We're dead."

"Maybe he'll realize the situation and go back to the station and call for help."

"There can be such a thing as too much optimism, too. My young friend, he's not going to get to the station."

"What? Why not?"

"Because the only laser tube not already in the station able to trigger the cobweb launchers is right here on my equipment clip. That's another reason I think he's a nut. He should have thought of that and pried it away from me somehow."

"Maybe it just means he wasn't serious about the whole thing."

"Never mind what it means about him. Whatever his intentions, I'd be willing to wait for him to come back to us with his tail between his legs if I thought he could find us. Since I don't think he can, we'd better get going ourselves."

"Huh? How?"

"Swim. How else?"

"But how do we navigate? Once we're out of sight of the core we'd be there in the dark with absolutely nothing to guide us. These little lights on our suits aren't—"

"I know they aren't. That wasn't the idea. Don't worry; I may not be able to swim in a straight line, but I can get us to the surface eventually. Come on; five miles is a long swim."

Silbert started away from the glow, and Bresnahan followed uneasily. He was not happy at the prospect of weightlessness and darkness combined; the doses on the trip down, when at least the sphere had been present for some sort of orientation, had been more than sufficient.

The glow of the core faded slowly behind them, but before it was too difficult to see Silbert stopped.

"All right, put your light on. I'll do the same; stay close to me." Bresnahan obeyed both orders gladly. "Now, watch."

The spaceman manipulated valves on his suit, and carefully ejected a bubble of air about two feet in diameter. "You noticed that waste gas from the electrolyzers in the diving suits didn't stay with us to be a nuisance. The bubbles drifted away, even when we were at the core," he pointed out. Bresnahan hadn't noticed, since he wasn't used to paying attention to the fate of the air he exhaled, but was able to remember the fact once it was mentioned.

"That of course, was not due to buoyancy, so close to the core. The regular convection currents started by solar heat at the skin must be responsible. Therefore, those currents must extend all the way between skin and core. We'll follow this bubble."

"If the current goes all the way, why not just drift?"

"For two reasons. One is that the currents are slow— judging by their speed near the skin, the cycle must take over a day. Once we get away from the core, the buoyancy of this bubble will help; we can swim after it.

"The other reason is that if we simply drift we might start down again with the current before we got close enough to the skin to see daylight.

"Another trick we might try if this takes too long is to have one of us drift while the other follows the bubble to the limit of vision. That would establish the up-down line, and we could swim in that direction for a while and then repeat. I'm afraid we probably couldn't hold swimming direction for long enough to be useful, though, and it would be hard on the reserve air supply. We'd have to make a new bubble each time we checked. These suits have recyclers, but a spacesuit isn't built to get its oxygen from the surrounding water the way that diving gear is."

"Let's just follow this bubble," Bresnahan said fervently.

At first, of course, the two merely drifted. There simply was no detectable buoyancy near the core. However, in a surprisingly short time the shimmering globule of gas began to show a tendency to drift away from them.

The direction of drift was seldom the one which Bresnahan was thinking of as "up" at the moment, but the spaceman nodded approval and carefully followed their only guide. Bresnahan wished that his training had given him more confidence in instrument readings as opposed to his own senses, but followed Silbert hopefully.

VIII

The fourteen hours he spent drifting weightless in the dark made an experience Bresnahan was never to forget, and his friends were never to ignore. He always liked crowds afterward, and preferred to be in cities or at least buildings where straight, clearly outlined walls, windows, and doors marked an unequivocal up-and-down direction.

Even Silbert was bothered. He was more used to weightlessness, but the darkness he was used to seeing around him at such times was normally pocked with stars which provide orientation. The depths of Raindrop provided *nothing*. Both men were almost too far gone to believe their senses when they finally realized that the bubble they were still following could be seen by a glow not from their suits' lights.

It was a faintly blue-green illumination, still impossible to define as to source, but unmistakably sunlight filtered through hundreds of feet of water. Only minutes later their helmets met the tough, elastic skin of the satellite.

It took Silbert only a few moments to orient himself. The sun and the station were both visible—at least they had not come out on the opposite side of the satellite—and he knew the time. The first and last factors were merely checks; all that was really necessary to find the lock was to swim toward the point under the orbiting station.

"I don't want to use the sonar locater unless I have to," he pointed out. "There is sonar gear on the sphere. I should be able to get us close enough by sighting on the station so that the magnetic compass will work. Judging by where the station seems to be, we have four or five miles to swim. Let's get going."

"And let's follow the great circle course," added Bresnahan. "Never mind cutting across inside just because it's shorter. I've had all I ever want of swimming in the dark."

"My feeling exactly. Come on."

The distance was considerably greater than Silbert had estimated, since he was not used to doing his sighting from under water and had not allowed for refraction; but finally the needle of the gimballed compass showed signs of making up its mind, and with nothing wrong that food and sleep would not repair the two men came at last in sight of the big lock cylinder.

For a moment, Silbert wondered whether they should try to make their approach secretly. Then he decided that if the Weisanens were there waiting for them the effort would be impractical, and if they weren't it would be futile.

He simply swam up to the small hatch followed by Bresnahan, and they entered the big chamber together. It proved to be full of water, but the sphere was nowhere in sight. With no words they headed for the outer personnel lock, entered it, pumped back the water, and emerged on Raindrop's surface. Silbert used his laser, and ten minutes later they were inside the station. Bresnahan's jump had been a little more skillful than before.

"Now let's get on the radio!" snapped Silbert as he shed his space helmet.

"Why? Whom would you call, and what would you tell them? Remember that our normal Earth-end contacts are part of the same group the Weisanens belong to, and you can't issue a general broadcast to the universe at large screaming about a plot against mankind in the hope that someone will take you seriously. Someone might."

"But—"

"My turn, Bert. You've turned what I still think was just a potentially tragic mistake of Weisanen's into something almost funny, and incidentally saved both our lives. Now will you follow my lead? Things could still be serious if we don't follow up properly."

"But what are you going to do?"

"You'll see. Take it from me, compromise is still possible. It will take a little time; Aino Weisanen will have to learn something I can't teach him myself. Tell me, is there any way to monitor what goes on in Raindrop? For example, can you tell from here when the lock down there is opened, so we would know when they come back."

"No."

"Then we'll just have to watch for them. I assume that if we see them, we can call them from here on regular radio."

"Of course."

"Then let's eat, sleep, and wait. They'll be back after a while, and when they come Aino will listen to reason, believe me. But we can sleep right now, I'm sure; it will be a while yet before they show up. They should still be looking for us—getting more worried by the minute."

"Why should they appear at all? They must have found out long ago that they can't get back to the station on their own. They obviously haven't found us, and won't. Maybe they've simply decided they're already fugitive murderers and have settled down to a permanent life in Raindrop."

"That's possible, I suppose. Well, if we don't see them in a couple of weeks, we can go back down and give them a call in some fashion. I'd rather they came to us, though, and not too soon.

"But let's forget that; I'm starved. What's in your culture tanks besides liver?"

IX

It did not take two weeks. Nine days and eight hours after the men had returned to the station, Silbert saw two spacesuited figures standing on the lock half a mile away, and called his companion's attention to them.

"They must be desperate by this time," remarked Bresnahan. "We'd better call them before they decide to risk the jump anyway." He activated the transmitter which Silbert indicated, and spoke.

"Hello, Mr. and Mrs. Weisanen. Do you want us to send the cobweb down?"

The voice that answered was female.

"Thank God you're there! Yes, please. We'd like to come up for a while." Silbert expected some qualifying remarks from her husband, but none were forthcoming. At Bresnahan's gesture, he activated the spring gun which launched the web toward the satellite.

"Maybe you'd better suit up and go meet them," suggested the computerman. "I don't suppose either of them is very good at folding the web, to say nothing of killing angular speed."

"I'm not sure I care whether they go off on their own orbit anyway," growled the spaceman rising with some reluctance to his feet.

"Still bitter? And both of them?" queried Bresnahan.

"Well—I suppose not. And it would take forever to repair the web if it hit the station unfolded. I'll be back." Silbert vanished toward the hub, and the younger man turned back to watch his employers make the leap from Raindrop. He was not too surprised to see them hold hands as they did so, with the natural result that they spun madly on the way to the web and came close to missing it altogether.

When his own stomach had stopped whirling in sympathy, he decided that maybe the incident was for the best. Anything which tended to cut down Weisanen's self-assurance should be helpful, even though there was good reason to suspect that the battle was already won. He wondered whether he should summon the pair to his and Silbert's quarters for the interview which was about to ensue, but decided that there was such a thing as going too far.

He awaited the invitation to the Weisanens' rooms with eagerness.

It came within minutes of the couple's arrival at the air lock. When Bresnahan arrived he found Silbert already in the room where they had first reported on their brief visit to Raindrop. All three were still in spacesuits; they had removed only the helmets.

"We're going back down as soon as possible, Mr. Bresnahan," Weisanen began without preliminary. "I have a rather lengthy set of messages here which I would like you and Mr. Silbert to transmit as soon as possible. You will note that they contain my urgent recommendation for a policy change. Your suggestion starting construction of smaller farms from Raindrop's outer layers is sound, and I think the Company will follow it. I am also advising that material be collected from the vicinity of the giant planets —Saturn's rings seem a likely source—for constructing additional satellites like Raindrop as private undertakings. Financing can be worked out. There should be enough profit from the farms, and that's the logical direction for some of it to flow.

"Once other sources of farm material are available, Raindrop will not be used further for the purpose. It will serve as Company headquarters—it will be more convenient to have that in orbit anyway. The closest possible commercial relations are to be maintained with Earth."

"I'm glad you feel that way, sir," replied Bresnahan. "We'll get the messages off as soon as possible. I take it that more of the Company's officials will be coming up here to live, then?"

"Probably all of them, within the next two years or so. Brenda and I will go back and resume surveying now, as soon as we stock up with some food. I'll be back occasionally, but I'd rather she kept away from high weight for the next few months, as you know."

"Yes, sir," Bresnahan managed, by a heroic effort, to control his smile—almost. Weisanen saw the flicker of his lip, and froze for a moment. Then his own sober features loosened into a broad grin.

"Maybe another hour won't hurt Brenda," he remarked. "Let's have a meal together before we go back."

He paused, and added almost diffidently, "Sorry about what happened. We're human, you know."

"I know," replied Bresnahan. "That's what I was counting on."

"And that," remarked Silbert as he shed his helmet, "is that. They're aboard and bound for the core again, happy as clams. And speaking of clams, if you don't tell me why that stubborn Finn changed his mind, and why you were so sure he'd do it, there'll be mayhem around here. Don't try to make me believe that he got scared about what he'd nearly done to us. I know his wife was on our side, basically, but she wasn't about to wage open war for us. She was as worried about their kid as he was. Come on; make with the words, chum."

"Simple enough. Didn't you notice what he wanted before going back to Raindrop?"

"Not particularly—oh; food. So what? He could live on the food down there—or couldn't he? Don't you believe what he said?"

"Sure I believe him. He and his wife can digest cellulose, Heaven help them, and they can live off Raindrop's seaweed. As I remarked to him, though—you heard me, and he understood me—they're human. I can digest kale and cauliflower, too, and could probably live off them as well as that pair could live off the weeds. But did you ever stop to think what the stuff must taste like? Neither did they. I knew they'd be back with open mouths—and open minds. Let's eat—anything but liver!"

Drifting idly, the *Shark* tended to look more like a manta ray than her name suggested; but at high cruise, as she was now, she bore more resemblance to a flying fish. She was entirely out of the water except for the four struts that carried her hydroplanes; the air propellers which drove her were high enough above the surface to raise very little spray. An orbiting monitor satellite could have seen the vessel herself from a hundred miles up, since her upper hull was painted in a vividly fluorescent pattern of red and yellow; but there was not enough wake to suggest to such a watcher that the wedge-shaped machine was traveling at nearly sixty-five knots.

Chester V. Winkle—everyone knew what the middle initial stood for, but no one mentioned it in his presence— sat behind the left bow port of his command with his fingers resting lightly on the pressure controls. He was looking ahead, but knew better than to trust his eyes alone. Most of his attention was devoted to the voice of the smaller man seated four feet to his right, behind the other "eye" of the manta. Yoshii Ishihara was not looking outside at all; his eyes were directed steadily at the sonar display screen which was all that stood between the *Shark* and disaster at her present speed among the ice floes and zeowhales of the Labrador Sea.

"Twenty-two targets in the sweep; about fourteen thousand meters to the middle of the group," he said softly.

"Heading?" Winkle knew the question was superfluous; had a change been in order, the sonarman would have given it.

"As we go, for thirty-two hundred meters. Then twenty-two mils starboard. There's ice in the way."

"Good. Any data on target condition yet?"

"No. It will be easier to read them when we stop, and will cost little time to wait. Four of the twenty-two are drifting, but the sea is rich here and they might be digesting. Stand by for change of heading."

"Ready on your call." There was silence for about a minute.

"Starboard ten."

"Starboard ten." The hydroplanes submerged near the ends of the *Shark*'s bow struts banked in response to the pressure of Winkle's fingers, though the hull remained nearly level. The compass needle on the panel between the view ports moved smoothly through ten divisions. As it reached the tenth Ishihara, without looking up from his screen, called, "Steady."

"Steady she is," replied the commander.

"Stand by for twelve more to starboard—now." The *Shark* swung again and steadied on the new heading.

"That leaves us a clear path in," said the sonarman. "Time to engine cut is four minutes."

In spite of his assurance that the way was clear, Ishihara kept his eyes on his instrument—his standards of professional competence would permit nothing less while the *Shark* had way on her. Winkle, in spite of the sleepy appearance which combined with his name to produce a constant spate of bad jokes, was equally alert for visible obstructions ahead. Several ice floes could be seen; but none were directly in the vessel's path, and Winkle's fingers remained idle until his second officer gave the expected signal.

Then the whine of turbines began to drop in pitch, and the *Shark*'s broad form eased toward the swell below as the hydrofoils lost their lift. The hull extensions well out on her "wings" which gave the vessel catamaran-type stability when drifting kissed the surface gently, their added drag slowing the machine more abruptly; and twenty feet aft of the conning ports the four remaining members of the crew tensed for action.

"Slow enough for readings?" asked Winkle.

"Yes, sir. The homing signal is going out now. I'll have counts in the next thirty seconds." Ishihara paused. "One of the four drifters is underway and turning toward us. No visible response from the others."

"Which is the nearest of the dead ones?"

"Fifteen hundred meters, eight hundred forty mils port." Winkle's fingers moved again. The turbines that drove the big, counter-rotating air propellers remained idle, but water jets playing from ducts on the hydrofoil struts swung the ship in the indicated direction and set her traveling slowly toward the drifter. Winkle called an order over his shoulder.

"Winches and divers ready. The trap is unsafetied. Contact in five minutes."

"Winch ready," Dandridge's deep voice reported as he swept his chessboard to one side and closed a master switch. Mancini, who had been facing him across the board, slipped farther aft to the laboratory which occupied over half of the *Shark*'s habitable part. He said nothing, since no order had been directed at him, and made no move to uncage any of his apparatus while the vessel was still in motion.

"Divers standing by." Farrell spoke for himself and his assistant after a brief check of masks and valves—both were already dressed for Arctic water. They took their places at either side of the red-checkered deck area, just forward of the lab section, which marked the main hatch. Dandridge, glancing up to make sure that no one was standing on it, opened the trap from his control console. Its halves slid smoothly apart, revealing the chill green liquid slipping between the hulls. At the *Shark*'s present speed she was floating at displacement depth, so that the water averaged about four meters down from the hatch; but this distance was varied by a swell of a meter or so. Farrell stood looking down at it, waiting patiently for the vessel to stop; his younger assistant dropped prone by the edge of the opening and craned his neck through it in an effort to see forward.

Ishihara's voice was barely audible over the wind now that the hatch was open, but occasional words drifted back to the divers. "Six hundred . . . as you go . . . four . . . three . . ."

"I see it," Winkle cut in. "I'll take her." He called over his shoulder again, "Farrell . . . Stubbs . . . we're coming up on one. You'll spot it in a minute. I'll tell you when I lose it under the bow."

"Yes, sir," acknowledged Farrell. "See it yet, Rick?"

"Not yet," was the response. "Nothing but jellyfish."

"Fifty meters," called the captain. "Now thirty." He cut the water jets to a point where steerage way would have been lost if such a term had meant anything to the *Shark*, and continued to inch forward. "Twenty."

"I see it," called Stubbs.

"All right," answered the captain. "Ten meters. Five. It's right under me; I've lost it. Con me, diver."

"About five meters, sir. It's dead center . . . four . . . three . . . two . . . all right, it's right under the hatch. Magnets ready, Gil?"

The magnetic grapple was at the forward end of its rail, directly over the hatch, so Dandridge was ready; but Winkle was not.

"Hold up . . . don't latch on yet. Stubbs, watch the fish; are we drifting?"

"A little, sir. It's going forward and a little to port . . . now you're stopping it . . . there."

"Quite a bit of wind," remarked the captain as his fingers lifted from the hydrojet controls. "All right. Pick it up."

"Think the magnets will be all right, Marco?" asked Dandridge. "That whale looks funny to me." The mechanic joined the winchman and divers at the hatch and looked down at their floating problem.

At first glance the "whale" was ordinary enough. It was about two meters long, and perfectly cigar-shaped except where the intake ring broke the curve some forty centimeters back of the nose. The exhaust ports, about equally far from the tail end, were less visible since they were merely openings in the dark gray skin. Integument and openings alike were hard to see in detail, however; the entire organism was overgrown with a brownish, slimy-looking mass of filaments reminiscent both of mold and sealskin.

"It's picked up something, all right," Mancini conceded. "I don't see why your magnets shouldn't work, though . . . unless you'd rather they didn't get dirty."

"All right. Get down the ladder and steer 'em, Rick." Dandridge caused a light alloy ladder to extend from the bow edge of the hatch as he spoke; then he fingered another switch which sent the grapples themselves slowly downward. Stubbs easily beat them to the foot of the ladder, hooked one leg through a rung, reached out with both arms and tried to steady the descending mass of metal. The *Shark* was pitching somewhat in the swell, and the eighty pounds of electromagnet and associated wiring was slightly rebellious. The youngest of the crew and the only nonspecialist among its members—he was still working off the two-year labor draft requirement which preceded higher education—Rick Stubbs got at least his share of the dirty work. He was not so young as to complain about it.

"Slower . . . slower . . . twenty c's to go . . . ten . . . hold it now . . . just a touch lower . . . all right, juice!" Dandridge followed the instructions, fed current to the magnets, and started to lift.

"Wait!" the boy on the ladder called almost instantly. "It's not holding!"

The mechanic reacted almost as fast.

"Bring it up anyway!" he called. "The infection is sticking to the magnets. Let me get a sample!" Stubbs shrank back against the ladder as the slimy mass rose past him in response to Mancini's command. Dandridge grimaced with distaste as it came above deck level and into his view.

"You can have it!" he remarked, not very originally.

Mancini gave no answer, and showed no sign of any emotion but interest. He had slipped back into his lab as the material was ascending, and now returned with a two-liter flask and the biggest funnel he possessed.

"Run it aft a little," he said briefly. "That's enough . . . I'll miss some, and it might as well fall into the water as onto the deck." The grapple, which had crawled a few inches toward him on its overhead rail, stopped just short of the after edge of the hatch. Mancini, standing unconcernedly at the edge of the opening with the wind ruffling his clothes, held funnel and flask under the magnets.

"All right, Gil, drop it," he ordered. Dandridge obeyed.

Most of the mess fell obediently away from the grapple. Some landed in the funnel and proceeded to ooze down into the flask; some hit Mancini's extended arm without appearing to bother him; a little dropped onto the deck, to the winchman's visible disgust. Most fell past Stubbs back into the sea.

The mechanic took up some of the material from his arm and rubbed it between thumb and forefinger. "Gritty," he remarked. "And the magnets held this stuff, but not the whale's skeleton. That means that most of the skeleton must be gone, and I bet this grit is magnetite. I'll risk a dollar that this infection comes from that old 775-Fe-DE6 culture that got loose a few years ago from Passamaquoddy. I'll give it the works to make sure, though. You divers will have to use slings to get the fish aboard, I'm afraid."

"Rick, I'll send the magnets down first and you can rinse

'em off a bit in the water. Then I'll run out the sling and
you can get it around the whale."

"All right, sir. Standing by." As the grapple went down
again Dandridge called to the mechanic, who had turned
back toward the lab.

"I suppose the whale is ruined, if you're right about the
infection. Can we collect damages?" Mancini shook his
head negatively.

"No one could collect from DE; they went broke
years ago—from paying damages. Besides, the courts decided years ago that injury or destruction of a piece of
pseudolife was recoverable property damage only if an
original model was involved. This fish is a descendant of a
model ten years old; it was born at sea. We didn't make it,
and can't recover for it." He turned to his bench, but
flung a last thought over his shoulder. "My guess that this
pest is a DE escapee could be wrong, too. They worked
out a virus for that strain a few months after it escaped,
and I haven't heard of an iron infection in four years.
This may be a mutation of it—that's still my best guess—
but it could also be something entirely new." He settled
himself onto a stool and began dividing the material from
the flask into the dozens of tiny containers which fed the
analyzers.

In the water below, Stubbs had plunged from the ladder
and was removing slime from the grapple magnets. The
stuff was not too sticky, and the grit which might be
magnetite slightly offset the feeling of revulsion which the
boy normally had for slimy materials, so he was able to
finish the job quickly enough to keep Dandridge happy. At
Rick's call, the grapple was retracted; a few moments later
the hoist cable came down again with an ordinary sling at
its extremity. Stubbs was still in the water, and Farrell had
come part way down the ladder. The chief diver guided
the cable down to his young assistant, who began working
the straps around the torpedo-like form which still bobbed
between the *Shark*'s hulls.

It was quite a job. The zeowhale was still slippery, since
the magnets had not come even close to removing all the
foreign growth. When the boy tried to reach around it to
fasten the straps it slithered away from him. He called for
more slack and tried to pin it against one of the hulls as he
worked, but still it escaped him. He was too stubborn to

ask for help, and by this time Farrell was laughing too hard to have provided much anyway.

"Ride him, Buster!" the chief diver called as Stubbs finally managed to scissor the slippery cylinder with his legs. "That's it . . . you've got him dogged now!"

The boy hadn't quite finished, actually, but one strap did seem secure around the forward part of the hull. "Take up slack!" he called up to the hatch, without answering Farrell's remark.

Dandridge had been looking through the trap and could see what was needed; he reached to his control console and the hoist cable tightened.

"That's enough!" called Stubbs as the nose of the zeo-whale began to lift from the water. "Hold it until I get another strap on, or this one will slip free!"

Winches obediently ceased purring. With its motion re-strained somewhat, the little machine offered less opposition to the attachment of a second band near its stern. The young swimmer called, somewhat breathlessly, "Take it up!" and paddled himself slowly back to the ladder. Farrell gave him a hand up, and they reached the deck almost as quickly as the specimen.

Dandridge closed the hatch without waiting for orders, though he left the ladder down—there would be other pickups in the next few minutes, but the wind was cold and loud. Stubbs paid no attention; he barely heard the soft "Eight hundred meters, seventy-five mils to starboard," as he made his way around the closing hatch to Mancini's work station. The mechanic's job was much more fascinating than the pilot's.

He knew better than to interrupt a busy professional with questions, but the mechanic didn't need any. Like several other men, not only on the *Shark* but among the crew of her mother ship, Mancini had come to like the youngster and respect his general competence; and like most professionals, his attitude toward an intelligent labor draftee was a desire to recruit him before someone else did. The man, therefore, began to talk as soon as he noticed the boy's presence.

"You know much about either chemical or field analysis, Rick?"

"A little. I can recognize most of your gear—untracentrifuge, chromatographic and electrophoretic stuff, NMR equipment, and so on. Is that," he pointed to a cylindrical machine on another bench, "a deffraction camera?"

"Good guess. It's a hybrid that a friend of mine dreamed up which can be used either for electron micro-photography or diffraction work. All that comes a bit later, though. One thing about analysis hasn't changed since the beginning; you try to get your initial sample into as many different homogeneous parts as possible before you get down to the molecular scale."

"So each of these little tubes you're filling goes through centrifuge, or solvation, or electrophoresis—"

"More usually, through all of them, in different orders."

"I should think that just looking at the original, undamaged specimen would tell you *something*. Don't you ever do that?"

"Sure. The good old light microscope will never disappear; as you imply, it's helpful to see a machine in its assembled state, too. I'll have some slides in a few more seconds; the mike is in that cabinet. Slide it out, will you?"

Stubbs obeyed, literally since the instrument was mounted on a track. The designers of the *Shark*'s laboratory had made it as immune to rough weather as they could. Mancini took the first of his slides, clipped it under the objective, and took one look.

"Thought so," he grunted. "Here, see for yourself."

Stubbs applied an eye to the instrument, played briefly with the fine focus—he had the normal basic training in fundamental apparatus—and looked for several seconds.

"Just a mess of living cells that don't mean much to me, and a lot of little octahedra. Are they what you mean?"

"Yep. Magnetite crystals, or I'm a draft-dodger." (His remark had no military significance; the term now referred to individuals who declined the unskilled-labor draft, voluntarily giving up their rights to higher education and, in effect, committing themselves to living on basic relief.) "We'll make sure, though." The mechanic slid another piece of equipment into position on the microscope stage, and peered once more into the field of view. Stubbs recognized a micromanipulator, and was not surprised when Mancini, after two minutes or so of silent work, straightened up and removed a small strip of metal from it. Presumably one of the tiny crystals was now mounted on the strip.

The mechanic turned to the diffraction camera, mounted the bit of metal in a clamp attached to it, and touched a button which started specimen and strip on a journey into the camera's interior. Moments later a pump started to whine.

"Five minutes to vacuum, five more for scanning," he remarked. "We might as well have a look at the fish itself while we wait; even naked-eye examination has its uses." He got up from his seat, stretched, and turned to the bench on which the ruined zeowhale lay. "How much do you know about these things, Rick? Can you recognize this type?"

"I think so. I'd say it was a copper-feeder of about '35 model. This one would be about two years old."

"Good. I'd say you were about right. You've been doing some reading, I take it."

"Some. And the *Guppy*'s shop is a pretty good museum."

"True enough. Do you know where the access regions are on this model?"

"I've seen some of them opened up, but I wouldn't feel sure enough to do it myself."

"It probably wouldn't matter if you did it wrong in this case; this one is safely dead. Still, I'll show you; better see it right than do it wrong." He had removed the straps of the sling once the "fish" had been lowered onto a rack on the bench, so nothing interfered with the demonstration. "Here," he pointed, "the reference is the centerline of scales along the back, just a little lighter in color than the rest. Start at the intake ring and count eight scales back; then down six on either side, like that. That puts you on this scale . . . so . . . which you can get under with a scalpel at the start of the main opening." He picked up an instrument about the size of a surgical scalpel, but with a blunt, rounded blade. This he inserted under the indicated scale. "See, it comes apart here with very light pressure, and you can run the cut back to just in front of the exhaust vents—like that. If this were a living specimen, the cut would heal under sealant spray in about an hour after the fish was back in the water. This one . . . hm-m-m. No wonder it passed out. I wonder what this stuff is?"

The body cavity of the zeowhale was filled with a dead-black jelly, quite different in appearance from the growth which had covered the skin. The mechanic applied retrac-

tors to the incision, and began silently poking into the
material with a variety of "surgical" tools. He seemed
indifferent to the feelings which were tending to bring
Stubbs' stomach almost as much into daylight as that of the
whale.

Pieces of rubbery internal machinery began to litter the
bench top. Another set of tiny test tubes took samples of
the black jelly, and followed their predecessors into the
automatic analyzers. These began to hum and sputter as
they went to work on the new material—they had long
since finished with the first load, and a pile of diagrams
and numerical tables awaited Mancini's attention in their
various delivery baskets. He had not even taken time to see
whether his guess about magnetite had been good.

Some of the organs on the desk were recognizable to the
boy—for any large animal, of course, a heart is fairly
obviously a heart when it has been dissected sufficiently to
show its valve structure. A four-kilogram copper nugget
had come from the factory section; the organism had at
least started to fulfill its intended purpose before disease
had ended its pseudolife. It had also been developing normally in other respects, as a twenty-five centimeter em-
bryo indicated. The zeowhales and their kindred devices
reproduced asexually; the genetic variation magnification,
which is the biological advantage of sex, was just what the
users of the pseudo-organisms did not want, at least until
some factor could be developed which would tend to select
for the characteristics they wanted most.

Mancini spent more than an hour at his rather revolt-
ing task before he finally laid down his instruments. Stubbs
had not been able to watch him the whole time, since the
Shark had picked up the other two unresponsive whales
while the job was going on. Both had been infected in the
same way as the first. The boy was back in the lab, though,
when the gross dissection of the original one was finished.
So was Winkle, since nothing more could be planned until
Mancini produced some sort of report.

"The skeleton was gone completely," was the mechanic's
terse beginning. "Even the unborn one hadn't a trace of
metallic iron in it. That was why the magnets didn't hold,
of course. I haven't had time to look at any of the analysis
reports, but I'm pretty certain that the jelly in the body
cavity and the moldy stuff outside are part of the same life

form, and that organism dissolved the metallic skeleton and precipitated the iron as magnetite in its own tissues. Presumably it's a mutant from one of the regular iron-feeding strains. Judging by its general cellular conformation, its genetic tape is a purine-pyrimidine nucleotide quite similar to that of natural life—"

"Just another of the original artificial forms coming home to roost?" interjected Winkle.

"I suppose so. I've isolated some of the nuclear material, but it will have to go back to the big field analyzer on the *Guppy* to make sure."

"There seem to be no more damaged fish in the neighborhood. Is there any other material you need before we go back?"

"No. Might as well wind her up, as far as I'm concerned—unless it would be a good idea to call the ship first while we're out here to find out whether any other schools this way need checking."

"You can't carry any more specimens in your lab even if they do," Winkle pointed out, glancing around the littered bench tops.

"True enough. Maybe there's something which wouldn't need a major checkup, though. But you're the captain; play it as you think best. I'll be busy with this lot until we get back to the *Guppy* whether we go straight there or not."

"I'll call." The captain turned away to his own station.

"I wonder why they made the first pseudolife machines with gene tapes so much like the real thing," Stubbs remarked when Winkle was back in his seat. "You'd think they'd foresee what mutations could do, and that organisms too similar to genuine life might even give rise to forms which could cause disease in us as well as in other artificial forms."

"They thought of it, all right," replied Mancini. "That possibility was a favorite theme of the opponents of the whole process—at least, of the ones who weren't driven by frankly religious motives. Unfortunately, there was no other way the business could have developed. The original research of course had to be carried out on what you call 'real' life. That led to the specific knowledge that the cytosine-thymine-adenine-guanine foursome of ordinary DNA could form a pattern which was both self-replicating and able to control polypeptide and polysaccharide synthesis—"

"But I thought it was more complex than that; there are phosphates and sugars in the chain, and the DNA imprints RNA, and—"

"You're quite right, but I wasn't giving a chemistry lecture; I was trying to make an historical point. I'm saying that at first, no one realized that anything except those four specific bases could do the genetic job. Then they found that quite a lot of natural life forms had variations of those bases in their nucleotides, and gradually the reasons *why* those structures, or rather their potential fields, had the polymermolding ability they do became clear. Then, and only then, was it obvious that 'natural' genes aren't the only possible ones; they're simply the ones which got a head start on this planet. There are as many ways of building a gene as there are of writing a poem—or of making an airplane if you prefer to stay on the physical plane. As you seem to know, using the channels of a synthetic zeolite as the backbone for a genetic tape happens to be a very convenient technique when we want to grow a machine like the one we've just taken apart here. It's bulkier than the phosphate-sugar-base tape, but a good deal more stable.

"It's still handy, though, to know how to work with the real thing—after all, you know as well as I do that the reason you have a life expectancy of about a hundred and fifty years is that your particular gene pattern is on file in half a cubic meter of zeolite mesh in Denver under a nice file number . . ."

"026-18-5633" muttered the boy under his breath.

" . . . which will let any halfway competent molecular mechanic like me grow replacement parts and tissues if and when you happen to need them."

"I know all that, but it still seems dangerous to poke around making little changes in ordinary life forms," replied Rick. "There must be fifty thousand people like you in the world, who could tailor a dangerous virus, or germ, or crop fungus in a couple of weeks of lab and computer work, and whose regular activities produce things like that iron-feeder which can mutate into dangerous by-products."

"It's also dangerous to have seven billion people on the planet, practically every one of whom knows how to light a fire," replied Mancini. "Dangerous or not, it was no more possible to go from Watson and Crick and the DNA structure to this zeowhale without the intermediate development than it would have been to get from the Wright brothers and their powered kite to the two-hour transatlantic ramjet without building Ford tri-motors and DC-3's in between. We have the knowledge, it's an historical fact that no one can effectively destroy it, so we might as well use it. The fact that so many competent practitioners of the art exist is our best safeguard if it does get a little out of hand at times."

The boy looked thoughtful.

"Maybe you have something there," he said slowly. "But with all that knowledge, why only a hundred and fifty years? Why can't you keep people going indefinitely?"

"Do you think we should?" Mancini countered with a straight face. Rick grinned.

"Stop ducking. If you could, you would—for some people anyway. Why can't you?" Mancini shrugged.

"Several hundred million people undoubtedly know the rules of chess." He nodded toward the board on Dandridge's control table. "Why aren't they all good players? You know, don't you, why doctors were reluctant to use hormones as therapeutic agents even when they became available in quantity?"

"I think so. If you gave someone cortisone it might do what you wanted, but it might also set other glands going or slow them down, which would alter the levels of other hormones, which in turn . . . well, it was a sort of chain reaction which could end anywhere."

"Precisely. And gene-juggling is the same only more so. If you were to sit at the edge of the hatch there and let Gil close it on you, I could rig the factors in your gene pattern so as to let you grow new legs; but there would be a distinct risk of affecting other things in your system at the same time. In effect, I would be taking certain *restraints* which caused your legs to stop growing when they were completed *off* your cell-dividing control mechanisms—the sort of thing that used to happen as a natural, random effect in cancer. I'd probably get away with it—or rather, you would—since you're only about nineteen and still pretty deep in what we call the stability well. As you get older, though, with more and more factors interfering with that stability, the job gets harder—it's a literal juggling act, with more and more balls being tossed to the juggler every year you live.

"You were born with a deep enough stability reserve to keep yourself operating for a few decades without any applied biochemical knowledge; you might live twenty years or ninety. Using the knowledge we have, we can play the game longer; but sooner or later we drop the ball. It's not that we don't know the rules; to go back to the chess analogy, it's just that there are too many pieces on the board to keep track of all at once."

Stubbs shook his head. "I've never thought of it quite that way. To me, it's always been just a repair job, and I couldn't see why it should be so difficult."

Mancini grinned. "Maybe your cultural grounding didn't include a poem called the 'Wonderful One-Hoss Shay.' Well, we'll be a couple of hours getting back to the *Guppy*. There are a couple of sets of analysis runs sitting with us here. Maybe, if I start trying to turn those into language you can follow, you'll have some idea of why the game is so hard before we get there. Maybe, too"—his face sobered somewhat—"you'll start to see why, even though we always lose in the end, the game is so much fun. It isn't just that our own lives are at stake, you know; men have been playing that kind of game for two million years or so. Come on."

He turned to the bench top on which the various analyzers had been depositing their results; and since Stubbs had a good grounding in mathematical and chemical fundamentals, their language ceased to resemble Basic English. Neither paid any attention as the main driving turbines of the *Shark* came up to quarter speed and the vessel began to pick her way out of the patch of ice floes where the zeowhales had been collecting metal.

By the time Winkle had reached open water and Ishihara had given him the clearance for high cruise, the other four had lost all contact with the outside world. Dandridge's chess board was in use again, with Farrell now his opponent. The molecular mechanic and his possible apprentice were deeply buried in a task roughly equivalent to explaining to a forty-piece orchestra how to produce "Aida" from overture to finale—without the use of written music. Stubbs' basic math was, for this problem, equivalent to having learned just barely his "do, re, mi."

There was nothing to distract the players of either game. The wind had freshened somewhat, but the swells had increased little if at all. With the *Shark* riding on her hydrofoils there was only the faintest of tremors as her struts cut the waves. The sun was still high and the sky almost cloudless. Between visual pilotage and sonar, life seemed as uncomplicated as it ever gets for the operator of a high-speed vehicle.

The *Guppy* was nearly two hundred kilometers to the south, far beyond sonar range. Four of her other boats were out on business, and Winkle occasionally passed a word or two with their commanders; but no one had anything of real importance to say. The desultory conversations were a matter of habit, to make sure that everyone was still on the air. No pilot, whether of aircraft, space vessel, surface ship, or submarine, attaches any weight to the proverb that no news is good news.

Just who was to blame for the interruption of this idyll remains moot. Certainly Mancini had given the captain his preliminary ideas about the pest which had killed their first whale. Just as certainly he had failed to report the confirmation of that opinion after going through the lab results with Stubbs. Winkle himself made no request for such confirmation—there was no particular reason why he should, and if he had it is hard to believe that he would either have realized all the implications or been able to do anything about them. The fact remains that everyone from Winkle at the top of the ladder of command to Stubbs at the bottom was taken completely by surprise when the *Shark*'s starboard after hydrofoil strut snapped cleanly off just below the mean planing water line.

At sixty-five knots, no human reflexes could have coped with the result. The electronic ones of the *Shark* tried, but the vessel's mechanical I.Q. was not up to the task of allowing for the lost strut. As the gyros sensed the drop in the right rear quadrant of their field of perception, the autopilot issued commands to increase the angle of attack of the control foils on that strut. Naturally there was no response. The dip increased. By the time it got beyond the point where the machine thought it could be handled by a single set of foils, so that orders went out to decrease lift on the port-bow leg, it was much too late. The after portion of the starboard flotation hull smacked a wave top at sixty-five knots and, of course, bounced. The bounce was just in time to reinforce the letdown command to the port-bow control foils. The box curve of the port hull struck in its turn, with almost undiminished speed and with two principal results.

About a third of the *Shark*'s forward speed vanished in less than the same fraction of a second as she gave up kinetic energy to the water in front, raising a cloud of spray more than a hundred meters and subjecting hull and contents to about four gravities of acceleration in a most unusual direction. The rebound was high enough to cause the starboard "wing" to dip into the waves, and the *Shark* did a complete double cartwheel. For a moment she seemed to poise motionless with port wing and hull entirely submerged and the opposite wing tip pointing at the sky; then, grudgingly, she settled back to a nearly horizontal position on her flotation hulls and lay rocking on the swell.

Externally she showed little sign of damage. The missing strut was, of course, under water anyway, and her main structure had taken only a few dents. The propellers had been twisted off by gyroscopic action during the cartwheel. Aside from this, the sleek form looked ready for service.

Inside, things were different. Most of the apparatus, and even some of the men, had been more or less firmly fixed in place; but the few exceptions had raised a good deal of mayhem.

Winkle and Ishihara were unconscious, though still buckled in their seats. Both had been snapped forward against their respective panels, and were draped with sundry unappetizing fragments of the dissected zeowhale. Ishihara's head had shattered the screen of his sonar instrument, and no one could have told at first glance how many cuts were supplying the blood on his face.

The chess players had both left impressions on the control panel of the winch and handling system, and now lay crumpled beside it. Neither was bleeding visibly, but Farrell's arms were both twisted at angles impossible to intact bones. Dandridge was moaning and just starting to try to get to his feet; he and Mancini were the only ones conscious.

The mechanic had been seated at one of his benches facing the starboard side of the ship when the impact came. He had not been strapped in his seat, and the four-G jerk had started to hurl him toward the bow. His right leg had stopped him almost as suddenly by getting entangled in the underpinning of the seat. The limb was not quite detached from its owner; oddly enough, its skin was intact. This was about the only bit of tissue below the knee for which this statement could be made.

Stubbs had been standing at the mechanic's side. They were to argue later whether it had been good or bad luck that the side in question had been the left. It depended largely on personal viewpoint. There had been nothing for Rick to seize as he was snatched toward the bow or, if there was, he had not been quick enough or strong enough to get it. He never knew just what hit him in flight; the motions of the *Shark* were so wild that it might have been deck, overhead, or the back of one of the pilot seats. It was evident enough that his path had intersected that of the big flask in which Mancini had first collected the iron-feeding tissue, but whether the flask was still whole at the time remains unclear. It is hard to see how he could have managed to absorb so many of its fragments had it already shattered, but it is equally hard to understand how he could have scattered them so widely over his anatomy if it had been whole.

It was Stubbs, or rather the sight of him, that got Mancini moving. Getting his own shattered leg disentangled from the chair was a distracting task, but not distracting enough to let him take his eyes from the boy a few meters away. Arterial bleeding is a sign that tends to focus attention.

He felt sick, over and above the pain of his leg; whether it was the sight of Rick or incipient shock he couldn't tell. He did his best to ignore the leg as he inched across the deck, though the limb itself seemed to have other ideas. Unfortunately these weren't very consistent; sometimes it wanted—demanded—his whole mind, at others it seemed to have gone off somewhere on its own and hidden. He did not look back to see whether it was still with him; what was in front was more important.

The boy still had blood when Mancini reached him, as well as a functioning heart to pump it. He was not losing the fluid as fast as had appeared from a distance, but something would obviously have to be done about what was left of his right hand—the thumb and about half of the palm. The mechanic had been raised during one of the periods when first-aiders were taught to abjure the tourniquet, but had reached an age where judgment stands a chance against rules. He had a belt and used it.

A close look at the boy's other injuries showed that nothing could be done about them on the spot; they were bleeding slowly, but any sort of first aid would be complicated by the slivers of glass protruding from most of them. Face, chest, and even legs were slashed freely, but the rate of bleeding was not—Mancini hoped—really serious. The smaller ones were clotting already.

Dandridge was on his feet by now, badly bruised but apparently in the best shape of the six.

"What can I do, Marco?" he asked. "Everyone else is out cold. Should I use—"

"Don't use anything on them until we're sure there are no broken necks or backs; they may be better off unconscious. I know I would be."

"Isn't there dope in the first-aid kit? I could give you a shot of painkiller."

"Not yet, anyway. Anything that would stop this leg from hurting would knock me out, and I've got to stay awake if at all possible until help comes. The lab equipment isn't really meant for repair work, but if anything needs to be improvised from it I'll have to be the one to do it. I could move around better, though, if this leg were splinted. Use the raft foam from the handling locker."

Five minutes later Mancini's leg, from mid-thigh down, was encased in a bulky, light, but reasonably rigid block of foamed resin whose original purpose was to provide on-the-spot flotation for objects which were inconvenient or impossible to bring aboard. It still hurt, but he could move around without much fear of doing the limb further damage.

"Good. Now you'd better see what communication gear, if any, stood up under this bump. I'll do what I can for the others. Don't move Ishi or the captain; work around them until I've done what I can."

Dandridge went forward to the conning section and began to manipulate switches. He was not a trained radioman—the *Shark* didn't carry one—but like any competent crew member he could operate all the vessel's equipment under routine conditions. He found quickly that no receivers were working, but that the regular transmitter drew current when its switches were closed. An emergency low-frequency beacon, entirely separate from the other communication equipment, also seemed intact; so he set this operating and began to broadcast the plight of the *Shark* on the regular transmitter. He had no way of telling whether either signal was getting out, but was not particularly worried for himself. The *Shark* was theoretically unsinkable—enough of her volume was filled with resin foam to buoy her entire weight even in fresh water. The main question was whether help would arrive before some of the injured men were beyond it.

After ten minutes of steady broadcasting—he hoped—Dandridge turned back to the mechanic, to find him lying motionless on the deck. For a moment the winchman thought he might have lost consciousness; then Mancini spoke.

"I've done all I can for the time being. I've splinted Joe's arms and pretty well stopped Rick's bleeding. Ishi has a skull fracture and the captain at least a concussion; don't move either one. If you've managed to get in touch with the *Guppy*, tell them about the injuries. We'll need gene records from Denver for Rick, probably for Ishi, and possibly for the captain. They should start making blood for Rick right away, the second enough gene data is through; he's lost quite a bit."

"I don't know whether I'm getting out or not, but I'll say it all anyway," replied Dandridge, turning back to the board. "Won't you need some pretty extensive repair work yourself, though?"

"Not unless these bone fragments do more nerve damage than I think they have," replied Mancini. "Just tell them that I have a multiple leg fracture. If I know Bert Jellinge, he'll have gene blocks on all six of us growing into the machines before we get back to the *Guppy* anyway."

Dandridge eyed him more closely. "Hadn't I better give you a shot now?" he asked. "You said you'd done all you could, and it might be better to pass out from a sleepy shot than from pain. How about it?"

"Get that message out first. I can hold on, and what I've done is the flimsiest of patchwork. With the deck tossing as it is any of those splints may be inadequate. We can't strap any of the fellows down, and if the wave motion rolls one of them over I'll have the patching to do all over again.

When you get that call off, look at Rick once more; I think his bleeding has stopped, but until he's on a repair table I won't be happy about him."

"So you'd rather stay awake."

"Not exactly, but if you were in the kid's place, wouldn't *you* prefer me to?" Dandridge had no answer to that one; he talked into the transmitter instead.

His words, as it happened, were getting out. The *Conger,* the nearest of the *Shark*'s sister fish-tenders, had already started toward them; she had about forty kilometers to come. On the *Guppy* the senior mechanic had fulfilled Mancini's prediction; he had already made contact with Denver, and Rick Stubbs' gene code was about to start through the multiple-redundant communication channels used for the purpose—channels which, fortunately, had just been freed of the saturation caused by a serious explosion in Pittsburgh, which had left over five hundred people in need of major repair. The full transmission would take over an hour at the highest safe scanning rate; but the first ten minutes would give enough information, when combined with the basic human data already in the *Guppy*'s computers, to permit the synthesis of replacement blood.

The big mother-ship was heading toward the site of the accident so as to shorten the *Conger*'s journey with the victims. The operations center at Cape Farewell had offered a "mastodon"—one of the gigantic helicopters capable of lifting the entire weight of a ship like the *Shark.* After a little slide-rule work, the *Guppy*'s commander had declined; no time would have been saved, and the elimination of one ship-to-ship transfer for the injured men was probably less important than economy of minutes.

Mancini would have agreed with this, had he been able to join in the discussion. By the time Dandridge had finished his second transmission, however, the mechanic had fainted from the pain of his leg.

Objectively, the winchman supposed that it was probably good for his friend to be unconscious. He was not too happy, though, at being the only one aboard who could take responsibility for anything. The half hour it took for the *Conger* to arrive was not a restful one for him, though it could not have been less eventful. Even sixty years later, when the story as his grandchildren heard it included complications like a North Atlantic winter gale, he was never able to paint an adequate word picture of his feelings during those thirty minutes—much less an exaggerated one.

The manta-like structure of the tenders made trans-shipping most practical from bow-to-bow contact, but it was practical at all only on a smooth sea. In the present case, the *Conger*'s commander could not bring her bow closer than ten meters to that of the crippled ship, and both were pitching too heavily even for lines to be used.

One of the *Conger*'s divers plunged into the water and swam to the helpless vessel. Dandridge saw him coming through the bow ports, went back to his console, and rather to his surprise found that the hatch and ladder responded to their control switches. Moments later the other man was on the deck beside him.

The diver took in the situation after ten seconds of explanation by Dandridge and two of direct examination, and spoke into the transmitter which was part of his equipment. A few seconds later a raft dropped from the *Conger*'s hatch and two more men clambered down into it. One of these proved on arrival to be Mancini's opposite number, who wasted no time.

"Use the foam," he directed. "Case them all up except for faces; that way we can get them to the bench without any more limb motion. You say Marco thought there might be skull or spine fractures?"

"He said Ishi had a fractured skull and Winkle might have. All he said about spines was that we'd have to be careful in case it had happened."

"Right. You relax; I'll take care of it." The newcomer took up the foam generator and went to work.

Twenty minutes later the *Conger* was on her hydroplanes once more, heading for rendezvous with the *Guppy*.

In spite of tradition, Rick Stubbs knew where he was when he opened his eyes. The catch was that he hadn't the faintest idea how he had gotten there. He could see that he was surrounded by blood-transfusion equipment, electronic circulatory and nervous system monitoring gear, and the needle-capillary-and-computer maze of a regeneration unit, though none of the stuff seemed to be in operation. He was willing to grant from all this that he had been hurt somehow; the fact that he was unable to move his head or his right arm supported this notion. He couldn't begin to guess, however, what sort of injury it might be or how it had happened.

He remembered talking and working with Mancini at the latter's lab bench. He could not recall for certain just what the last thing said or done might be, though; somehow the picture merged with the foggy struggle back to consciousness which had culminated in recognition of his surroundings.

He could see no one near him, but this might be because his head wouldn't turn. Could he talk? Only one way to find out.

"Is anyone here? What's happened to me?" It didn't sound very much like his own voice, and the effort of speech hurt his chest and abdomen; but apparently words got out.

"We're all here, Rick. I thought you'd be switching back on about now." Mancini's face appeared in Stubbs' narrow field of vision.

"We're *all* here? Did everyone get hurt somehow? What happened?"

"Slight correction—most of us are here, one's been and gone. I'll tell you as much as I can; don't bother to ask questions, I know it must hurt you to talk. Gil was here for a while, but he had just had a few bruises and is back on the job. The rest of us were banged up more thoroughly. My right leg was a jigsaw puzzle; Bert had an interesting time with it. I thought he ought to take if off and start over, but he stuck with it, so I got off with five hours of manual repair and two in regeneration instead of a couple of months hooked up to a computer. I'm still splinted, but that will be for only a few more days.

"No one knows yet just what happened. Apparently the *Shark* hit something going at full clip, but no one knows yet what it was. They're towing her in; I trust there'll be enough evidence to tell us the whole story."

"How about the other fellows?"

"Ishi is plugged in. He may need a week with computer regeneration control, or ten times that. We won't be able to assess brain damage until we find how close to consciousness he can come. He had a bad skull fracture. The captain was knocked out, and some broken ribs I missed on the first-aid check did internal damage. Bert is still trying to get him off without regeneration, but I don't think he'll manage it."

"You didn't think he could manage it with you, either."

"True. Maybe it's just that I don't think I could do it myself, and hate to admit that Jellinge is better at my own job than I am."

"How about Joe?"

"Both arms broken and a lot of bruises. He'll be all right. That leaves you, young fellow. You're not exactly a critical case, but you are certainly going to call for professional competence. How fond are you of your fingerprints?"

"What? I don't track."

"Most of your right hand was sliced off, apparently by flying glass from my big culture flask. Ben Tulley from the *Conger*, which picked us up, found the missing section and brought it back; it's in culture now."

"What has that to do with fingerprints? Why didn't you or Mr. Jellinge graft it back?"

"Because there's a good deal of doubt about its condition. It was well over an hour after the accident before it got into culture. You know the sort of brain damage a few minutes without oxygen can do. I know the bone, tendon, and connective tissue in a limb is much less sensitive to that sort of damage, but an hour is a long time, chemically speaking. Grafting calls for healing powers which are nearly as dependent on genetic integrity as is nerve activity; we're just not sure whether grafting is the right thing to do in your case. It's a toss-up whether we should fasten the hand back on and work to make it take, or discard it and grow you a new one. That's why I asked how much you loved your fingerprints."

"Wouldn't a new hand have the same prints?"

"The same print classification, which is determined genetically, but not the same details, which are random."

"Which would take longer?"

"If the hand is in shape to take properly, grafting would be quicker—say a week. If it isn't, we might be six or eight times as long repairing secondary damage. That's longer than complete regeneration would take."

"When are you going to make up your minds?"

"Soon. I wondered whether you'd have a preference."

"How could I know which is better when you don't? Why ask me at all?"

"I had a reason—several, in fact. I'll tell you what they were after you've had two years of professional training in molecular mechanics, if you decide to come into the field. You still haven't told me which you prefer."

The boy looked up silently for a full minute. Actually, he spent very little of that time trying to make his mind up; he was wondering what Mancini's reasons might be. He gave up, flipped a mental coin, and said, "I think I'd prefer the original hand, if there's a real chance of getting it back and it won't keep me plugged in to these machines any longer than growing a new one would."

"All right, we'll try it that way. Of course, you'll be plugged in for quite a while anyway, so if we do have trouble with the hand it won't make so much difference with your time."

"What do you mean? What's wrong besides the hand?"

"You hadn't noticed that your head is clamped?"

"Well, yes; I knew I couldn't move it, but I can't feel anything wrong. What's happened there?"

"Your face stopped most of the rest of the flask, apparently."

"Then how can I be seeing at all, and how is it that I talk so easily?"

"If I knew that much about probability, I'd stop working for a living and take up professional gambling. When I first saw you after your face had been cleaned off and before the glass had been taken out I wondered for a moment whether there hadn't been something planned about the arrangement of the slivers. It was unbelievable, but that's the way it happened. They say anything can happen once, but I'd advise you not to catch any more articles of glassware with your face."

"Just what was it like, Marco? Give me the details."

"Frankly, I'd rather not. There are record photos, of course, but if I have anything to say about it you won't see them until the rebuilding is done. Then you can look in a mirror to reassure yourself when the photos get your stomach. No"—as Stubbs tried to interrupt—"I respect what you probably think of as your clinical detachment, but I doubt very strongly that you could maintain it in the face of the real thing. I'm pretty sure that I couldn't, if it were my face." Mancini's thoughts flashed back to the long moments when he had been dragging his ruined leg across the Shark's deck toward the bleeding boy, and felt a momentary glow—maybe that disclaimer had been a little too modest. He stuck to his position, however.

Rick didn't argue too hard, for another thought had suddenly struck his mind. "You're using regeneration on my face, without asking me whether I want it the way you did with my hand. Right?"

"That's right," Mancini said.

"That means I'm so badly damaged that ordinary healing won't take care of it."

Mancini pursed his lips and thought carefully before answering. "You'd heal, all right," he admitted at last. "You might just possibly, considering your age, heal without too much scarring. I'd hesitate to bet on that, though, and the scars you could come up with would leave you quite a mess."

Stubbs lay silent for a time, staring at the featureless ceiling. The mechanic was sure his expression would have been thoughtful had enough of the young face been visible to make one. He could not, however, guess at what was bothering the boy. As far as Mancini could guess from their work together there was no question of personal cowardice—for that matter, the mechanic could not see what there might be to fear. His profession made him quite casual about growing tissue, natural or artificial, on human bodies or anywhere else. Stubbs was in no danger of permanent disfigurement, crippling damage, or even severe pain; but something was obviously bothering the kid.

"Marco," the question came finally, "just where does detailed genetic control end, in tissue growth, and statistical effects take over?"

"There's no way to answer that both exactly and generally. Genetic factors are basically probability ones, but they're characterized by regions of high probability which we call stability wells. I told you about fingerprints, but each different situation would call for a different specific answer."

"It was what you said about prints that made me think of it. You're going to rebuild my face, you say. You won't tell me just how much rebuilding has to be done, but you admitted I *could* heal normally. If you rebuild, how closely will you match my original face? Does that statistical factor of yours take over somewhere along the line?"

"Statistical factors are everywhere, and work through-out the whole process," replied Mancini without in the least meaning to be evasive. "I told you that. By rights, your new face should match the old as closely as the faces of identical twins match each other, and for the same reason. I grant that someone who knows the twins really well can usually tell them apart, but no one will have your old face around for close comparison. No one will have any doubt that it's you, I promise."

"Unless something goes wrong."

"If it goes wrong enough to bother you, we can always do it over."

"But it *might* go really wrong."

Mancini, who would have admitted that the sun might not rise the next day if enough possible events all happened at once, did not deny this, though he was beginning to feel irritated. "Does this mean that you don't want us to do the job? Just take your chances on the scars?" he asked.

"Why do scars form, anyway?" was the counter. "Why can't regular, normal genetic material reproduce the tis-sue it produced in the first place? It certainly does some-times; why not always?"

"That's pretty hard to explain in words. It has to do with the factors which stopped your nose growing before it became an elephant's trunk—or more accurately, with the factors which stopped your overall growth where they did. I can describe them quite completely, and I believe quite accurately, but not in Basic English."

"Can you measure those factors in a particular case?"

"Hm-m-m, yes; fairly accurately, anyway." Stubbs pounced on this with an eagerness which should have told the mechanic something.

"Then can't you tell whether these injuries, in my partic-ular case will heal completely or leave scars?"

"I . . . well, I suppose so. Let's see; it would take . . . hm-m-m; I'll have to give it some thought. It's not regular technique. We usually just rebuild. What's your objection, anyway? All rebuilding really means is that we set things going and then watch the process, practically cell by cell, and correct what's happening if it isn't right—following the plans you used in the first place."

"I still don't see why my body can't follow them without your help."

"Well, no analogy is perfect; but roughly speaking, it's

because the cells which will have to divide to produce the replacement tissue had the blueprints which they used for the original construction stamped 'production complete; file in reference storage' some years ago, and the stamp marks covered some of the lines on the plans." Mancini's temper was getting a little short, as his tone showed. Theoretically his leg should not have been hurting him, but he had been standing on it longer than any repairman would have advised at its present stage of healing. And why did the kid keep beating around the bush?

Stubbs either didn't notice the tone or didn't care.

"But the plans—the information—that's still there; even I know that much molecular biology. I haven't learned how to use your analysis gear yet, much less to reduce the readings; but I can't see why you'd figure it much harder to read the plans under the 'file' stamp than to work out the ability of that magnetite slime to digest iron from the base configuration of a single cell's genes."

"Your question was why your body couldn't do it; don't change the rules in the middle of the game. I didn't say that *I* couldn't; I could. What I said was that it isn't usual, and I can't see what will be gained by it; you'd at least double the work. I'm not exactly lazy, but the work at best is difficult, precise, and time-consuming. If someone were to paint your portrait and had asked you whether you wanted it on canvas or paper, would you dither along asking about the brand of paint and the sizes of brushes he was going to use?"

"I don't think that's a very good analogy. I just want to know what to expect—"

"You can't *know* what to expect. No one can. Ever. You have to play the odds. At the moment, the odds are so high in your favor that you'd almost be justified in saying that you know what's going to happen. All I'm asking is that you tell me straight whether or not you want Bert and me to ride control as your face heals, or let it go its own way."

"But if you can grow a vine that produces ham sandwiches instead of pumpkins, why—" Mancini made a gesture of impatience. He liked the youngster and still hoped to recruit him, but there are limits.

"Will you stop sounding like an anti-vivisectionist who's been asked for a statement on heart surgery and give me a straight answer to a straight question? The chances are all I can give you. They are much less than fifty-fifty that your face will come out of this without scars on its own. They are much better than a hundred to one that even your mother will never know there's been a controlled regeneration job done on you unless you tell her. You're through general education, legally qualified to make decisions involving your own life and health, and morally obligated to make them instead of lying there dithering. Let's have an answer."

For fully two minutes, he did not get it. Rick lay still, his expression hidden in dressings, eyes refusing to meet those of the man who stood by the repair table. Finally, however, he gave in.

"All right, do your best. How long did you say it would take?"

"I don't remember saying, but probably about two weeks for your face. You'll be able to enjoy using a mirror long before we get that hand unplugged, unless we're remarkably lucky with the graft."

"When will you start?"

"As soon as I've had some sleep. Your blood is back to normal, your general pattern is in the machine; there's nothing else to hold us up. What sort of books do you like?"

"Huh?"

"That head's going to be in a clamp for quite a while. You may or may not like reading, but the only direction you can look comfortably is straight up. Your left hand can work a remote control, and the tape reader can project on the ceiling. I can't think of anything else to occupy you. Do you want some refreshing light fiction, or shall I start you on Volume One of 'Garwood's Elementary Matrix Algebra for Biochemists?' "

A regeneration controller is a bulky machine, even though most of it has the delicacy and structural intricacy possible only to pseudolife—and, of course, to "real" life. It's sensors are smaller in diameter than human red blood cells, and there are literally millions of them. Injectors and samplers are only enough larger to take entire cells into their tubes, and these also exist in numbers which would make the device a hopeless one to construct mechanically. Its computer-controller occupies more than two cubic meters of molecular-scale "machinery" based on a synthetic zeolite framework. Mating the individual gene record needed for a particular job to the basic computer itself takes nearly a day; it would take a lifetime if the job had to be done manually, instead of persuading the two to "grow" together.

Closing the gap between the optical microscope and the test tube, which was blanketed under the word "protoplasm" for so many decades, also blurred the boundary between such initially different fields as medicine and factory design. Marco Mancini and Bert Jellinge regarded themselves as mechanics; what they would have been called a few decades earlier is hard to say. Even at the time the two had been born, no ten Ph.D.'s could have supplied the information which now formed the grounding of their professional practice.

When their preliminary work—the "prepping"—on Rick Stubbs was done, some five million sensing tendrils formed a beard on the boy's face, most of them entering the skin near the edges of the injured portions. Every five hundred or so of these formed a unit with a pair of larger tubes. The sensors kept the computer informed of the genetic patterns actually active from moment to moment in the healing tissue—or at least, a statistically significant number of them. Whenever that activity failed to match within narrow limits what the computer thought should be happening, one of the larger tubes ingested a single cell from the area in question and transferred it to a large incubator—"large" in the sense that it could be seen without a microscope—just outside Rick's skin. There the cell was cultured through five divisions, and some of the product cells analyzed more completely than they could be inside a human body. If all were well after all, which was quite possible because of the limitations of the small sensors, nothing more happened.

If things were really not going according to plan, however, others of the new cells were modified. Active parts of their genetic material which should have been inert were inerted, quiet parts which should have been active were activated. The repaired cells were cultivated for several more divisions; if they bred true, one or more of them was returned to the original site—or at least, to within a few microns of it. Cell division and tissue building went on according to the modified plan until some new discrepancy was detected.

Most of this was, of course, automatic; too many millions of operations were going on simultaneously for detailed manual control. Nevertheless, Mancini and Jellinge were busy. Neither life nor pseudolife is infallible; mutations occur even in triply redundant records. Computation errors occur even—or especially—in digital machines which must by their nature work by successive-approximation methods. It is much better to have a human operator, who knows his business, actually see that connective tissue instead of epidermis is being grown in one spot, or nerve instead of muscle cells in another.

Hence, a random selection of cells, not only from areas which had aroused the computer's interest but from those where all was presumably going well, also traveled out through the tubes. These went farther than just to the incubators; they came out to a joint where gross microscopic study of them by a human observer was possible. This went on twenty-four hours a day, the two mechanics chiefly concerned and four others of their profession taking two-hour shifts at the microscope. The number of man-hours involved in treating major bodily injury had gone up several orders of magnitude since the time when a sick man could get away with a bill for ten dollars from his doctor, plus possibly another for fifty from his undertaker.

The tendrils and tubes farthest from the damaged tissue were constantly withdrawing, groping their way to the action front, and implanting themselves anew, guided by the same chemical clues which brought leukocytes to the same area. Early versions of the technique had involved complex methods of warding off or removing the crowd of white cells from the neighborhood; the present idea was to let them alone. They were good scavengers, and the controller could easily allow for the occasional one which was taken in by the samplers.

So, as days crawled by, skin and fat and muscle and blood vessels, nerves and bones and tendons, gradually extended into their proper places in Stubbs' face and hand. The face, as Mancini had predicted, was done first; the severed hand had deteriorated so that most of its cells needed replacement, though it served as a useful guide.

With his head out of the clamp, the boy fulfilled another of the mechanic's implied predictions. He asked for a mirror. The man had it waiting, and produced it with a grin; but the grin faded as he watched the boy turn his face this way and that, checking his appearance from every possible angle. He would have expected a girl to act that way; but why should this youngster?

"Are you still the same fellow?" Mancini asked finally. "At least, you've kept your fingerprints." Rick put the mirror down.

"Maybe I should have taken a new hand," he said. "With new prints I might have gotten away with a bank robbery, and cut short the time leading to my well-earned retired leisure."

"Don't you believe it," returned Mancini grimly. "Your new prints would be on file along with your gene record and retinal pattern back in Denver before I could legally have unplugged you from the machine. I had to submit a written summary of this operation before I could start, even as it was. Forget about losing your legal identity and taking up crime."

Stubbs shrugged. "I'm not really disappointed. How much longer before I can write a letter with this hand, though?"

"About ten days; but why bother with a letter? You can talk to anyone you want; haven't your parents been on the 'visor every day?"

"Yes. Say, did you ever find out what made the *Shark* pile up?"

Mancini grimaced. "We did indeed. She got infected by the same growth that killed the zeowhale we first picked up. Did you by any chance run that fish into any part of the hull while you were attaching the sling?"

Rich stared aghast. "My gosh! Yes, I did. I held it against one of the side hulls because it was so slippery . . . I'm sorry . . . I didn't know—"

"Relax. Of course you didn't. Neither did I, then; and I never thought of the possibility later. One of the struts was weakened enough to fall at high cruise, though, and Newton's Laws did the rest."

"But does that mean that the other ships are in danger? How about the *Guppy* here? Can anything be done?"

"Oh, sure. It was done long ago. A virus for that growth was designed within a few weeks of its original escape; its gene structure is on file. The mutation is enough like the original to be susceptible to the virus. We've made up a supply of it, and will be sowing it around the area for the next few weeks wherever one of the tenders goes. But why change the subject, young fellow? Your folks *have* been phoning, because I couldn't help hearing their talk when I was on watch. Why all this burning need to write letters? I begin to smell the proverbial rat."

He noticed with professional approval that the blush on Rick's face was quite uniform; evidently a good job had been done on the capillaries and their auxiliary nerves and mucles. "Give, son!"

"It's . . . it's not important," muttered the boy.

"Not important . . . oh, I see. Not important enough to turn you into a dithering nincompoop at the possibility of having your handsome features changed slightly, or make you drop back to second-grade level when it came to the responsibility for making a simple decision. I see. Well, it doesn't matter; she'll probably do all the deciding for you."

The blush burned deeper. "All right, Marco, don't sound like an ascetic; I know you aren't. Just do your job and get this hand fixed so I can write—at least there's still one form of communication you won't be unable to avoid overhearing while you're on watch."

"What a sentence! Are you sure you really finished school? But it's all right, Rick—the hand will be back in service soon, and it shouldn't take you many weeks to learn to write with it again—"

"What?"

"It is a new set of nerves, remember. They're connected with the old ones higher up in your hand and arm, but even with the old hand as a guide they probably won't go to exactly the same places to make contact with touch transducers and the like. Things will feel different, and you'll have to learn to use a pen all over again." The boy stared at him in dismay. "But don't worry. I'll do my best, which is very good, and it will only be a few more weeks. One thing, though—don't call your letter-writing problem my business; I'm just a mechanic. If you're really in love, you'd better get in touch with a doctor."

How many of these Dell bestsellers have you read?

The **Money Game** by "Adam Smith" $1.25

The **Madonna Complex** by Norman Bogner $1.25

The **Manor** by Isaac Bashevis Singer $1.25

The **Beastly Beatitudes of Balthazar B** by J. P. Donleavy $1.25

Soul On Ice (A Delta Edition) by Eldridge Cleaver $1.95

The **Hundred Yard War** by Gary Cartwright   95c

The **Other Side** by James A. Pike   95c

Tell Me How Long The Train's Been Gone
by James Baldwin $1.25

An American Melodrama
by Lewis Chester, Godfrey Hodgson, Bruce Page $1.65

The **Brand-Name Calorie Counter** by Corinne T. Netzer   95c

The **Doctor's Quick Weight-Loss Diet**
by I. Maxwell Stillman M.D., and S. Sinclair Baker   95c

The **Beatles** by Hunter Davies   95c

The **Movie Maker** by Herbert Kastle $1.25

The **Secret of Santa Vittoria** by Robert Crichton   95c

Pretty Maids All In A Row by Francis Pollini   95c

The big shock-it-to-'em bestseller

THE PRESIDENT'S PLANE IS MISSING

by Robert J. Serling

On a calm night in a nervous world, Air Force One jets off from Andrews Air Force Base. Aboard is the President of the United States, an idolized leader whose image combines the best qualities of John Kennedy and Lyndon Johnson—but whose inner thoughts remain a dark secret even to his closest aides.

The flight is normal—until the plane is high over Arizona. Then, suddenly, before a horrified controller's eyes, the plane vanishes from the radar screen . . .

"The shock of screaming headlines—a runaway bestseller that is tense . . . frightening . . . superb."—Kansas City Star

A DELL BOOK 95c